NEXT TRAIN OUT

Sallie Showalter

Tanya,
Thanks for going
on this ride
with us! Sallie
2023

Murky Press

Cover design by Barbara Grinnell
Book design by Sallie Showalter

© 2020 by Sallie Showalter
All rights reserved.
ISBN: 978-0-9992540-3-5

Murky Press
www.murkypress.com

For Mary Marrs

The truth was that for some months he had been going through that partitioning of the things of youth wherein it is decided whether or not to die for what one no longer believes . . . He used to think that he wanted to be good, he wanted to be kind, he wanted to be brave and wise, but it was all pretty difficult. He wanted to be loved, too, if he could fit it in.

—F. Scott Fitzgerald
Tender Is the Night

Contents

NEXT
TRAIN
OUT

1961

*M*y mother lifted the top of the heavy wooden chest tucked away in a dark corner of our basement. The hinges groaned with the weight. Straining on tiptoe, my fingers grasping the front edge of the chest, I tried to peer inside. Exotic smells—cedar, mothballs, the peculiar scent of pattern paper used in sewing—tickled my nose. I watched as she pulled out the large box and placed it on the floor. She turned back to the chest, looking for something else.

My sister and I dropped to our knees and timidly folded back the flimsy cardboard to reveal the box's contents. I felt my breath catch as I once again glimpsed the strings of pearls mounded on top of the wedding dress, patiently awaiting the chance to hang free from the modest neckline and drape the bosom of yet another enchanted bride. My fingers grazed the pearls first, and then the heavy fabric, sturdy enough to withstand gravity's pull on hundreds of beads. The material had aged to a creamy amber, darker in places, but I could still see the swirling effect of the fabric finish, easily visible only when the dim light caught it a certain way.

Mesmerized, I leaned back on my heels and stared. My mother, having found what she needed, bent over and closed the top of the box and then gently laid it back in the chest, entombing it once again.

Effie Mae
Saturday, December 6, 1941

I collapsed in a heap on the floor, books scattered around me like broken headstones. *What's that man gone and done?* I stared at the tiny newspaper clipping still in my grip until my thoughts disappeared in a settling fog.

ME AND LYONS, WE'VE been together a long time. At least for me it feels like a long time. Seven years. That's forever after your last husband was kilt within a year of your marrying him, and your first husband proved to be a scoundrel after you birthed him four children. Well, maybe that marriage lasted longer than I remember. I just know I was ready to be rid of him. The traitor.

So, I thought I knew most everything about my current husband. The one I've moved all over this blessed country with. But I reckon I was wrong.

Granted, we didn't marry til I was well into my forties, so we'd both done a heap a living before that. And maybe there was a few details he forgot to tell me. Or thought I wouldn't want to know. Or thought was best kept to hisself.

It's hard to know what's going on in a man's head. We women, we tend to lay all our cards on the table. I know in my case, I'm a simple person. And I don't want to try to keep track of a bunch of stories or a bunch of lies or a bunch of secrets. I'd rather just tell you straight up what's what and let you deal with it. I ain't interested in knotting a bunch of fancy tales together like some heirloom crocheted lap throw I have to worry about keeping all nice and neat.

And Lyons gets that about me. Sure, sometimes he'll just sit and watch me with that lopsided grin of his when I start going off about something that happened at Logmont or Yellow Creek, back when I was living in them coal camps in Kentucky with my kids, back before all the bloody fighting in the '30s. He just sits there and looks at me as if to say, *Effie Mae, is there any truth to them tales you tell?* But they're all true, of course. I don't know how to lie. And why would I make stuff up? The truth is harder to believe than most lies, if you ever stop and think about it.

I let out a snort, as I fingered the fragment of newsprint whose words had done made my legs buckle. Thoughts continued swooping through my head like colorful kites rising and dropping on a windy day. In all that jumble, I caught sight of Lyons when we first met, and I frantically reeled in them memories to try to quiet my mind.

I was living at Yellow Creek back then, with my first husband, Wilson. I'd done had two of my four children, so it musta been 1912, maybe '13. I'd bundle up the oldest, Valarie, who was hardly more than a toddler at the time, and we'd walk or hitch a ride into the big city of Middlesboro ever now and then, just to get away from the coal dust and see some different faces. The first time we walked by the drugstore, which towered over the main corner of town, Valarie come to a dead stop, staring at the dragon and serpent carved in stone above the main entrance. She seemed more curious than frightened. We had all kinds of critters in them hills.

"You wanna go inside and get a cherry phosphate?" I asked. I had tied a few coins in a handkerchief before we left home, and I put my hand in my coat pocket to make sure they was still there.

She looked up at me and beamed. I don't reckon she had any clue what a cherry phosphate was, but I figgered it was time I introduced her to the type of treat we could only get in town.

When I pulled open the door, I heard his whistling right away. It was a cheery tune, with a clear beat and bright, brassy notes. I looked down the long aisle of ointments and liver pills and saw a dark-haired young man working behind the main counter, lips pursed as he leaned over a white ceramic bowl, pressing hard on the tool he hid in his hand. At the sound of the door closing behind us, the whistling stopped and he looked up, a crooked smile creasing his face.

I pulled Valarie toward him, trying to keep her fingers from all the mysterious packages at her eye level.

"Howdy," I said.

On closer inspection, I noted that his ears stuck out a little too much underneath that wavy hair, but his watery blue eyes danced in the shadows of them dark brows, seemingly full of mischief.

"And what can I do for you two young ladies today?" he asked, still smiling.

I nodded toward the sody fountain to my right and winked at him. "I was hoping to get my little girl a cherry phosphate. Could you help us out?"

"I'd be happy to, ma'am," he said, wiping his hands on his crisp white apron as he stepped from behind the counter. I noticed he was dressed right smart. His trousers was pressed, his shoes shone. I felt a little self-conscious about my drab dress and my nearly threadbare gray coat. But I had taken care to pin up my thick auburn hair and, despite the two children, I knew my figure could still draw a look or two when I walked through town. As usual, I had let that wink escape before I realized its potential for stirring up trouble.

I lifted Valarie up on a stool and gave it a twirl. She shrieked with glee.

"Can I make that two, one for you both?" he asked.

I settled on the stool next to her. "No sir. I only have the change for one."

"Well, then, the second one's on the house," he said. "For my newest and currently most favorite customers."

I'm sure I blushed as he busied himself with the preparations, occasionally glancing at me with that grin.

"What's that you was whistling?" I asked, trying to still my suddenly jangled nerves.

He put the two glasses in front of us and looked at me with amusement. "You heard that, huh? I've had this Sousa march in my head all week for some reason. Maybe I should come up with something more attuned to accompanying a female voice. Do you sing?"

"Only when I think there ain't nobody around. But everybody in my family is musical. It's hard not to be around here."

And just like that we was off and running. In no time I felt like we'd knowed each other all our lives. We talked about our families—I shared a lot more than he did, I realize now—and about music and about them flickers they'd just started showing in town, both of us gushing over Lillian Gish. He talked about Kentucky's own Champ Clark, who had gotten beat by President Wilson in the Democratic primary. I talked about the union's battles in the coal camp and he talked about the other pharmacies where he'd worked in Corbin and LaGrange—D. W. Griffith's hometown. I was hypnotized by his words. He seemed like an exotic creature dropped in the middle of our hardscrabble life.

I reckon I was smitten right then. Here I was a married woman with children mooning over some drugstore clerk who could string together pretty words. I didn't have no dishonorable intentions, and I knew he was just chatting up a friendly customer, but over the next several months me and Valarie made that trip into town a little more frequently.

Then, one day, we went to see him, and Mr. Sprague, the owner, was the only one there.

"Morning, Mr. Sprague. Is Lyons around today?"

"Morning to you, Mrs. Noble. No, I'm afraid Lyons has been called home to Hopewell. His father is bad sick. I felt real sorry for the young man. I think he hated to leave. And I sure hated to lose his help. I'm still looking for someone to replace him."

I stood frozen in place. It hit me hard. I squeezed Valarie's hand. I felt like a corner of my heart had done been torn away and flung to the moon.

"Would you and the young missus like a cherry phosphate today?" he asked.

I barely heard him. "No, thank you. We'd best be moving on." And I pointed little Valarie toward the door and pert near shoved her out to the street.

I figgered I'd never see him again. It's kind of silly, I know. I had no claim to him. But I felt like I'd been abandoned. One day—poof—he was just gone.

It was nearly twenty years later when our paths crossed again, in another city, in another world. We had both lived two lifetimes by then. Everything was different. But we picked up right where we left off, talking so easy, wanting to intertwine our lives.

So I thought we'd done shared everything over the years. But looking down at that newspaper clipping, as I sat on the musty-smelling braided rug, I realized there must be a lot he'd never told me. Sure, there was times when I felt maybe he was holding something back. But I just chalked it up to him being a man of some breeding who come from a very different background than me.

I closed my eyes and tried to recollect everything he'd told me about his early life. All I really knew was he'd growed up in a small town in central Kentucky where everybody knew everybody's business. The way he described it, they was all trying to cling to some status that had been bequeathed em by George Washington or the King of Prussia or someone. I figger it took a lot of energy to keep up appearances and shrug off life's certain miseries. I think it plum wore him out. He never told me what happened, but he obviously left that all behind.

By the time we married, he'd been working for some years as a cook. Or a "chef," as he sometimes says. I don't really see no difference. Seems like in both cases you're just putting food on the table. He seems to like the work. And it meant he could find jobs even when times was hard. And sometimes those jobs was in some pretty swanky places—big fancy hotels, for instance. We worked at the Roney Plaza in Miami in '34 and '35, for instance, until the big Labor Day hurricane spooked us enough we moved on north. We landed at the Roney in part because Lyons had worked at the Waldorf up in Toledo before I married him, and the Waldorf people had some connection to the Roney. So it was the type of job that could take you places, if you let it.

And that's more or less how we ended up here. I opened my eyes and looked around the cramped living room—the upholstered rocker by the window, the lumpy sofa that had seen better days, the dust rag lying by my feet—trying to get my bearings.

"Here" is very different from the Roney or, I imagine, the Waldorf. Sparrows Point is another company town, similar to the company towns I knowed when I was younger. But rather than being walled up by the mountains that hide the horizon from your view, here the land is flat as a tobacco field and you might actually catch a sunset if you peer between the giant smokestacks west of town. It makes me chuckle when I think how I traded the dreary coal dust that blackened every surface for the choking red dust that the open-hearth furnaces cough up twenty-four hours a day. You pick your laundry days carefully here. If the wind is from the east, any washing on the clothesline will get covered in black soot; if the wind is coming from the west, over the open hearths, your clothes come off the lines the color of a shiny penny.

Here the old Bessemer converters stretch into the sky like the giant chestnuts and beeches of my youth. Leaping flames scorch the air. The smell of sulfur burns the nose. The earth seems to rumble as the heavy machinery groans and the sheet metal crashes and the fire roars. Overhead pipes snake around the town sizzling with steam and other gases. An orange haze settles like fog. "Hell with the lid off" someone once called it. All so the rolling mills and metal shops can turn out raw material for everything from automobiles to skyscrapers to pipes to nails to beer cans. Some of the steel goes directly to the nearby ship-building yard, where I understand we're already assembling freighters and cargo ships for the fighting overseas.

When I need a hint of fresh air, it's just a short walk to the harbor. In fact, water laps around nearly all four sides of this little kingdom. Back in the mountains, our freshwater streams was narrow and talk-ative, gurgling and chirping as they tumbled over rocks in the steep terrain, rushing downhill. Here the river heading out to the Chesa-peake Bay, carrying the scents and sins of Baltimore, looks more like an ocean to me, wide and flat with the wind whipping up something like waves on its surface. As you get closer to the edge of land, the wind helps deaden the commotion coming from the blast furnaces. Sometimes the gusts are strong enough you have to work mighty hard just to stay put.

I reckon I shouldn't be surprised at the similarities of these compa-ny towns I've knowed. After all, they was all built by the steel compa-nies. They all had the same purpose: increasing profits. And at each of these towns, whether in the mountains of Kentucky or the shores of Maryland, they owned us. They controlled where we lived and how we lived and how much money we had and where we could spend it. If we lived or died, it was of little concern to em, as long as them dollars kept flowing upstream.

I looked down at the clipping. I rubbed my thumb over the words, hoping maybe they was counterfeit. I felt a huge sigh stick in my throat, and I couldn't figger out how to release it.

I thought me and Lyons had settled in real nice here after leaving our jobs at the Commercial House down in Charleston. I like the ash and maple and sycamore trees that line the neighborhood streets and the pretty wood and brick and stucco houses the company built for the workers. I like this little apartment on the third floor of Mr. Wallace Fowler's handsome frame boardinghouse with the contrasting shutters and the gingerbread trim. I have me a tiny kitchen and a living room with a dormer window that looks out on the street.

Lyons has charge of the big kitchen on the main floor where, with the help of a couple of boys, he prepares three meals a day for the boarders. The big furnaces never shut down here, so the men work seven days a week. Thank goodness they finally managed to vote the union in back in September, despite the Bethlehem bosses forbidding em from doing any organizing here at the Point. Things should get better. As it is, nearly all the families occupying the small private homes a couple of streets down still rent a room or two to the single workers. It's tight quarters for everyone, but it helps pay the bills.

It's my job to tackle the orange grit that finds its way inside our boardinghouse. I scrub and clean all week long, but it's a losing battle. My real job, as far as I'm concerned, is creating a home for them young boys and older men who's away from their families. They're all wore out at the end of their shifts. I just wanna give em a clean place to lay their heads after Lyons fills their bellies.

I guess I've been feeling pretty smug in this comfortable little world. We both had work. I had my son Doug living here in the boardinghouse, working as an electrician for the steel company. I was getting on to an age where I was ready to settle down and quit roaming the whole damn country.

And then, moments ago, I felt the person I trusted the most in the world yank that well-worn rug right out from under me.

Lyons had gone next door to our local community center—the Clubhouse—earlier in the day to fix some fancy food for a company Christmas party. I had cleaned the grand Clubhouse parlors that morning so the place would be spic-and-span for the big shots. Soon after, I was here in our apartment, going through the motions of a weekly cleaning. I was humming "O Holy Night," fitting in the words whenever I could remember em. Mostly I was thinking about hunting for a little Christmas tree to put by our window.

I reached over my head to wrastle a handful of books from the little shelf Doug had put up by the kitchen door, planning to dust behind em. Now I ain't a reader, but just recently Lyons had taken to acquiring a few books. To me, him keeping em around was a good sign. Maybe we wasn't going to pick up and go again right away. Maybe he was planning to settle for a while.

The cold had my rheumatism flaring up and my hands was cranky, and evidently I didn't get a good grip on them books. As I slid em off the shelf they tumbled directly to the floor. One landed prone, its backbone arched, splayed out like a turkey vulture testing its wings before flight.

The title of the book caught my eye: *Tender Is the Night* by that fella with the fancy name that Lyons said he'd knowed back in Kentucky, during training camp before he was sent off to war. Lyons had said he was an odd bird, with his hand-tailored uniforms and his uppity manners, but that he sure knew how to write. The title didn't really make no sense to me, but it stuck in my head.

When I reached down to pick up the book, I discovered the newspaper clipping, which musta been hidden among its pages, on the floor beneath it.

I picked it up and squinted to make out the words. Then I felt all the strength in my legs give out. Next thing I knew I was sitting on the floor surrounded by the books.

I stared again at the little piece of yellowed newsprint between my thumb and forefinger, both fingers and paper burnished to nearly the same golden hue.

> The *Bedford County News*, Hopewell, Kentucky,
> Tuesday, November 1, 1921
>
> *"Mr. and Mrs. Lyons Board, of Hopewell, are the happy*
> *parents of a fine daughter, born at the home of Mrs. Board's*
> *parents, in Lawrenceburg, last week. Mrs. Board, before her*
> *marriage, was Miss Nell Marrs, a member of the Hopewell*
> *High School faculty."*

I don't know how long I sat on that floor, but I still hadn't moved when Doug came in after handling an emergency call, his hands and face still black from the blast furnace he'd been working on.

"What's the matter, Ma?" His eyes surveyed the mess on the floor. "You hurt?"

I couldn't answer. I didn't know what to say. I still couldn't understand what I'd read.

I handed him the newspaper clipping.

He read it and was silent a moment. "Did you know Lyons done been married before?"

I shook my head.

"That he had a daughter?"

I shook my head again.

He reached down to help me up and led me into the kitchen. He pulled out a chair at the little table covered with the red checked oilcloth and I sat down. He busied himself making us some coffee.

As I begun to come to my senses, I fumbled in my apron pocket and pulled out my Camels. I tapped one out of the packet. Doug was right there with a match as he set a cup of coffee in front of me. I pulled hard on my cigarette and blew the smoke out the corner of my mouth, away from Doug, who had taken a seat at the table, coffee cup in hand. I pushed a wayward curl behind my ear and then I looked over at him, to see if I could read his face. The kitchen was quiet, and I listened to the second hand on the wall clock as it marched on.

"How can a man hide a secret like that?" I demanded.

Doug lifted his cup and took a noisy sip. "You sure it's him?"

"Well, it says 'Mr. and Mrs. Lyons Board.' And the date's November 1, 1921. He would've been 29 years old—unless he done lied to me about that, too. If you do the figuring, that means he would've been back from serving overseas for a coupla years—time to get married and have a kid. It all fits together."

The room turned quiet again, but my thoughts was swirling like a child's pinwheel caught in a gusty breeze. I didn't know how to slow em down, how to focus on what was real.

"What am I gonna do, Doug?"

Doug shifted in his seat. This was not the kind of conversation he particularly liked. He was good at fixing things, but that usually meant big machinery or my crotchety appliances. I could tell he was uneasy with this type of breakdown. How do you mend something you never knew was broke?

"I reckon you have to talk to him," he finally said. "Confront him with it. What else can you do? You can't pretend you never saw it. Not now."

I looked at the announcement again. The baby would now be 20. A young woman. I looked at Doug. He had just turned 25. I was a mess when he was overseas for four years with the Navy. That's why I convinced Lyons to move up here, so I could be closer to my boy. How long had it been since Lyons had seen his daughter? How could he stand it?

"You think he has other children?" I asked Doug.

He took another sip of coffee and looked at me out of the corner of his eye. He was always a quiet boy, the most serious of all my children. They say that's usually the oldest, but in my case it was the youngest. Lord knows what he saw on them ships around Shanghai as he tended them submarines. I imagine he was hiding stuff from me, too.

He shrugged. "Does it bother you that he's been married before? And you didn't know?" he asked.

I'd been so focused on the child that I'd hardly paid no mind to the fact that he'd had another wife. "Well, I've been married twice before, but he knows all about that. I ain't kept no secrets from him."

I stubbed out my cigarette, with a little more force than needed. "I wonder if she still lives in Kentucky."

We was quiet again. Then I felt a shiver, starting deep in my bowels and quickly moving through my chest and into my shoulders.

"What if the child died, and that's why he's kept this all these years? That might explain why he never said nothin." I felt an odd sense of relief as I uttered those words. I knew it weren't right, but I couldn't help myself.

I watched Doug as he rubbed his finger around the rim of the coffee cup. "Well, that's possible, of course," he said. "Maybe they both died in some horrible accident."

"And he's been a grieving their deaths all these years and just couldn't bear to mention it." I found myself fabricating a story that I could live with, even if it meant that my husband had endured some unspeakable loss. But I also had had my own experience with how a tragic accident could rip apart a happy home. That was something I could wrap my head around.

I got up and poured myself a little more coffee. I knew better than to drink so much that late in the day, but it felt comforting somehow.

Doug finally spoke, somewhat hesitatingly. "You know, he's

always seemed like the kind of guy, at least to me, who might have something up his sleeve."

"What d'you mean by that?" I snapped, more sharply than I meant to.

He took a minute to respond, piecing his thoughts together. "Well, he seems to have a foot in two worlds. From what I can tell, he appears to be happy working as a cook, but when he's around the bosses he seems to naturally elevate himself to their level. It's almost as if they don't notice that he's edged into their conversation. I sometimes wonder if he ain't hiding something. He's a good man, I think, Mama. There's just something..."

I could see Doug either wasn't sure how to finish the sentence or didn't want to. I let it dissipate with the rest of the smoke in the room.

"If his daughter is still alive, do you think they stay in touch?" I asked.

He looked up at me. "Seems unlikely. Don't you think we'd know?"

I got up and put my cup in the sink. "Well, I've got a few hours before he gets home to figger out how to approach him. How do you think he'll react?"

Doug smiled sheepishly. "Let's just say I'll be down at Mickey's meditating on my beer while you two are talking. I don't plan to be anywhere in the vicinity when you have that conversation."

Lyons
Wednesday, October 26, 1921

I shifted the big Oakland sedan into gear and roared out of Hopewell, eager to get out of town before someone recognized me in Johnny's car.

I was a twentieth-century Jesse James ensconced in my gasoline-powered stagecoach, racing away from the havoc I had just bestowed upon the Deposit and Loan. When I looked in the side mirror, I half expected to see a cluster of downtown businessmen illuminated by the streetlights, shaking their fists at me as I sped away with the town's riches.

On the bench seat beside me, however, was not a bag of loot and a shotgun, but a bouquet of red roses for my beloved. The telegram had come earlier that day from Nell's mother, who had presided over the delivery at her home in Lawrenceburg, west of Hopewell:

BABY GIRL BORN 0903 [STOP] ARDUOUS LABOR BUT
ALL IS WELL [STOP]

I had to smile. Reading between the cryptic lines, I grasped the message she would probably relay to me later in person: "Having that baby was no joyride. You should be happy that menfolk have been spared the agony of labor and childbirth." Too many words for the telegram, thank goodness.

I dragged my thoughts back to the real matter at hand. Nell and I had a baby girl. *How did that happen?* I wanted to ask. We had only been married a year, but I suspect Nell was always precocious in everything she tackled. Frankly, parenthood was a bit of a shock to me, the gadabout who never really saw himself settling down. But then the last year—the last three years—had been full of surprises, some more agreeable than others. Sitting in the unfamiliar sedan, rolling through the liquid darkness toward my in-laws' home, I tried to recall how I had gotten myself into this startling situation.

The dominoes started falling in 1918, when record cold made tough work for the gravediggers after my father rather thoughtlessly departed this world at the end of January. My mother thereupon announced she was leaving Hopewell, despite her family's moldering roots there, and moving to Louisville to be near her most cherished—and only living—son, yours truly. Before she could attend her first whist party, the ever solicitous Uncle Sam declared that I must forthwith cancel any plans I had for the next year: he had arranged a little overseas trip for me.

While all of this family drama was unfolding, the rest of the world was watching with bated breath as Spanish influenza galloped from port to port and home to home in a relentless competition with the Great War to garner the most innocent souls. Fortunately, my soul was not deemed a sufficiently innocent target, so after four months of building camaraderie with my fellow recruits at a lovely flu-ridden hideaway outside Louisville, followed by more disciplined languishing at a bucolic retreat up in Ohio, I found myself in New York City awaiting my luxury liner to an uncertain future.

When I finally made it back to the States, six months after the end of the war—the war to end all wars, if you're simple enough to believe one of our revered pundits—I had planned to go back to my glamorous job repairing automobile tires at a Louisville Gulf station. At that time, admittedly, my ambitions were few, and I had absolutely no intention of returning to the town where I had grown up and where all the memories were safely buried. But when I accompanied Mother to Hopewell to take care of those loose ends that inevitably fray after a community pillar's demise, I discovered my rather pedestrian military career had transformed me, and my prospects, in the eyes of many of the good townspeople. I wouldn't exactly call it a hero's welcome, not like Reuben Hutchcraft or Bishop Batterton would have gotten if they'd managed to outrun those bullets, but folks were surprisingly deferential and willing to help any way they could.

So when the general manager at the Gas and Electric Company offered me a bookkeeping job, I decided that trading in my dirty coveralls for a white collar and starched shirt might be the best path to take. I had inherited my father's knack for figures, and I calculated that every home would eventually need gas or electric service or both, whereas every household may not have the means to trade in their buggy for a shiny motorcar that required regular tire repair. At least not yet.

By that time, Nell, a new faculty member at Hopewell High, had already won over her wide-eyed students and spellbound colleagues alike with her expertise in ladies' hats and the mysteries of angel food cake. I had to work a little harder at wooing her than I had those cheeky Hello Girls manning the switchboards over in France, who seemed delighted to find themselves surrounded by desperate men far away from their moral arbiters. But I liked the challenge Nell presented. Even more, though, I liked that I won.

That victory, however, seemed highly dubious on the day we met. It was a beautiful July afternoon, hot without being wilting, and I was engaging the lovelies at a high-society boating party along Stoner Creek. In hindsight, preening might be a better word for it. Barely two months after my discharge from the service, and a month after resettling in Hopewell, I was still strutting like the undecorated corporal I was. Imagining that my worldly experiences magnified my natural allure, I worked hard to maintain my ironic smile as I wandered the broad lawn in front of the stately brick mansion, exchanging banalities with young ladies I had last known as adolescent girls. In those days, I had accompanied Miss Hettie Hutchcraft to a number of parties at my mother's request, since Mr. Hutchcraft and my father were business associates. But watching Hettie now, it was clear why my parents had to intervene on her behalf. I allowed my eyes to drift elsewhere.

I spotted my cousin Hiram—a massive man who had regularly astonished the girls at Hopewell cotillions and Threlkeld School mixers with his grace on the dance floor—standing amid a group of familiar faces: his lovely new wife, Isobel, his sister, Caroline—who was as tiny as her brother was immense and whose sparkling personality beautifully masked her disappointing countenance—and my old friend Dan Peed and his very proper wife. Towering over this small crowd, Hiram reminded me of newly appointed Chief Justice Taft surrounded by diminutive women's suffrage supplicants hoping to change his mind.

I sauntered in their direction. As I approached, making sure my chest was sufficiently puffed, I noticed a smartly dressed wisp of a woman who disappeared beneath her broad summer hat festooned with excitable flowers barely contained by purple ribbon. I had to stop myself from bending at the waist and peering under the brim to determine just what she might be hiding.

I composed myself, dropped my gaze, and noticed her tiny feet in elegant white slippers. I dared allow my eyes to inch upward, noting shapely ankles covered by white silk stockings. Hiram interceded before my inspection continued its natural course.

"Lyons! It's about time you joined us. Let me introduce you to Hopewell's most adored schoolmarm."

I rearranged my face to erase all traces of prurience and don the bonhomie the occasion required. Then, smiling, I quickly turned to Hiram and gave his hand a firm shake, my other hand reaching to grasp his shoulder. I tipped my hat to Isobel, feeling some surprise as I grasped a light-as-a-feather summer boater rather than my military-issued campaign hat, and then leaned toward Caroline and kissed her cheek. "Hello, cousin." I nodded at Dan, who seemed absorbed in conversation with two others, whom I did not recognize.

Only then did I allow my eyes to once again light on the mysterious woman beneath the hat.

"Lyons, this is Nell Marrs, our new maven of domestic sciences at Hopewell High. Nell, this is my cousin Lyons Board, fresh from the fields of France."

I extended my hand. She tilted her head back to peer into my face, and only then did I see the finely chiseled features and the warm smile.

"Mr. Board. So happy to meet you. I believe I have had the pleasure of chatting with your mother on several occasions."

Of course. Mother had written breathless descriptions of this recent arrival who had sparked the imaginations of the townspeople, relieving them of the boredom of gossiping about the same familiar rakes and harpies. Around Hopewell, mothers of eligible sons had lined up to make the necessary introductions. I sensed my mother's exasperation that I was still roaming Europe with the 110th, even though the war was over, and I couldn't be here to compete for this woman's prodigious charms. I'm sure my mother felt she had failed to uphold the proper standards of intrusive matchmaking.

"Enchantée," I said. "My mother mentioned you in her letters each time she had the good fortune of your company."

"So you and your mother corresponded regularly while you were overseas?"

"As frequently as the circumstances allowed—although I will admit that her missives were generally more engaging than mine."

"And has the adjustment to civilian life gone smoothly?"

I felt the blood drain momentarily from my face. A most innocent question, indeed, but my immediate response felt neither innocent nor rational. I absently reached for my breast pocket, expecting to find a pack of cigarettes secured in my wool tunic, but instead fingered a smooth silk-lined vest.

After accepting the job in Hopewell, I had discovered through a number of conversations that many in town mistakenly believed I had served in battle with the 110th Field Signal Corps, whose bravery during the bloodbath in the Meuse-Argonne—exceptional valor tested by incompetent leaders and insufficient equipment as much as by the enemy—was already becoming legend. Initially I saw no need to correct that assumption, which I finally understood came from an article that had appeared in the unimpeachable *Bedford County News*. I had indeed been assigned to the 110th but not until *December*, after the Armistice was signed. And, yes, I was a part of that battalion when I was discharged in May, a fact that the local newspaper evidently found noteworthy and deserving of a little editorializing.

So I had bunked and trained with those fine men for months and listened acutely to their harrowing stories. At times I felt I had stood beside them in battle. But, in actuality, during the war I had been attached to the 309th Field Signal Corps. We roamed along the front providing replacements where needed. My courage had been tested, but my experience would have seemed like a Boy Scout jamboree to the men of the 110th.

I had already learned that civilians had no interest in the details of the war, and there was no use trying to sort out these niceties. They clung to their myths and denied the truth. In the end, I simply nodded when acquaintances droned on about how brave I was and what horrors I must have seen. After a while, I started to believe it myself.

Nell's voice interrupted my ruminations. "Oh, I'm afraid I may have said something indelicate," she said, placing her decidedly delicate fingertips gently on her lips. "Forgive me if I've overstepped some boundary. I meant no harm." She lowered her head again, briefly hiding her face.

Hiram looked at me curiously. I flushed again, but then felt the life force renew its circulation.

"Have you been down to the water yet?" I asked no one in particular in a tone distressingly jocular.

"I was just telling Hiram I wanted him to row Isobel and me a short way up the creek," said Caroline. "Why don't you take Nell out?"

"What a splendid idea." I turned to the intriguing waif at my side. "Nell, would you be interested in a jaunt upstream?"

She hesitated. "I fear I may have offended you. Are you sure you want my company?"

"Of course!" I said a little too gaily, offering her my arm.

She acquiesced, and we strolled to the edge of the lawn, across the road, and down the metal stairway our hosts had conveniently installed against the sloping bank. Nell and I remained silent as we listened to Caroline and Isobel chatter. A pontoon full of merrymakers was just leaving the shore, and three skiffs with oars awaited the intrepid. Hiram and I each wrestled one into the water and then helped the ladies into the boats. I noted that Nell managed the entire embarkation without dirtying her shoes.

She settled onto her seat and secured her hat. I unbuttoned the cuffs on my shirt, pushed the sleeves up to my elbows, and dipped the oars in the water. With gentle strokes, I pulled us away from the shore.

Momentarily, I heard the unmistakable sound of a Great Blue Heron muscling its enormous wings into flight. I looked to my left and pointed him out to Nell.

She watched the bird glide just above the boat carrying the other three, screeching as he went. "So ungainly yet so graceful," she said.

"Our ancestors believed they spread a sort of luminous pixie dust on the water to better see their prey. Seems to me that might be a useful adaptation for all of us."

I suspected a wry smile was hidden under the broad brim of her hat. Her rather curious comment, however, made me wonder which of us she identified as the hunter.

The sun was intense, and I felt the sweat forming on my brow. I smiled at Nell. She seemed comfortable on the water. I expected she would be comfortable anywhere. She would always know the right thing to do and precisely what needed to be said. No wonder my mother had been taken with her.

We followed the other boat upstream, pulling against the gentle current.

As I steered us around a bend, I looked over my shoulder for any snags or downed trees. The light breeze seemed to intensify as we turned, and I heard a quiet "Ooh." When I turned back to Nell, I saw that her extraordinary hat covered with the feisty flowers had leapt from her head and into the water. I found myself mesmerized by her classic visage, now fully visible and surrounded by newly loosened soft curls. I was reminded of a cameo brooch I recalled my mother wearing.

"Lyons!" she yelled. "Grab it! Grab my hat before it floats away!"

I broke my stare and pulled the right oar hard to position the boat a little closer to the frolicsome hat. I dropped the oar back in the boat and reached for it—futilely. The current was carrying the hat downstream as our rather unwieldy boat slowed its forward momentum upstream. I grabbed both oars and attempted to row backwards, moving the boat back downstream in the direction I was facing. Two good strokes and I had the hat once again within reach. I lunged for it.

I heard the splash before I realized I was in the water. I surfaced, flustered, but caught the prey in my sights. A few quick strokes and I plucked the hat from the surface and, in a single flourish, handed it to Nell—who I then realized had already repositioned herself next to the oars and taken control of the boat. She dropped one oar long enough to daintily shake the water from her hat, none the worse for its maiden voyage, and place it in her lap. Taking up the oars once again, she held the boat steady as I nabbed my straw boater as it floated by and then reached for the gunwale and heaved myself in like a gasping flounder. At that point, Nell was unable to suppress her laughter. With few other options, I grinned back. The others had pulled on upstream, unaware of my ridiculous performance.

This whole scene replayed in my mind as I drove toward her and our newborn daughter. I felt that same sheepish grin spread across my face. When I eventually offered her my hand in marriage, we both knew who was going to steer that ship.

Having surmounted all initial obstacles, I, like all nervous suitors, then faced the vexing scrutiny of her family. That was the challenge I wasn't fully prepared for.

Her family, solid and respected merchants in their community, was skeptical about me from the beginning. After all, I had no clear profession, no obvious means to take care of their elder daughter. Like many other returning servicemen—and many scoundrels, I'm sure—I was living at the local YMCA. I can see why I did not appear to be a good bet. But Nell worked hard to convince them that I was a perfect complement to her traditional, ordered view of the world.

I could just imagine how that conversation went.

Mrs. Marrs: "What? You're seriously thinking about marrying him? Are you sure that's a smart move, Nell? I know he has an appealing manner, and he's certainly a fine looking man. But are you certain he's the man you want to settle down with, to have a family with?"

Mr. Marrs: "Can he take care of you, sweetheart? I mean, financially. Is his position at the Gas and Electric Company stable?"

Nell: "Yes, Daddy. He's doing just fine. I know he might seem a little reckless or cavalier at times, but he's intent on a fresh start. You know he comes from a good family. I'm fully confident he'll find his footing. And I can nudge him along. We'll be good for each other."

Mrs. Marrs: "You're certain you're not rushing into this? You've only known him a year. And won't you have to give up your teaching position? Does the Hopewell Board of Education allow married women to teach?"

Nell: "Mother, I'm 30 years old. I've enjoyed teaching, but if I want to have a family, I can't wait much longer. Besides, I love Lyons. *And he just makes me tingle all over.*"

OK, I doubt she uttered that last line. But I like to think that my beguiling charisma had some effect on her decision.

As I continued my drive west, I was relieved I hadn't been there for the birth, and not only because hearing my wife suffer was not necessarily how I typically liked to spend my day. As I have said, my in-laws are fine people, paragons of all the social graces, but sometimes I feel like they're watching my every move, just waiting for me to slip up. And that's guaranteed to happen. I've been called a bonehead before.

Growing up, I chafed at the burdens of privilege that others around me embraced. As my friends scattered to prestigious prep schools like Andover or Woodberry Forest or dour military academies in Millersburg or Staunton—where they expected to endure tedious time in the classroom while laying the groundwork for a lifetime of cozy business deals—my devoted mother couldn't bear to completely release me from her clutches. I instead took the local interurban to Nicholasville each week to benefit from the instruction of the widely esteemed Professor T. B. Threlkeld at his private academy for boys and, thankfully, a few audacious girls. Colleges across the state clamored for his students, recognizing that much of their work had already been done.

The old man tried his best to fill my head with Latin and classic literature and higher mathematics, but I was a stubborn student who always assumed charm would take me farther than erudition. I secretly suspected my mother chose Threlkeld Select School less for the rigorous academics and more because I would be living under the watchful eye and instruction of Mr. Threlkeld's educated and cultured and nonetheless universally adored wife, Annette, who with her husband paid especial attention to the proper development of each student's manners and character. A tall order, I assure you.

The Threlkelds' son, Logan, and I became fast friends and occasional co-conspirators. We challenged each other on the tennis courts for the school's highest ranking but steered clear of the football field, where one's life was always at risk. We thought too much of ourselves and our futures to play at that game. Logan was by far the superior student, and neither he nor his father ever let me forget it.

I remember the last of Mrs. Threlkeld's annual parties I attended at the Nicholasville Opera House—a mandatory soirée for the students to honor those who had completed their studies. She and Professor Threlkeld stood in their usual spot in a darkened corner, assessing the students' social skills in such a setting. I was waltzing with the beautiful but utterly unattainable Annabelle Shipley, my right hand resting assuredly at the small of her back just beneath her cascade of blond curls, and my left hand pressed lightly against her palm. I spotted the Threlkelds watching us and deftly steered my partner around the other couples toward them.

"What elegance," I heard Mrs. Threlkeld say quietly to her husband. "Mr. Board certainly knows how to carry himself on the dance floor."

The professor watched us a moment and frowned. "Too bad he doesn't bring that grace and precision to Latin class."

"Does he not apply himself to his studies?" his wife asked.

"He seems interested only in polishing his oratorical skills, but has little patience for learning the particular mechanics of the language."

"Ah. Then he'll be a man of some success and esteem."

"Yes, my dear. A fool. A preposterous fool."

I suppressed a smile and led my lovely partner back toward the middle of the floor.

So I was aware I hadn't taken full advantage of the benefits my family's situation had bestowed upon me. When I decided to marry Nell, I knew I needed to shore up my respectability. As if on cue, I was invited to be a partner with Big Four Motors, a new enterprise in Hopewell created to meet the public's growing need for a shiny symbol of a man's success. We planned to sell Chalmers and Oaklands and somehow compete with the Fords and Buicks and Studebakers already being heavily discounted around town. Nell's brother-in-law's family had been in the buggy and automobile business for decades, and they seemed cozy with the Marrs family. I figured this was my ticket into their good graces.

Which brings me to why I wandered over to the Central Garage on Main Street shortly after I got the telegram. I hadn't yet drummed up the funds to purchase that Chalmers roadster I'd been eyeing, and I wasn't too keen on driving my beat-up 1916 Maxwell "Wonder Car" over to Lawrenceburg on this special occasion. It just seemed disrespectful somehow. Besides, I had a better idea.

When I got to the garage, I walked through the small front office to the back bay. As my eyes slowly adjusted to the gloom, the exhilarating aroma of grease and worn rubber and dirty engines took me back to my days at the Gulf station in Louisville, before my involuntary tour of France. I could almost feel my forearms straining as I struggled to release a tire from the wheel rim.

"You gotta put some muscle into it, Lyons," I heard Russell call out to me. I looked over my shoulder and saw his mouth pulled into a wide smile, his dark face slick with motor oil and sweat. He was a big man, strong. He must have found the sight of my back bowed over the wheel, tire iron gripped firmly in my uncallused hand, highly comical.

"Give him a break, Russell," Eddie chimed in. "He spent his formative years making malts and handing out pills. It's gonna take him a while to get hardened to this work. Maybe we can bring him some tea and crumpets to help him get through the day."

They laughed as they leaned back over the engine they were working on. I smiled and shook my head. The ribbing hadn't stopped since I had started working with these fellas. I had found a certain satisfaction in the manual labor and the constancy of the work. The automobile was still an intoxicating novelty for most people, and that allure had initially prompted me to seek employment on the fringes of the industry. But the nuisance of repeated flats and blowouts had made driving a frustrating and sometimes perilous adventure. And the high-pressure clincher tires had an annoying habit of popping off the rims whenever the driver picked up speed. By the time I had begun my ad-hoc apprenticeship in the industry, many owners had found their way to the more reliable Goodyear No-Rim-Cut model, but there was still plenty of business to fill my day.

"How many wheels you got stacked up over there, Lyons?" Russell asked. "You need me to send Eddie over to help you? He ain't doing much here with this engine. I don't think he knows a spark plug from a magneto coil."

"Whoa! You're not demoting me, are you, Russell?" Eddie asked, his eyes wide with mock insult. "Maybe you can bring your 10-year-old in to give Lyons a hand. He might not be much bigger than that wheel, but I bet he could show Lyons a thing or two."

If they gave me a chance, I'd finally try to get in a lick or two. "You two boys need to cut your ragging and get some work done," I said. "Last I checked we had a waiting room full of customers. You want me to go out there and sweet-talk them before they get fighting mad about the delay? I have a few skills it's clear you haven't perfected yet."

And so it went for most of the day. In the middle of our sparkling repartee, a customer might come in carrying a wheel from his Model T abandoned a mile or more down the road. If the wheel appeared undamaged and the tires were still good, I'd pop the tire off the rim, search the inside of the tire for a horseshoe nail or piece of glass, patch or replace the punctured tube, secure the tire back on the wheel, and fully inflate. When I handed the repaired wheel back to the customer, you'd think I'd handed him the golden goose. Occasionally I considered suggesting they carry a tire repair kit with them, but I liked the work too much to reduce my customer volume.

As my eyes finally adjusted inside Johnny's garage back in Hopewell, I looked to my left and saw a big Oakland with all four wheels removed. Glancing to the right, I saw Johnny's lower legs sticking out from under an old Studebaker touring car.

"Hey, Johnny. Is that Doc Hume's Oakland? You waiting on some tires?"

Johnny rolled out from under the car, wiping his hands on a cloth. "Yeah, can't get em until tomorrow afternoon. Can't figure out how that man wears em out so fast."

Most everyone around town knew how the good doctor managed to accomplish that mildly herculean feat, and it wasn't from making house calls. Rumors of the money he wagered on the horses up at Latonia and down on Race Street in Lexington and over at Churchill Downs and Douglas Park in Louisville had circulated for years. He put a lot of miles on that car sneaking out of town for all those heart-pumping demonstrations of equine athleticism while his unsuspecting wife thought he was delivering some poor woman's baby out near North Middletown. But if Johnny hadn't picked up on that, I didn't think it was my responsibility to enlighten him.

"What're you doing here, Lyons?" he asked. "You got a car that needs some work?"

"Nah. I was hoping you could do me a favor, Johnny. Nell had the baby—a girl—and I need to go to Lawrenceburg tonight and face the in-laws. Any chance you'd let me borrow that shiny new vehicle of yours? I thought I might make a better appearance if I showed up in that beauty."

Johnny was still on his back. He stared up at me. "Uhh...I don't think so. It's not that I don't trust you or nothin, Lyons. I'm just not keen on anyone else driving my car. Not yet anyway. I've only had it a couple of months. Let me at least break it in a bit."

I stubbed the toe of my boot at some debris on the concrete floor to give Johnny time to come up with a different answer. "Come on, Johnny. You know I'll take good care of it. I just want to show that I'm up to the task of being a responsible husband and father. A good provider. You know, the whole deal. What do you say? Do an Army buddy a favor."

Johnny looked at me hard. We'd covered for each other since we were in the same unit in France, Johnny doing the dangerous work of running wires right up to the troops at the front and me usually getting to hang back well behind the trenches managing the radio. Ah, the advantages of a fancy education.

"I'm sorry, pal. I'm just not ready to loan it out yet. You're not going over until tonight, are ya? It'll be dark. They won't even see your car. Besides, what does it matter how you get there as long as you're in for the long haul, right?"

Johnny slid back under the car, letting me know the conversation was over.

As I walked back through the office, I noticed Johnny's car key hanging next to the others by the door. Any struggle between my conscience and my larcenous impulse was brief. I grabbed the key and stuffed it in my pocket. I knew the car would still be parked out front later that afternoon. Johnny liked having it at work if he needed to run to Lexington or Maysville for parts—or tires. But there was no need for him to drive it two blocks to his house.

I hesitated just a moment, and then I moved the other Oakland key to the empty peg. If Johnny glanced at the peg on his way out the door that afternoon, he might not sense that anything was amiss. I could repeat the swap early the next morning, and he'd be none the wiser. I'd have my splendid chariot, and he'd have peace of mind.

Later that day, after closing up the dealership just as it got dark, I retraced my steps to the garage and drove off in Johnny's car. Jesse James on the run.

As I continued my cross-country trek, a curious sense of dread began to impede my little caper. The rising trepidation had little to do with taking Johnny's car against his wishes, or even the prospect of making small talk with my in-laws. What was seeping into my con- sciousness—a little belatedly—was the realization that I was heading to Lawrenceburg to meet my firstborn. I was now a father.

Stubborn questions trespassed the barriers I had carefully erected during my nine-month stupor. Did this happy event just upend life as I know it? What are the responsibilities of fatherhood? Am I capa- ble of handling a squalling infant? An exhausted wife? The financial obligations of both? After sacrificing a year of my life waging war for Uncle Sam, I had felt that I deserved a lifetime of peace. Nell, on the other hand, probably deserved more. And I expected she would demand it.

While in France, all us doughboys came face-to-face with how quickly our mother's plans for us could be quashed. I wasn't reck- less enough—or brave enough—to volunteer to be a runner and face death every night, dodging artillery shells and gas attacks in the smoky forests, but I saw the vacant stares of some who had. And that was enough to change a man, even a lout like me. I sometimes won- dered if I hadn't left part of my humanity buried in those rivers of mud. Was I even capable of loving a wife and daughter the way they should be loved? How do you know?

Once I was settled back in Hopewell, I got caught up in the same powerful wave that carries most young men toward a conventional life of marriage, family, and career. It was a relentless force, shrouding me in mildly sinister bourgeois deceit. Within a year, I had asked Nell to marry me, ready or not. Now I was heading west, to reunite our family of three.

Those thoughts pooled in my brain, mixing together like shades of gray on a palette. I felt myself break into an unseemly sweat, despite the October chill. Gripping the steering wheel a little tighter, I looked furtively around the cavernous front seat of the sedan for what was left of Jesse's cavalier insouciance.

I shifted my gaze to the road ahead, trying to focus on where my future was taking me. In an instant, I saw the beam from my headlight glance off something shiny. I instinctively jerked the wheel to the right, just as an approaching car with no headlights buzzed by me, the driver hurtling headlong down the middle of the road like the Headless Horseman. I felt the right wheels of the car slip off the edge of the road and the big sedan drop out from under me with a heart-stopping *thunk*. Before I could get my foot on the brake, the car swiped a gnarled black locust tree beside the road, metal screeching as the sedan's right-side door and the tree's bark vied to occupy the same space. The car lurched to the left, and I was somehow thrown clear like an insentient rag doll when the door latch gave way. As I tumbled into the shallow ditch beside the road, I heard the sickening crunch of metal and a sort of explosion. The ground beneath me seemed to shudder. I managed to wrap my arms around my head, trying to take cover. Then a shameful hissing shattered the night's wounded silence.

After a few moments, I lifted my face from the damp-smelling earth and pulled myself to my knees. I searched the immediate vicinity for crump-holes and tried to assess the human toll of the mortar strike. Instead, tilting my head back, I saw the long shiny nose of the beautiful blue Oakland accordioned against another tree about thirty yards ahead, smoke rising from its radiator signaling surrender.

I dropped back to the ground and lay there, unable to move, Jesse's bravado evaporating in the night air.

Effie Mae
Saturday, December 6, 1941

I pushed myself up from the table, putting one hand on my balky knee as if to shush it from its complaining, and set to fixing supper for Doug and me. I knew there was leftover stew in the main kitchen for the boarders since Lyons was working a special event, but I liked to spoil Doug with a meal just for the two of us when I could. He appreciated a simple meal, and I appreciated his company.

I pulled some ground beef out of the small icebox, along with a coupla eggs and some celery. I found an onion and some stale ends from a loaf of bread in the little cupboard. I dug around until I found the Worcestershire sauce.

As I kneaded the ingredients together in a bowl, I couldn't stop my mind from wandering back to the newspaper clipping. Doug was right. I wasn't going to be able to set it aside and pretend like it'd never happened, as if I'd never seen the birth announcement. Something had changed. I could feel it in my bones. My understanding of who my husband was had shifted. I wasn't sure yet just how much. But I had to figger out how I was going to confront him about it.

Would I learn about a loss he had suffered long ago? Or a marriage that done broke apart for one reason or another?

I knew something about both of those. My marriage to my first husband, Wilson, had ended badly. We had fought like angry jays. As each of our four children come into the world, the strain of keeping us all clothed and fed had set every last nerve he had afire. Each morning he'd board the cart at the mouth of the mine and head 300 feet underground to the blackest part of Hades, where his ears would ring with the sound of the sledgehammers clanging around him as sweat carried the grime into his eyes. And what did he get for enduring that hell? Barely enough to keep his family whole. Sometimes, around the camp, you could just feel the frustration of the hardworking men oozing out of their grit-plugged pores.

When he'd lash out, my redheaded temper would flare. I knew it weren't aimed at us, but I didn't get why we had to bear the brunt of it. The children would retreat as far as they could in that little house, to a cot in the corner or the small patch of grass out back. I'd stand up to him, matching fierce word with fierce word, getting louder and louder. It weren't good for nobody, including the neighbors.

Then one night, he came home with an eerie sense of quiet about him and a grim smile on his face.

"Things are about to change for us," he said.

I remember feeling uneasy. Fearful, even.

"I made arrangements to take a foreman's job up at Benham, where they've held off the union and a man knows if he's gonna have work from one day to the next. I'll make an extra five dollars a week. It's a nice camp up there. All the houses have running water and electricity. Things should be easier for us."

I steadied myself on the arm of the sofa, hoping it would hold my weight. Then I slowly slid onto the threadbare cushion.

I looked hard at him. "What if I don't want their blood money?" I said.

He scowled. "This ain't about you, Effie. This is about the kids. This is about me getting a chance to get a leg up. We can't continue the way things are going. The union promised nearly two years ago that things would get better, that they could convince the operators to pay us a decent wage so we could at least put food on the table. But that ain't happened. And it looks more and more like we're headed toward another strike. Maybe a big one this time. That won't be good for none of us."

I couldn't believe what I was hearing. The mining families in Bell County had always stuck together. Me and Wilson had gotten through a heap a strikes there at Yellow Creek over the last six or seven years. And now he was telling me he was throwing in the towel, going to work in a mine where they had kept the union out?

I tried to suppress the fury rising inside me. I really did. But my blood was curdling as I thought about his betrayal.

"So you're gonna switch sides, just like that?" I asked. "How could you? People have died fighting them operators up in Harlan County. Look what happened to Luther Shipman, just cause he was a union man. And that posse that kilt him was headed by Harlan County officials. What are you thinking going up there to work? You're just gonna become one of em?"

Wilson sat down next to me, a look of defeat crossing his face. "You know how it's been, Effie. During the war, there was so much demand, and the coal companies needed us. So they at least made a showing of working with us, and with the union. But now that the war's over, I can already see how they're going back on their word. It's just gonna get harder. And I can't go through these ups and downs no more. This is an opportunity for a better life, and I'm taking it."

I was quiet a moment. "Did you sign a yellow dog contract? Did you swear off the UMW?"

He didn't have to say nothin. I could tell by the way he hung his head that he had.

"You know the union ain't been able to get a foothold up there at Benham," he finally said. "It wouldn't have mattered whether I signed or not. International Harvester won't never let the union in."

Within a week, I had packed up the kids and moved in with my brother Virgil at the Crystal Coal camp near Logmont, about ten miles west of town. That don't seem that far now, but it felt like the end of the world at the time. The railroad spur from Middlesboro stretched just far enough to reach the camp's coal tipple, where men like my brother could load up their treasure into railroad cars that would take it somewhere that mattered.

It was a tiny camp, with only about seventy-five workers, isolated from everything I'd ever knowed. There weren't no luxuries, like what Wilson had described we'd have over at Benham. This was a new operation, and they was still trying to build up the camp and repair the old structures another coal operator had left behind. Virgil had responded to an ad looking for coal loaders that touted it as a "desirable place to locate." That was our running joke. There weren't nothin desirable about it. But he had a job and we had a leaky roof over our heads.

My brother was a saint. Doug was just three at the time. Valarie was ten, Lee eight, and Eileen six. We was a handful. But the Brady family had always stuck together, and Virgil saw it as his duty to help out. He went from feeding one mouth to feeding six, and his quiet bachelor nights come to an abrupt end.

In the mornings, I'd bundle the three oldest the best I could and send em trooping down to the little schoolhouse. Then Doug and me'd have the place to ourselves. He'd totter around behind me, imitating whatever I was doing. He was a good helper even then.

But we was hungry a lot of the time, and it was all I could do to keep the children properly clothed. During the coldest nights, we'd all pile into the one big bed to try to keep warm. Nobody wanted to get up and tend to the stove.

When the big strike finally come in the fall of '19, Virgil was out of work for three weeks. I ain't never seen times so tough. The Red Cross was feeding people over in Pineville and Middlesboro, but they wouldn't help out the union families—not that they would've made it all the way out to Logmont anyway. Of course, it tore all through me that Wilson was up there at Benham going to work ever day, earning his wages as a foreman. But I wouldn't second-guess my decision.

Mr. John L. Lewis finally called off the strike and the operators reached an agreement with the union. At least where we was, things got a little better. I started to see some relief in Virgil's face. The tightness around his mouth eased some, the creases in his brow began to disappear. He never did say much, so I had to look for signs where I could.

One evening, though, Virgil come home looking more beat down than usual. After I had cleared the few dishes from the supper table and shooed the children to the other room, I had to ask what was up.

"What's going on, Virgil?"

He glanced at me, as if calculating just how much to share.

"Things are getting really ugly up in Harlan County," he started, appearing slightly shocked at the words coming out of his mouth. "Men are talking. Word is that, at the smaller mines, union families are getting turned outta their homes. Those who manage to stick around are learning that the company check-weigh men are cheating on the amount of coal they're giving em credit for. So the wages the union negotiated are getting undercut. Nobody's enforcing the safety rules, and we hear stories nearly ever day about miners getting maimed and killed. I've even heard rumors that company-hired thugs are shooting at workers in broad daylight, but I don't know if I can believe that or not."

It was as if my simple question had opened a floodgate of anger and helplessness. He looked spent from spewing so many words.

I reached over and put my hand gently on his arm. I couldn't summon no speech of my own.

"Is it going to get like that here?" He looked up at me, and I felt his eyes pleading with me. "How long can we stand up to em, Effie?"

I watched him a moment, and then I gave in to a mother's

inclination. "We're going to be fine, Virgil. We are. We always get through these hard times. We'll do this together. Things ain't no worse here, at least for now. We'll just hang on like we always done."

None of them words reassured me, of course. I felt kinda foolish handing him empty hope. But that's what we do when there ain't nothin else to cling to.

As we talked, all I could think of was Wilson cozying up with them operators up at Benham while the union men outside his princely compound was giving up their lives.

I guess at some point Wilson found him another woman, cause he got word to me a few years later that he wanted a divorce. We filed some paperwork and he was out of my life for good.

I shaped the meatloaf in a pan and put it in the oven. I then rummaged around in the icebox until I found the green beans left over from the mess I'd prepared earlier in the week, and I put those on the stove to warm. I'd made some biscuits for breakfast that morning that I thought I could heat up. I figgered that would be enough—especially if there was still a little cobbler to finish off the meal.

I sat down at the table and lit a cigarette, pulling the Fort McHenry souvenir ashtray toward me. My heart felt like it done shrunk to half its normal size. I thought about Lyons and his mysteries. Why did I feel like I had lost something I couldn't never get back when, if I tried to think about it rationally, I had just discovered a stepdaughter I never knew I had? Why had Lyons kept it all such a secret? I tried to muddle through what I did know about this previous marriage of his.

If Lyons had gone through a hard breakup or a divorce that he never wanted to talk about, I reckon I could understand that. Why dredge up the past? I tried to recall if I'd ever asked him directly whether he had any children. Maybe I hadn't. I guess I just assumed it would have come up in conversation if he did. I wondered now how he would have answered that question.

Wilson never come around much after I moved in with Virgil.

Early on he'd try to make his way out there when one of the kids had a birthday, but those visits soon stopped. Maybe Lyons found hisself in a similar situation, where he tried to see his daughter, but his wife or her family made it hard on him. Or maybe his wife moved far away and took the child with her. Maybe that's how he eventually got so estranged from her that he never even mentioned em to me.

I had to admit, I sometimes felt ashamed about how I walked away from my older children a few years after that big strike. But that weren't because I didn't love em. Oh no. Not at all. It's just that they was well on their way to adulthood when I fell into an opportunity for a much better life for me and Doug. And with the two of us gone, Virgil had fewer mouths to feed.

I got up to set the table. I still had about a half hour before the meatloaf would be done, so I went back in the living room and sat in the upholstered rocker by the window. It was just beginning to get dark, and I noticed a few Christmas trees lit up down the street. I pulled the newspaper clipping out of my apron pocket and stared at it.

Lyons
Wednesday, October 26, 1921

I sat on the side of the road, head hung low, wondering what Jesse James would do in this situation. It appeared only my pride and perhaps my joie de vivre were seriously injured, but my pants and overcoat had taken a nasty beating, and I spied my fedora and one boot lying a few feet away. I pulled myself up and brushed away the impertinent mud and dirt the best I could. I then retrieved my other accoutrements and made myself as presentable as possible.

But for whom? It didn't look like I would exchange formal introductions with my daughter tonight after all. Of course, that meant I would also be spared an in-law interrogation. Perhaps driving off in Johnny's car ensured that Saint Christopher would be on a coffee break as I made my journey west. Chances are he was off telling Saint Peter that Lucifer had nabbed him another one.

I doubted too many cars would be traveling this far out of town after dark, so my options seemed few. Short of a *deus ex machina* delivered by an already irritated deity, I resigned myself to a long walk back to Hopewell.

Before I turned toward town, I reluctantly hazarded a glance at Johnny's cherished Oakland. Viewing the car from the rear, which appeared in fine form, I could almost convince myself that it was fully intact. But under a seemingly benevolent starlit sky, I could still see puffs of steam rising near the nose of the car, which had been short-ened by a good two feet. One front wheel had separated itself from the rest of the vehicle and was lying akimbo a few feet away, remind-ing me of my own unruly boot.

When I remembered the roses on the front seat of the car, I couldn't drum up the courage to approach the forlorn wreckage. I was afraid if I got too close its blight might transfer to me, rendering me damaged or inoperable in some way. I could get more roses tomorrow.

My valor untested, I turned to head back to Hopewell. I had only taken a step or two when I saw a flash of headlights coming my way. As the vehicle approached, I averted my eyes from the glare as it mo-mentarily bathed the shiny Oakland in a glorious spotlight, illuminat-ing my sins. Not sure whether I was ready to be center stage in this unfolding drama, I stepped back as the driver slowed to a stop along the edge of the road.

When I looked through the passenger's side window, I couldn't believe my rotten luck. James McWilliams, an in-law of Nell's sister and a legend in Hopewell for his skill cobbling ladies' fine shoes, was behind the wheel. He was probably heading to Lawrenceburg for the same reason I was.

"Lyons, is that you?" James called loudly as he peered through the passenger's window. "Looks like you got yourself into some trouble."

I sighed and walked slowly around to the driver's side, feeling a sharp pain in my hip.

He rolled down the window. "Yeah," I said, "some sonofabitch blew by me with no headlights and ran me right off the road. I was trying to get over to Lawrenceburg to see Nell and the baby."

"Well, that's where I'm headed. Ellen didn't want to come to-night, but I told George I wanted to see how everyone was doing. You wanna ride over with me?"

"I guess that's the best offer I'm going to get. It's getting kind of chilly out here."

I hobbled around the car again, tugged on the door, and climbed carefully into the front seat. James took a closer look.

"You hurt?"

"I don't think so. Not really. I might be a little sore for a day or two."

James put the car in gear and started to ease down the road. He glanced over at the tangled heap of shiny blue metal butted up against the tree.

"That's not your Maxwell, is it? Whose car were you driving?"

I winced. To my mother's chagrin, I had never mastered the art of confession. "It's Johnny Childers', from over at the garage. He let me borrow it to go see Nell. He's going to kill me. It took a good licking."

A half-truth seemed good enough.

James put the car into second. "Looks like it might need some costly repairs. Hope Johnny has some room on his dance card to work on his own car."

I stared out the window into the darkness, the unidentifiable landscape reflecting the blankness of my thoughts. I was afraid if I let the truth gain a foothold, I would see clearly the heap of trouble I was in. We drove in silence for a while, striking each unseen bump in the road with vigor.

A year ago my prospects seemed absurdly promising. To the surprise of nearly everyone who knew her, Nell had agreed to marry me. I played along in the charade, presenting her with a small but arguably handsome ring a jeweler in town had crafted from an antique gold setting that now cradled a tiny diamond. Nell, for her part, played the deferential daughter-in-law, agreeing to wear my mother's ivory silk moiré wedding gown with the heavy strings of pearls cascading across the bodice. The dress probably weighed more than she did, but we felt the goodwill she earned would balance the scale.

Professionally things were looking up, too. I had recently joined

Big Four Motors as a partner and was nicely filling out the mantle of business titan. Deaf to any arguments to take things slow in a fledgling industry that was beginning to show signs of a saturated market, we had plunged headlong into the construction of a two-story garage at High and Eighth streets. The grand opening had been scheduled to take place less than two weeks before the wedding, and my wise partners, recognizing that I was the man who could get all of Hopewell focused on our big gamble, put me in charge of planning the parade of new Chalmers and Oaklands down Main Street. To make sure no one missed the procession, I had even arranged to have a favorite jazz band—Johnny Hamp's Kentucky Serenaders—leading the way. We were convinced we had reason to celebrate, blind to the recession that was just around the corner racing to catch the tail end of our little parade.

I was even beginning to get the hang of civilian life again, as all these other distractions slowly suppressed the worst of my memories. In this shiny new decade, gas attacks and muddy trenches and unyielding boredom had no sovereignty. America was getting back to its own business.

And yet, here I was, just one short year later, losing the grip on my natural good cheer.

My thoughts shifted back to my current dilemma. "Do you think we can avoid telling Nell's family about my little accident tonight?" I asked James. "Let's just say you mentioned you wanted to stop by to see the baby, and we decided to drive together. That also gives me reason to get back to Hopewell tonight, so I can be at Johnny's first thing in the morning before he shows up at the garage and discovers his car is missing."

James glanced over at me. "Then how are you going to explain the condition of your clothes?"

I had momentarily forgotten about that. Nell knew I was

particular about my habiliments and I would never show up at her family's home with muddy britches.

"Oh, right." I factored in that variable. "Then I guess I'd better say I had some car trouble on the way over, and I had to get on the ground to take a look. Nell knows I love to tinker with that old car, so that story should pass muster."

"So why weren't you driving your Maxwell? That's still the car you have, right, the one you bought from J. P. and George?"

"Yeah. It needs a little work, and I wasn't sure I wanted to drive it all the way to Lawrenceburg at night. So I convinced Johnny to let me borrow his new Oakland." Nothing like reinforcing a white lie.

After another forty minutes, we pulled in front of the two-story white frame home on Woodford Street—the perfect backdrop for the upcoming scrutiny of my imperfections. The house was lit up, so I knew it would be full of well-wishers and curiosity-seekers. Nell's coldly elegant younger sister, Lydia, would certainly be there, as would her husband, the taciturn and mildly grumpy George. And, of course, Robert and Rosalie Marrs, Nell's parents, who had been taking care of her with the fierceness of a mama bear as they nervously awaited their first grandchild. And a couple of neighbors with nothing better to do might have arrived for a meal and a show. I imagine the one thing Nell needed most—a good nap—had been hard to come by.

The house was a few blocks east of Main Street in a section of town commonly referred to as Merchants Row, since many of the town's proprietors—some well-respected, some well-tolerated—made their homes there. Robert Marrs owned the hardware store on Main Street. J. P. McWilliams and his son, George, Lydia's husband, had the Maxwell dealership just up the street.

In a town of fewer than two thousand residents, everyone's business seemed intertwined, from the former bourbon barons still living in the mansions along Main Street to the clerks selling nuts and bolts.

From what Nell had told me, adults socialized together and children played together, with little thought of who owed whom.

As I sat in the car, my brain's directions to my recalcitrant limbs being steadfastly ignored, I realized that I was now even more inextricably tied to this family, a family in many ways just like my own. Nell and I were parents. We had a child to raise. This is the social contract my mother long hoped I would fumble into. Although I'm sure I disappointed her by not becoming a lawyer or a judge or a real estate developer or a bourbon tycoon like my cousins, at least I had married into an upstanding family and become a businessman like my father. And now we had given her a grandchild.

But that smug mirage lasted only a moment before reality booted it to the curb. For here I was, covered in mud, fabricating stories about how I got that way, incurious about my new daughter, and having no idea how I was going to face my wife.

James stood patiently on the sidewalk, waiting for me to join him, a solid bulwark against what was beginning to feel like impending doom. Although I had been annoyed at his discovery of my embarrassing misadventure, I was now grateful for his presence. His gentle demeanor seemed to relay some comfort, or some recognition of the way life can occasionally drop you to your knees. I took a deep breath and heaved my aching carcass out of the car.

I stood just a minute, feeling the sharp October air fill my lungs and clear my head as I braced for the awaiting congregation. By the time we had climbed the steps to the porch, Rosalie was smiling at us and pushing the door open.

"Oh, Lyons, come in, dear. You have a beautiful baby girl. She even has your dark hair."

I gave her a quick peck on the cheek. Even under these circumstances, she appeared refined, in control, warm but somehow reserved.

"Hello, Rosalie. How's Nell?"

She started to answer, but then stepped back and eyed me up and down.

"What happened to you?"

I didn't hesitate. "I had a little car trouble on my way over. I tried to make the repairs myself, but, thankfully, James rescued me."

"James, ever the Good Samaritan, I see," she said as he came in behind me. "Robert and J. P. and George are in the parlor if you want to get their take on the day's events. I think they're ready for some new diversion. There may even be a little celebratory bourbon flowing in there, though I can't say I know where they got it. I'll have some supper ready for us in just a few minutes."

"You're always the gracious hostess, Rosalie," said James. "I'm glad to hear all is well with your new grandbaby. Congratulations. I think Ellen may try to get over here on Friday. She had a couple of things on her calendar."

"That would be fine, James. You tell her we'd love to see her."

James disappeared into the parlor and Rosalie took my arm, steering me like a lost puppy toward the back bedroom. At that moment, a piercing wail came through the door.

"Uh-oh. Sounds like you've arrived at feeding time," said Rosalie. "That probably woke up Nell if she was dozing at all. She had a pretty rough go of it, but everything seems to be fine. Let me see if I can't help her get the baby feeding before you go in."

Rosalie hurried into the room while I waited dumbly outside the door as the baby continued to scream. When the wailing subsided, I heard low voices.

"Lyons?"

That was Nell. I softly pushed open the door. Nell was propped up in bed, looking even more tiny and frail than usual, with the newborn pressed against her breast. She smiled when she saw me, but I could see the exhaustion etched in her face.

I stood at her side grinning mutely. I scooted close to the bed, hoping she wouldn't notice the condition of my boots and trousers. When I heard Rosalie leave the room, I reached over and gently stroked Nell's hair.

"How are you doing? I hear this little thing couldn't decide if she really wanted to leave her cozy sanctuary."

"Well, it's over now," said Nell, ever pragmatic. "Look at her. It's almost too much to comprehend. She's beautiful, isn't she?"

"She sure is. Just like her mother." Damn, if only I had those roses to present to her with a dramatic flourish. That might have earned me a few points. "I hear she has my dark hair." I tugged on the blanket swaddling the baby just enough to ascertain that that was indeed the case.

"And your blue eyes," added Nell. "Let's just hope she hasn't inherited your charm. I'm not sure I would survive her teen years."

I smiled. "I expect she got your intelligence. And your stubbornness. With those two traits, she can rule the world."

"Looks and smarts. That sounds like a dangerous combination. Are we agreed on a name yet? I'm still thinking Mary Rose, after our mothers. What do you think?"

"Hello, Mary Rose," I said quietly, trying to still the quaver in my voice. A name seemed to solidify the reality of this chimera. "It's perfect."

We sat in silence a moment while the baby continued to suckle. When she had had her fill, Nell cradled her in her arms so I could get a better look. "Do you want to hold her?"

I involuntarily recoiled. Throughout this exchange, I had felt as if I were standing apart from the whole scene, simply an admirer of this Madonna and child. How did I fit into this? What role did I play? I desperately tried to plumb my heart, seeking a full reckoning of my feelings for this new member of my family.

"I'm going to let the two of you bond a little longer," I finally said. "You did all the work. You deserve the reward."

Coward, I said to myself.

"Well, I'm glad you're here," said Nell. She looked down at the baby. "Here's your daddy, Mary Rose."

I struggled to hold back a shudder.

"Look at her," cooed Nell. "There will be no mistaking who her daddy is."

The void I was feeling threatened to swallow me whole. I felt unchanged. Largely unmoved. My affection and tenderness for Nell were intact. And I recognized an inchoate sense of protectiveness for Mary Rose. But I thought I should be dissolving into a puddle of messy infatuation, bewitched by this tiny being, this pint-size mirror of myself.

And I wasn't.

To calm my increasing befuddlement, I shifted the conversation to business matters relating to the new arrival.

"Do you know when you two will be able to come home?" I asked.

"I'm not sure. Mother thinks I should rest a few days. She'd probably keep me here a month if she could. We may just need to see how it goes. I'll want to have the baby checked out again before I leave. Are you in a rush for us to get back to Hopewell? Do you miss my cooking?"

"Well, that's a given, of course. Eating like a bachelor again has been humbling. I really should pay more attention to the magic you conjure in the kitchen. But I'm in no rush. You take all the time you need. There are a few things I still need to do to get ready for the baby ... for Mary Rose."

I smiled, trying to relay a composure I didn't feel. I was supposed to be the commander, leading my troops into battle, disguising any trepidation about the mission or its toll. It was my job to soothe Nell, to reassure her that everything would be OK, that I was prepared for whatever lay ahead. But I sensed that she was the one who had everything under control. Much like her mother. I, on the other hand, was inwardly a wreck. Just like that car.

That damn car. I'd nearly forgotten about it as I was trying to figure out how to navigate this new situation. The longer Nell stayed in Lawrenceburg, the more time I'd have to straighten out that mess. Plus, Mother would surely arrive in Hopewell tomorrow, eager to see her first grandchild. Would she expect to stay with me, or would she choose to stay with her friends or cousins as she sometimes did? There was another wrinkle I needed to smooth out.

Momentarily Nell appeared to drift into a quiet slumber. I stared at the two, my emotions a jumble of contradictions. They seemed so peaceful, so at ease. What was I getting all worked up about? The vast majority of men have been fathers, raised children, survived it all with only a few battle scars. Surely I had the pluck to see this through.

After a few minutes, I got up and headed toward the parlor. Loud voices and cigar smoke emanated from the room.

"There he is. There's the new father," crowed J. P. as he approached with a cigar in one hand and slapped me on the back with the other. A longtime mayor in the city—a position he politely purchased by greasing the palms of loyal business partners—J. P. carried considerable weight around town on his slight, six-foot frame. I had the sense that those who didn't loathe him feared him.

Robert Marrs handed me a small glass of bourbon. "Congratulations, my boy," he said quietly. "You have one fine-looking daughter. I'm relying on you to take good care of her."

I nodded at the men. The events of the evening had left me in a state of utter confusion, and for one of the few times in my life I was at a loss for words.

I raised the bourbon to my nose and inhaled its woody scent, immediately feeling a hopeful sense of calm. I took a sip and allowed its warmth to burn my throat, singeing any words of protest I wanted to utter. Prohibition may have dented the livelihoods of the local bourbon magnates, but good old Irish-American ingenuity made sure the soothing spirit was still available—at least in a medicinal form, for those suffering from ailments typically unnamed but largely suspected to be thirst or boredom or overwork or, perhaps in my case, dread.

I waved off a cigar and took a seat in a nearby armchair, sensing the growing stiffness from my tumble earlier that evening.

"So, James tells me you're having a little trouble with that fine Maxwell I sold you a couple of years ago," said J. P. "Bring her in and I'll let my boys take a look at her."

I felt a prickly sensation wriggle up the back of my neck. Was it the bourbon, or a natural reaction to the smell of imminent danger?

"I think I can handle it, Mr. McWilliams. I've ordered a new back axle and I'm looking forward to getting my hands dirty."

"You bought that used, right?"

"Yes, sir. It's a 1916."

"Well, these Maxwells are standing the test of time. I'm real pleased George and I decided to take a chance on them. In fact, looks like Maxwell Motor Company is about to swallow up those Chalmers you've been selling over in Hopewell."

I felt my face redden. There was no doubt that J. P. had built a successful business, on both ambition and luck, but I secretly wondered what that success had cost him. Nell had told me that when he first came to Lawrenceburg as a tough-talking teenager, he apprenticed with his future father-in-law as a harness maker. He eventually brokered a humdinger of a deal by purchasing the buggy shop and marrying the man's daughter, Katie, to boot. Katie was a catch, but it was hard to tell whether it had been a marriage of opportunity or genuine affection for J. P., a man who many would say had never loved anyone but himself.

"It does sound like that might happen," I finally said. "But that's no surprise. Maxwell's been managing the Chalmers operations since we got into the war.

"Oakland sales are going strong, though," I added, "especially that new Sensible Six Sedan. The true blue color is hot right now." I took another sip of bourbon, trying hard to erase the image of Johnny's car wrapped around that tree.

"This damned recession has hit us all hard," said J. P. "Looks to me though like Harding is going to get this thing turned around. We've got Hoover over at Commerce and Mellon heading up Treasury. That sounds like a winning team to me."

I sneered, I hoped imperceptibly. Andrew Mellon had profited spectacularly from the war, and he was certain to find a way to profit from the recovery.

"You're a bit more optimistic than I'm feeling right now, J. P.," said Robert. "I had to let one more clerk go last week. I think they're calling this a depression now and I can't wait for it to ease up. The farmers are really suffering, and around here that hurts us all."

"Well, this whole thing is all because of young bucks like Lyons here," said J. P. That prickly sensation crept back down my spine, settling comfortably amid the pain in my hip.

"All these service heroes swarmed back home in 1919 expecting to find jobs," he continued. "We'd been living high while you boys were gone, working to provide you with food and vehicles and equipment and munitions. Thank goodness the Selective Service determined that George was needed here to keep our business going."

George looked sternly at his father but didn't say a word.

You miserable sonofabitch, I thought. You, too, managed to make a buck off my sacrifice. I was one of the lucky ones. I got to come home. But I got the sense he would have preferred to leave more corpses on those muddy fields to protect his profits.

Whether out of fatigue or uncharacteristic restraint, I decided not to take the bait. I looked down at my glass and, after a brief hesitation, took a rather generous gulp.

James stepped in, perhaps sensing that I was in no condition to defend myself. "Now, J. P., you know there were a lot of other factors at work in this downturn—rising interest rates, crashing commodity prices, nervous investors..."

"Yeah, my stock values have dropped nearly 50 percent. This had better turn around soon or we'll all be sunk."

Rosalie peered in the door and let us know the ladies had supper ready. I was relieved to see this discussion careen to a halt. The financial troubles at Big Four Motors were bigger than anyone else in the room knew, and I was in no condition to think about that this evening. As the intoxicating smell of Rosalie's creamy leek soup wafted through the open door, gently resting on the pillow of cigar smoke, I was surprised to discover that the evening's misadventures had not completely extinguished my appetite. I pulled myself gingerly to my feet and slowly followed the other men into the dining room.

Effie Mae
Saturday, December 6, 1941

Doug showed up in the kitchen, a little bleary-eyed from a nap, just as I took the meatloaf out of the oven. He got us a coupla bottles of Schlitz from the icebox. I put out my cigarette as we both sat down at the table.

"How many more cold ones we got in there?" I asked. "I may need more than one tonight."

Doug took a long pull on his beer and set it on the table. "You got a plan yet?"

"No. I cain't seem to focus. One minute I'm furious, the next I'm heartsick, then I'm furious again."

I stopped to catch my breath. "Mostly I'm just numb. And maybe a bit curious. My mind's been wandering all over the place. Instead of concentrating on this marriage Lyons never told me about, I've been recollecting my own. There ain't much to be proud about there neither. I was just thinking about when we lived with your Uncle Virgil up in Logmont. You remember them days?"

"Not too much. I remember running up and down the dirt road with some of the other kids. And always looking around the table for more to eat. We didn't have meals like this back then."

"Yeah, things was pretty scarce. I remember sometimes for breakfast I'd fix what we used to call water gravy: water and a little hog fat and some flour. If we had beans on the table we felt like we was living like kings. Sometimes I wonder how we all survived."

I looked at my plate and realized I couldn't eat a thing. I took a sip of beer. "Was you about ten when we moved to Cincinnati?" I asked.

"Yeah. I'd started school up in Logmont."

"What do you remember about Frank?"

Doug shoveled a coupla forks of food in his mouth. "I remember he was good to me. And to you. I remember being able to celebrate Christmas for the first time. We even had presents. I remember going to the department store in Cincinnati to see the model trains. I reckon I knew then it was too good to last."

It was early 1926 when I first laid eyes on Frank. I was in my late thirties, seemingly stuck in that godforsaken place. The Crystal Coal operation in Logmont was struggling, and the company officials was looking for a fast fix or a way out. As I come out of the company store one day, I saw a large man I ain't never seen around the camp before heading across the street. He was walking with confidence, like he had a purpose, not hunched over like he was used to being underground all day. And he was dressed in ordinary clothes, not the gray tattered uniforms of the miners. He held himself erect, hat firmly on his head.

Out of curiosity, or just plain boredom, I followed him a short way until he headed into the main office. It was late March, as I recall, and the sun had finally risen above the Cumberland Mountains. I found a spot in the sun's warmth and just stood there, staring at the door he had entered. I don't remember having no clear intentions. It was as if I was hypnotized by the warmth and the sight of a stranger.

When the man popped back out the door, I didn't have the good sense to turn right around and walk away. He saw me staring, tipped his hat, and headed up the street, in the other direction. Then, suddenly, he stopped, turned around, and come back toward me.

I didn't know what to do. Wilson always told me it was my eyes that done stopped him in his tracks. Sometimes I think my inner fire must leak out under my eyelashes when I least intend it.

"Pardon me, ma'am," he started. "Is there anywhere other than the company store here to get a bite to eat?"

I couldn't think of nothin to say. Here I was, a mother of four, tongue-tied with my heart leaping outta my chest.

"I don't rightly know," I stammered, "unless Aunt Mike's cooking up some beans and cornbread over at her boardinghouse by the bath house. She sometimes will sell ya a plate for five cents, if you've got the money. Most of us here don't have nothin but scrip though. It's only good at the company store, you know."

I rambled on, unable to stop myself. He just smiled, seemingly fancying how flustered I was.

"Well, since I don't know my way around, would you be willing to accompany me? I'll buy you an early lunch if we can come up with some grub."

I'm sure I blushed. Lord knows why. I didn't take no notice of the warning bells going off in my head. Them bells telling me that this man was dressed like a businessman and might be up to no good, for instance. That he might be a spy of some sort, trying to ingratiate hisself with us union folk. It was hard to tell what he was up to.

But I'd lost all sense, and I couldn't do nothin but nod and accept his offer.

Turns out he did buy me lunch and we had a long conversation. It felt good to talk to someone other than Virgil or the kids or the desperate wives in the camp. I learned his name was Frank Foster and he worked as a railroad detective. That poor man had been sent to the end of the rails, all the way up to Logmont, to look into how some of the coal freight up there kept going missing. I expect he'd made a few enemies already around the camp, so maybe I presented a friendly face. I didn't let on that some of the families up there would've froze to death if their children wasn't picking up scraps of coal along the rail line and near the tipple. Crystal Coal seemed to operate under the idea that the strong would survive, and there would always be just enough workers to get that black gold out of the mountain. I probably knew the fella orchestrating the bigger theft, too, but I wasn't going to be the one to rat him out. That was Frank's business to dig into, and I didn't pry too much. I lost my first husband cause I got too riled up about his business and which side he was on. I didn't even know this man. I just told myself he was working for the railroad, and they had their own interests to protect.

We sat in the cramped dining room of the boardinghouse, four mismatched tables practically pressed up against each other. We was there before any of the others would come in for lunch, so we had the room to ourselves. One little window on the east side let in a few rays of sunlight. Cozy smells of onions and greens and vinegar filled the room.

I could've listened to him talk all day. He had been places and seen things. I'd never been out of Bell County, but he could tell me about Nashville and Cincinnati and Louisville and Memphis. He'd even been to Atlanta and Birmingham. I could barely even imagine those places.

He told me just a little about his work, about the thieves and the vagrants he had to deal with. You could see by the way he carried hisself that he could be a tough guy when he needed to, but he seemed surprisingly soft-spoken as we chatted. He talked about working in northern Kentucky about ten years before when several railroad dicks had been kilt in separate incidents in the rail yards across from the Coney Island amusement park. I think he was testing me when he described one gruesome incident where a young detective was sent to that area and ended up being bludgeoned from behind with a pickax. The attacker then dragged the body across the tracks and rolled it down a cinder embankment. It was found the next day by a coupla teenage boys heading to the river for a swim. I didn't flinch though. I'd heard worse.

Frank seemed resigned to the dangers involved. I suspected he was pretty good at taking care of hisself. I also got the sense he was lonely. His work had him traveling all the time and he hadn't had a chance to think about settling down again since his wife had died about four years before. He seemed to like having a willing ear for his stories. I told him just a little about my family and how we ended up in Logmont. But mostly I just wanted to listen to his soothing, matter-of-fact voice. He made me feel like he could be in control of a situation no matter what sort of chaos was erupting around him.

We finished our soup beans and reluctantly got up from the table. He paid our meager bill and I winked at Aunt Mike as we headed toward the door. It bothered me that I was in a ratty old house dress and a hand-knit sweater with a big stain on it. But he didn't seem to notice.

Back out on the street he turned to me and said, "Mrs. Noble, if ever I'm back here in Logmont I hope our paths cross again. You have been delightful company. Thank you again for your hospitality." And then he quickly bowed his head before heading back up the street.

I thought I'd done died and gone to heaven. Granted, I didn't really think I'd ever see that man again, but that was more attention than I'd been paid in years. My head was full of the tales he told, and that alone was going to give me something else to study on besides the dreary day-to-day here at the camp.

I practically skipped back to our little ramshackle house. I had a rare burst of energy when I got inside, and I busied myself with chores I had put off for days.

When the two yougest got home from school later that afternoon, they could tell something had changed. I saw them steal glances at me as they settled in for an early supper. Finally, Eileen, the one with the mouth, couldn't stand it no longer.

"Mama? What's going on? Why are you smiling?"

"It's none of your business," I told her. "Come over here and help me find some clean bowls for this broth."

Of course, Frank did come back. It was never clear to me whether he had more business in Logmont, or whether he just decided to seek me out. Don't really matter, I guess. We couldn't do any traditional courting in that hellhole, but we fairly quickly decided we wanted to be together. I don't know what he saw in a poor old divorcée like me, but I sure was grateful. I think we gave each other life. I think that's what it was.

Right about the time we decided we was going to get hitched, he showed up from Middlesboro one warm summer evening with a long look on his face.

"What's the matter?" I asked, fear filling my heart. I shooed Eileen off the dirty front porch and waved for him to sit down on the step.

"I've been offered a job up in Cincinnati. I'll actually be working at several rail yards up there: B&O, C&O, and Penn, as well as L&N across the river. It's a bit of a promotion, and I don't see that I have much choice but to take it."

I held my tongue. I wasn't sure just yet what this meant for me.

Frank took my hand. "Would you be willing to move to the big city with me, Effie Mae? I know all your people are here in Bell County, and you're awfully close to them. It wouldn't be that hard to come back and visit. Cincinnati to Middlesboro is an easy trip, with brief stops in Hopewell and Corbin and a couple of towns in between. It's just a few hours on the train."

My heart was beating so fast I was certain he could feel it in my fingertips. My first thought was, *You know I'd follow you anywhere.* But I didn't say it out loud. Not yet. Which was probably a good thing because—and I'm ashamed to admit this—it took a few seconds for my second thought to find its way through the electrical storm in my brain. What about all them kids?

Could I cart four kids up to Cincinnati? Uproot em from their home, such as it was? My oldest son, Lee, had already started working as a loader with Virgil, even though he was only fifteen. Valarie was seventeen and had a steady boyfriend. I expected she'd be married soon. I doubted she would want to leave. And my guess was that Eileen wouldn't go nowhere without Valarie.

Frank was looking at me with such intensity that I almost laughed. He was a big man, all of six feet tall, broad through the chest and shoulders. But he seemed surprisingly vulnerable as he waited for my response.

"What about the kids?" I finally asked. I wasn't sure I wanted to hear his response. I wasn't sure I knew what the right answer was.

"We can load em all up and take em with us, if they want to come," Frank said.

I felt immense relief. That was the answer I needed. I knew it when I heard it. He was embracing all of us, whatever challenges that presented for him. I reached over and gave him a hug. I didn't want to let go, but Lee came out on the porch about that time.

"What's up?" he asked. "Eileen said there was some big pow-wow going on out here."

"Frank's job is taking him up to Cincinnati. He's inviting us all to go with him."

Lee stared at us, peering in one face and then the other. "That's mighty kind of you, Frank. But I've already started building a life here. I don't know nothin but these hills. I cain't even imagine living in a city."

"Well, the invitation is open, if you change your mind," Frank said. "I'll look for a place up there next week that will hold us all if we need it to." He smiled broadly. I could see he had started to relax.

"Lee, round up the others and let's see what they think," I said. "If you stay, I doubt I can pry Valarie away from that Donaldson boy. You two could look out for each other. Eileen and Doug might want to stick with Mommy though. Virgil certainly don't need to take care of all of you by hisself."

"Virgil and I can look after anyone who stays here," said Lee, standing up straighter and deepening his voice. "And we can always rely on Miss Lily next door if the girls need some help. We'll be OK."

It took a few days of hard conversations and some tears all around before we had our plan. Frank and me would take Doug to Cincinnati with us. He was reluctant to leave his brother and sisters at first, but he has my sense of adventure, so after Frank talked to him a bit about the size of the rail yards in Cincinnati and the skyscrapers downtown and the mighty Ohio, he was fully on board.

Eileen was the surprise. One morning as I was washing up after breakfast she sneaked up behind me.

"Mama, I done decided to stay here with Lee and Valarie. I like it here. I got friends at school. And I don't wanna leave."

I turned around and searched her face, trying to hide my own fear. "But, honey, you're only thirteen. Don't you think you'd better come with us?" I realized for the first time that I was looking up at her, that she had done outgrown me.

I saw her set her mouth. She flicked her thin brown hair over her shoulder and threw out her chest, which I noticed was more ample than it had been earlier that summer. "I ain't going. You cain't make me. I'll be just fine here."

This was my baby girl. I couldn't imagine leaving her behind. Surely she still needed her mama. But perhaps I just wanted to mother her. I could see that she was growing up. And I reckon she was just about that age where she needed to assert her independence. I wanted to fight her, but after a few words I realized I was only making things worse.

"Well," I finally said, "you know Frank said you can move up to Cincinnati with us any time you want if you change your mind. We'll get you right on that train and you'll be there in no time. You just let us know. I cain't hardly bear to leave you behind, honey, but I guess you're right. I cain't make you go."

Later that summer, me and Frank stood before the preacher and then boarded a train with Doug for our first ever trip outside the Kentucky mountains. We had no idea what awaited us.

Lyons

Thursday, October 27, 1921

I was sitting on the step in front of the door to the Central Garage smoking a cigarette, trying to mollify my nerves, when I looked up and saw Johnny walking down the street. It was a crisp fall morning and the sun was just beginning to cast away the early darkness. I had realized when I first got out of bed that my normally hearty constitution was AWOL, replaced instead with a weak-kneed, lily-livered, ill-humored sack o' bones. How much of that was attributable to my unrehearsed pratfall the night before and how much to my imminent engagement with Johnny Childers was hard to distinguish. But as I slowly dressed, wincing as I twisted to slide the other arm into my shirt sleeve, even the prospect of nibbling on a plain piece of toast threatened convulsions of protest. Wisely, I left my cup of coffee unfinished on the kitchen table.

As I sat on the stoop waiting for Johnny, I tried to imagine how I could extract a pleasant outcome from this little tête-à-tête. Many people in town gave Johnny a wide berth, a nod to his somewhat legendary pugnaciousness. I, on the other hand, recognized that his short fuse usually reflected his intolerance for fools or his refusal to accept unfair treatment as a matter of course. He felt he had proven himself on the battlefield, and there's no question he had. Few others in our unit had displayed his instinctive courage or ability to make the right decision under impossible conditions. I admired him, and I respected him.

But I had also taken advantage of him, and there would be a price to pay.

As I watched Johnny approach the garage, I happened to catch the moment of recognition, when his face changed from an indeterminate early morning fog to a pinched look of surprise. I could feel his heart drop into his stomach as his pace quickened. I put out my cigarette and stood up, bracing for the attack.

"Where's my car?" Johnny shouted when he was still about thirty yards away. "What did you do, Lyons?"

I straightened my coat as I stood up, and pressed my hat more firmly on my head.

In the moment, I decided to play it straight. Maybe my mother's admonishments had been right. Maybe a full-throated confession would spur Johnny toward leniency.

"I messed up, Johnny. I messed up big time," I began.

Johnny's eyes burned. He was a bit shorter than I was and squarely built. He stopped just in front of me and glared.

"What? What did you do?"

I steadied myself. "I took your car when I went to Lawrenceburg last night. I know you told me not to. But I didn't think you'd really care. And I planned to have it right back here by 10 o'clock. You never would have known."

"What do you mean you took my car? Did you hot-wire it?"

"No." I hesitated. "I saw the key hanging by the door as I left yesterday afternoon. I just slipped it in my pocket." I paused again. "I guess it's still in the ignition."

Johnny's face reddened. "What happened?" he demanded. "Where's my car?"

I tried to put my hand on Johnny's shoulder, but he knocked it off. "Just tell me, goddammit."

"It's on the side of the road, about eight miles west of town. It wasn't my fault, Johnny. A car came hurtling down the middle of the road and I snapped the steering wheel hard to avoid it. Your car slipped off the edge of the road." I couldn't go on. I could sense the archangels crowding around me, hands on hips, waiting to see how I would try to wheedle out of this one.

"How bad is it, Lyons?"

I couldn't look at him. "It's pretty bad. I got thrown out and the car smashed into a tree out there near the Shropshire place. I've already talked to Glenn and he's going to tow it in to town."

I saw Johnny tighten his fist, but I couldn't dodge it quick enough. I thought later that perhaps I had momentarily felt that a man should stand firm and take his punishment, that whatever Johnny doled out was a simple down payment on what I owed him. He caught me square in the left jaw, and I twirled on my heels before doubling over, my hand to my face, my hat on the ground in front of me. I felt Johnny push past me, open the door to the garage, and slam it behind him.

When the first blast of pain subsided, I picked up my hat and slowly straightened up. I shifted my lower jaw back and forth, then ran my tongue around the inside of my mouth to see if my teeth were all in their proper place. Everything seemed in order. It was a pretty good blow, but thankfully it didn't appear to have broken anything. I could only hope that the bruising or swelling wouldn't be too noticeable. I had already told Harlan I was taking the day off so I could meet my mother at the depot and take her to Lawrenceburg, but I still expected to see a lot of people who would want an explanation if my face looked like it had been inexpertly tenderized.

After a few moments, when it was clear Johnny wasn't interested in further negotiations, I turned up Main Street, then cut across Sixth heading toward home. Mother's train would arrive at 10:40, so I still had a little time to recover my composure and my good looks.

Back in the summer, Nell and I had moved from Mt. Airy Avenue, near where I had grown up, to a little house on Vine Street on the other side of town. It wasn't necessarily a step up; it was more like a step away. I was ready to leave behind the neighborhood where Mother and I had watched my father's decline, both from the rooms of her home at Houston and Second Street and at nearby Massie Memorial Hospital. I also had to admit that I was relieved I no longer needed to cross the Second Street bridge when heading from home to work and back again. Even though the incident on the bridge was a long time ago—I had only been eight years old—its aftermath still haunted me. I had no interest in riling any ghosts. And I hoped none wanted to exact revenge on me.

Nearly to Vine Street, I took my time walking past the handsome homes along Duncan Avenue as the morning sun filtered through the massive maple trees, enveloping the scene in golden light. I felt myself breathing deeply. The homes ranged from Italianate, brick with finely detailed white trim and broad lawns, to Romanesque, with stone pillars, arched porches, broad windows, and whimsical turrets. Whereas early Lawrenceburg families had discovered the local rivers were the resource they could mine to distill distinctive spirits and amass fortunes, settlers in Hopewell discovered rich agricultural land that was particularly salubrious for raising Thoroughbreds, a growing industry that was making a very few very rich. There might not have been gold in these parts, but it was another type of rock—the natural limestone lining the rivers and underlying the fields—that was helping fill the pockets of the region's mild-mannered robber barons.

Whatever the sources of the residents' money, I found the peculiarities of the street intriguing. In a moment, when I turned the corner onto Vine Street, I'd be back among the white clapboard houses more typical of Hopewell dwellings, all unquestionably satisfactory for the rest of us. But for a moment or two, I could imagine myself as a racehorse breeder or railroad magnate, sitting comfortably in my wood-paneled library behind the solid walls of one of these expansive homes.

I checked my watch as I stepped on the small front porch of our home. I had a little over an hour before I had to be at the station. As I closed the door behind me in the comfortable front room, I looked around with an eye for how Mother or Nell might assess my house-keeping skills. I wanted to straighten up a bit, but I first went to the icebox and chipped some ice into a dish towel. I then collapsed on the sofa, ice to jaw, and tried to map out the day.

Since it was such a beautiful morning, I decided to walk the short distance to the train station to meet my mother. It was my under-standing that she planned to stay only until Sunday, so her small va-lise shouldn't require a motorized pack mule. I expected she would welcome the brief walk back to the house, where she could rest for a while before we got back on the road. Despite the story I had told last night, I felt fairly confident the Maxwell would get us to Lawrence-burg without trouble. It did need some routine repairs, but there had been no signs of an impending breakdown. Once at the Marrs home, we could play it by ear and see how long we should stay.

I tried to think back to the brief interaction with Nell the night before, and to what lay ahead. Of course, I'd had the standard issue amount of time to prepare for fatherhood, but I'd been so busy tak-ing care of my business responsibilities that I hadn't fully considered the potential complications of a tiny termagant storming our castle's walls and impatiently barking orders. What else should I have been doing to plan for this assault? As the day of reckoning approached, I had watched from afar as Nell handled the pregnancy in her usual soldierly way. Nothing seemed to flummox her—not the temporary sickness, not her growing girth, not the physical awkwardness during the late stages. She had been at the center of a social frenzy, as her many friends in Hopewell threw her one party after another. In many ways, all of that seemed remote to me, as if I had been a shell-shocked bystander.

But now it was real. The baby was here, and it was time for me to buck up. My parenting savvy, however, had already proven to be akin to my familiarity with china patterns.

"Do we have a piece of furniture we could move into the nursery for a changing table?" Nell asked about a month before the baby arrived, as we tried to prepare the small back bedroom for the new arrival. The room already boasted my crib, which my mother had stored with a relative for just such a propitious occasion, and a beautiful bentwood rocker that Nell's family had loaned to us. Diapers and other mysterious paraphernalia were stacked neatly on a shelf.

I stared at her with the blankness of a vast snow field. "A what?" I asked, with both genuine innocence and poorly masked annoyance.

She stared back without changing her expression. There was work to do, after all. If I couldn't step up to the plate, I needed to move aside and let the experts go to bat.

"We'll need a sturdy place to change the baby's diapers," she said. "With a broad enough surface that I can safely lay the baby down, and preferably at a height where I don't have to bend over too much." She moved toward a blank wall. "We could put something here, I think. Do we have a spare chest of drawers or a table that would work?"

I had no response. I tried to recall the stories that Jamie Day, the youngest partner at Big Four Motors, had shared about the birth of his son barely a year before and what it was like adjusting to being a new father. He seemed to have taken it all with good humor. Perhaps I should have paid more attention to his rather elaborate and most often tedious stories. But, at the time, they seemed to have no connection to me. And, quite frankly, I hadn't been interested.

I shifted the ice on my jaw and thought about my mother and the two children she had lost when they were infants before I had been born. I always had the sense that she had never fully gotten past that sorrow, and that she somehow expected me to fulfill her hopes for all three of her sons. That was a burden I never carried well. I knew I had disappointed her in many ways, chiefly in deciding not to pursue medicine after I had shown some aptitude while working at the pharmacies. But Dad's illness just seemed to wipe away any ambition I'd ever had. Or perhaps it provided a convenient excuse for my natural indolence.

My father had come to Hopewell from Harrodsburg in the early 1880s as the town's intrepid Adams Express agent. Handling the parcels and shipments and wire transmissions and financial transactions for an entire community provided the perfect opportunity for him to elbow his way into a seat at the local table. As Mother tells it, his affable manner immediately earned him friends and allies among the local businessmen, and he charmed his way into the best social circles. My mother's cousin Belle once shed a little more light on the story. She said Bill Board had charged into town and swept my mother off her feet, eventually leading her to break off her engagement to a young man from Louisville. I still remembered a line from a newspaper story about their wedding that Mother kept in her scrapbook: "The young gentlemen of Hopewell, while regretting that some one of them did not win her hand, have, however, learned to greatly esteem Mr. Board," it declared.

It had once been hard for me to imagine my rather flinty mother as the target of all those young men's affections. But a wedding photo of the striking couple changed my mind. She with her dark hair and intelligent air in the elaborate wedding gown. He looking dashing with his handlebar mustache, aquiline nose, and piercing, almost laughing eyes, as if he knew he had stolen the prize.

As I was helping Mother pack for the move to Louisville after Dad's death, I happened upon a letter from her first fiancé, a memento she had held onto all those years. Whether out of well-disguised sentimentality or vain triumph, I wasn't sure. She had evidently written to him to let him know she had to break off the engagement and to ask how she should return the ring.

"You do yourself an injustice by thinking you have done wrong, for you have done exactly right in everything," he had written back to her. Since it was clear to him that she no longer loved him, "It would have been far more wrong if you were to marry me than to do as you have done. Your action is that of a true woman and instead of blaming, I admire you for it," he added. He signed his name at the bottom of the page: Lyons—Lyons Simmons.

Four months later Mary Lake Barnes married William Ellery Board. That act of mild rebellion seems completely uncharacteristic of the woman whose hawkish governance I lived under for the first eighteen years of my life. I wondered if she would have made those choices had her father, the esteemed Dr. L. D. Barnes, still been alive. I sometimes suspected that accepting a proposal of marriage from Bill Board was one of the few times she had acted on emotion. I now wondered whether the relentless cold pragmatism I always associated with her reflected in any way regret for that rash decision.

Dad eventually took a position at the Deposit Bank, a natural progression from his job with the express office. His new position gave him even more opportunities to engage with other people's money—until his mentor there retired, perhaps costing my father the cover he had had for any heedless bungling that had occurred on his watch. Dad's personal financial affairs always seemed in unseemly disarray. He would buy and sell parcels of land around town and sign bank notes for the questionable activities of his brother. When I was a teenager, at least two local businessmen—including the grocer—had the temerity to file suits against my mother for not keeping up her accounts. My poor mother's good fortune was that Dr. Barnes, when she was still a young girl, had seen to it that his daughter had some property of her own that no future husband could get his hands on.

But somehow all of Dad's pecuniary peccadilloes never seemed to diminish my parents' status in Hopewell. They were still socializing with the other pioneer families who tightly held the reins to the community. Together they were all complicit in a five-gaited minuet that preserved everyone's place.

One of the most significant social events occurred each May, when the Grand Commandery of the Knights Templar held its annual conclave. The good townspeople in the community chosen to host the event exulted in this opportunity to show off their hospitality and their commitment to the original Knights' virtues—poverty, chastity, and obedience—by staging the biggest parade, the grandest receptions, and the most extravagant city-wide decorations. Everyone in the community seemed giddy as they joined the hosts in welcoming hundreds if not thousands of humble Knights and Ladies who gathered to renew their vows as faithful Christian servants.

"The Maltese Cross Waves O'er Our Captured City," crowed the Maysville *Daily Public Ledger* in 1907, according to clippings my father had preserved from that conclave. The year before, Hopewell had been the blessed site of the event and "the town was turned over to the plumed army," as I recall the newspaper describing it.

It was before the Maysville event, I believe, that I caught my father preening in front of the mirror in full costume. With the military cut and styling of the uniform, he did indeed resemble a Christian soldier marching as to war. In this case, however, the only threat of a casualty might spring from a fall off the dais or a flaring of gout.

"Don't you look striking," I said to him with a teenage churlish grin I hoped he was too preoccupied to notice.

He stood a little straighter, turning to one side to assess his reflection in profile. "It's important that I wear the uniform properly, and soberly represent all that it stands for."

It seemed to me that the uniform's panache might be the main attraction, that perhaps his faith to the cause served only to magnify his own glory. Or, as I later mused, to conceal his infamy.

"What goes on at one of these things?" I asked, trying to appear interested.

"In the morning, we'll meet at the Masonic Temple and conduct all of our business. That's when I'll be named the Eminent Grand Captain of the Guard. That evening there will be a festive reception at the home of Grand Commander Keith. Hundreds will attend, and I understand Weber's Orchestra from Cincinnati will perform. The next day will be the parade. All of the commanderies from all across the state will participate, bringing their own bands and guests. The Hopewell Military Band will march with us. It will be quite the scene, son, quite the scene."

Over the years, I recognized that my father appeared to invest all his energy in three pursuits: his career, which eventually had him traveling the state wooing new clients for Unity Insurance of Pittsburgh; his increasing responsibilities with the Knights Templar, for which he finally served as the Eminent Grand Warder for the Kentucky Grand Commandery; and his obligations to the Hopewell Christian Church. It occurred to me that perhaps his pious do-goodism evolved from his efforts to validate his worth to the family he had married into. His wife was inordinately proud of her family's august lineage. Everyone who knew her knew she was a charter member of the Jemima Johnson Chapter of the Daughters of the American Revolution there in Hopewell. Although my father's ancestors had also received a land grant to come to Kentucky after volunteering to get shot at by the Brits, I had the sense that Dad's actions and many of his decisions all were part of an effort to claim his rightful spot in Hopewell society.

That, I later realized, revealed in part why my father and mother tried so hard to disguise the symptoms of Dad's illness for so long. It became the family's unified purpose. We would tell friends and acquaintances little lies to explain away the limp he had developed or the tremors or the slurred speech or the erratic behavior. He would vacillate between a withdrawn state of depression and overbearing excitement and grandiose delusions. Finally, shortly after I had returned to Hopewell from Middlesboro, we could no longer hide the truth. Paralysis was beginning to overtake him and his eyesight was failing. He was spending long stretches of time in the hospital.

By late 1914, Bill Board had become an invalid, and the effects of syphilis were slowly destroying his mind and his body.

As a young adult, I watched my father disappear. I watched my mother maintain her stiff upper lip and stand uncowed amidst the neighbors' chatter. Only once did she share her deepening despair with me.

"Lyons, isn't there anything that can be done? You work in a pharmacy. Aren't there treatments? Something to reverse these awful symptoms?"

I wasn't sure how much to share. "There is a new drug that doctors are just beginning to try," I finally said. "But it's only been available a short time. My understanding is it's difficult to administer, so doctors haven't been too keen on it just yet."

Her eyes caught mine. "Shouldn't we ask Dr. Amburgey about it? Why hasn't he mentioned it? He told me there was nothing we could do. Why didn't you tell me about this?"

I hesitated, having already stirred those false hopes I had wanted to avoid. "I think you have to start treatments fairly early in the progression of the disease. And, you know, Dad's been sick a long time."

"What's the name of the drug? Shouldn't I at least ask about it?"

Then I second-guessed myself. Perhaps I should have pushed the doctor on this subject as soon as I was aware of the diagnosis. But by the time my father had sought qualified medical care for his symptoms, by the time he could admit to himself what was probably already clear to others, I was fairly certain it was too late for the treatment to do him any good. The blood test for diagnosing syphilis had only recently become available. I was away from home, in

Middlesboro. I assumed the doctor was doing all he felt he could. It didn't seem my place to intrude on my parents' very personal difficulties. If there had been an opportunity for me to play the messiah, I never auditioned for the role.

But sometimes I have wondered if I could have done more, if I could have changed the way it played out if I had just spoken up. Perhaps if I had been home, keeping a closer eye on my family, I would have recognized the symptoms earlier and urged him to get help. But after leaving school, I was ready to launch my own life, and I didn't expect it would be in Hopewell. If there was a train heading out of town, I was ready to hop it.

"It's called Salvarsan," I said somewhat reluctantly. "You can ask Doc Amburgey, of course, but I doubt he will recommend it at this point."

I had delivered the fatal blow. I have no idea if she asked about the drug. She never brought it up again. From all I could tell, she simply returned to the unrelenting chore of caring for an invalid.

I tried to be a dutiful son. I really did. For as long as I could, I remained in Hopewell and helped with my father's care. And when I couldn't stand to watch what was happening any more, I escaped to Louisville, where I eventually took that job at the Gulf station near downtown. Fixing flats seemed immeasurably better than witnessing a deteriorating situation that had no remedy.

I wasn't proud that I had run away, that I had essentially left my mother to care for a blind, paralyzed husband on her own. A husband who had betrayed her and whom she now tended to despite his visible shame. I never questioned that she loved him. I never questioned her loyalty to him. But I did wonder sometimes about that other young suitor she had let go, and I wondered whether she still thought of him.

I did what I could from Louisville, but by that time Dad spent most of his days in the hospital in Hopewell or in Lexington. By the end, he had lost his mind, and he died at the Lexington hospital I had always known as the Eastern Kentucky Asylum for the Insane.

I never confronted my father about how he got the disease. I didn't really want to know. And I tried hard to suppress any anger I felt toward him. But somewhere in the darkest recesses of my brain perhaps I filed away what can happen when you pursue the appearance of propriety at all costs, when you suppress the man you are to fit the mold of the man your wife wants you to be. Some part of you will find a release valve, an escape hatch, or else you will find your soul seeping out of some invisible wound.

Water dripping down my arm from the melted ice roused me from my stupor. I quickly checked my watch and realized I needed to hustle to get to the train station in time. Mother hadn't raised a son who could tolerate tardiness. I put the soggy dish towel in the kitchen and walked in the bathroom to check my jaw. The swelling wasn't too noticeable, and I figured it would take several more hours for any discoloration to become too obvious. I hoped I had at least a small window of time before I would have to explain what had happened. But I needed to have a ready answer, just in case.

I grabbed my coat and hat and headed down the street to meet the train.

Effie Mae
Saturday, December 6, 1941

After Doug headed over to Mickey's just beyond the entrance to Sparrows Point, I started straightening up the kitchen. I preserved what I could of the food left on my plate and scraped the rest into the garbage. I put the other leftovers in the fridge and then started washing dishes, hoping to get my thoughts straight before Lyons got home. But my mind was still racing, flitting from one memory to the next, trying to figure out what clues I might have missed.

I guess I ain't never really pried into my husband's past. I'm more interested in making the most out of today, and Lyons and I certainly have had some good times together. I always figgered, why mess that up by digging into the pain and sorrows we all carry? What good does that do? What's done is done. So I reckon there was important questions I just never asked.

When he came to my aid that night in Cincinnati several years after Frank died, I ain't laid eyes on him for twenty years. His was certainly the last face I expected to see when I looked up from that awkward position on my hands and knees and saw him walking towards me with my pocketbook in his hands, the would-be thief scurrying away behind him with his tail tucked between his legs. I guess Lyons had heard my screams after the man had come up behind me and snatched my pocketbook and shoved me to the sidewalk. I knew the neighborhood had gotten rougher after me and Doug had moved away, what with the Depression and all the hobos who had set up house in them boxcars and in the weeds along the tracks. But I had made it a Christmas tradition to stop in and see Edna and Claire, my two neighbors from that brief year Doug and I spent with Frank. And I wasn't about to let the threat of a run-in with some riffraff keep me from visiting with em and bringing em homemade cobbler.

Fate had to have intervened to put Lyons on that very street corner that evening. There's no other way to explain it. And I don't see no reason to question these things. I just accept em. The good and the bad. Just like when Frank suddenly showed up in Logmont, and just as suddenly was taken away. It's all part of life's road map that I have no way of reading. I just take the turns as they come.

I had made the trip on the streetcar all the way from Hyde Park east of the city where Doug and I was still living at the home of Mr. Thomas King. Doug was in his senior year in high school by that time, and he was out and about with some friends that evening. So I was by myself as I left Edna's house on Freeman Street, hustling to catch the streetcar back home.

I cain't imagine why I looked like a good victim to that vagrant, but I reckon when you're desperate you don't take time to evaluate all your options. Maybe he was just hoping for a warm night in jail and a square meal. My overcoat wasn't doing much to protect me from the cold, and I remember the familiar smell of coal smoke lingering in the air from a train that had just trundled through. As I tried to wrap my scarf tighter around my neck, I was hit from behind.

I cried out as I fell to the sidewalk, more out of surprise than pain. When I realized what had just happened, I started yelling at the top of my lungs, hoping the ruckus would make him drop my pocketbook as he ran. I didn't have nothing much of value in it, of course, but I didn't want to make it easy for him to get away with it neither. As I looked down to check the condition of my stockings and my knees, I heard the shouts of a male voice and a brief scuffle just ahead. When I looked up, it appeared a man had pushed the thief to the ground and had successfully wrenched my pocketbook from his grasp. He had his knee on the man's back and I saw him cock his arm ready to slug him, but he appeared to change his mind and instead backed onto his heels and stood up. The smaller man staggered to his feet and took off. It all happened real quick and the fast-settling darkness made it hard to make out exactly what was going on. Then I saw the man who had intervened heading toward me.

He was wrapped in a heavy overcoat, a muffler, and a hat, so I had trouble making out his face at first. But as he got closer, there was something about them eyes that made me catch my breath.

"Are you all right?" he called out. And then I knew for sure.

I stood up and allowed a smile to spread across my face. It made no sense that he was there. But, like I said, I had long given up trying to explain how these things happen. Or why. I pulled the scarf away from my mouth.

"Lyons? Is that really Lyons Board?"

He stopped in his tracks. He looked down at the pocketbook, as if that would give him a clue as to who was calling his name. Then he looked back at me. He took another step or two closer, as he peered into my face.

"Effie Mae? How on earth?" he started.

"You remember me?" I asked, surprised.

"How could I forget that voice? And if I'm not mistaken, I see a bit of that glorious auburn hair peeping out from under your hat."

I reached up to tuck the wayward curls back in place. I imagine I blushed all the way down to my toes.

"Did he hurt you?" he asked, turning serious again.

"No, I'm fine. Just bruised my pride a little. And I may have to buy me a new pair of stockings. I cain't thank you enough for running him off."

"Well, I wanted to do more than that, but I thought better of it. Hopefully he'll know not to come into this neighborhood again looking for an easy target. I thought they had cleaned up this area when they opened Union Terminal back in the spring. You'd think he'd have better luck pickpocketing the travelers coming in and out of the station."

"Yeah, that big concrete dome is quite the sight on the horizon now. I haven't been inside yet, but I hear it's something else."

I hesitated a moment. "Do you think I should call the police?" I was thinking about Frank, and his final night near them railroad tracks. I watched Lyons tuck his chin and grow quiet. He looked nearly as shaken as I was.

"No," he finally answered. "I think he got the message. I can't say he won't try it again, but let's don't get the officials involved since no harm was done. He looked like he's been suffering enough in this cold."

I watched a wave of darkness cross his face, as if he had been blindsided by a memory he couldn't keep at bay. "You OK?" I asked.

"Oh, yeah. I'm just a little winded. I'm not as young as I used to be, you know. So what are you doing in Cincinnati? I guess you didn't just get off the train, since you said you haven't been inside the terminal."

"No, I live here. Well, not here, really, at least not now. I used to live right there at the corner of Gest Street. Now I live in the east end."

Lyons looked at me. "Is that right? Well you have moved up in the world. I live in a boardinghouse around the corner on Pine. I had the night off and thought I'd stroll around the block and have a smoke before I went in for the evening. When I came around the corner I heard you yelling. Then I saw the guy running in the opposite direction, and I guessed what had happened. Are you sure you're OK?"

"Yeah, yeah," I said, smoothing my skirt. "Really. I'm fine. How long you been living in Cincinnati?"

"A little over a year. I was up in Toledo, but things got bad up there, so I headed back here to find work." He paused, and then grinned. "I'm a lot like all these other bindle stiffs, I suppose. What are you doing here?"

"Oh, Lyons, it's a long story. And it's too cold to tell it out here on the street. Ain't there somewhere we can duck inside and chat? I have a little time before I need to head back home."

"Well, there was a fire roaring in the sitting room at the boarding-house when I left. It's a short walk, if you're up for it. Let's head over there and you can warm up. Then we'll get you on your way. But first you need to tell me what made you leave God's country."

I couldn't pass up that offer, of course. He handed me my pocket-book, and we headed toward Gest Street to cut over to Pine. During previous visits back to the west end, I had avoided walking past the little house we had shared with Frank. It was just too painful. But walking by with Lyons was almost comforting. I took his elbow as we rounded the corner and I felt I had the strength to walk on by, to look up the street to what was to come.

We spent an hour or so in the sitting room catching up and reminiscing. I reckon I talked more than he did, telling him about my kids, what had happened to my husbands. Maybe it didn't occur to me then that his story seemed to lack details.

He talked about jobs that had taken him here and yonder, and a little about the war, but he didn't share much that was personal. Perhaps I should've paid more attention then. Perhaps I should've asked more questions. But I guess it just didn't seem important to me. We seemed to pick up right where we had left off way back when, and I was mighty happy. I had had so much heartache, so many highs and lows, that I just wanted to latch onto this person who had always made my heart sing. He could've spent the past twenty years in prison for all I knew. I never asked, and I didn't care.

I finished up the dishes and sat down at the table to light a cigarette. I guess I ain't never spent much time thinking about how my life turned out or what brung me here to Sparrows Point. Sifting through all that seemed a luxury left to folks whose circumstances done gave them more choices. I just took what come at me and done the best I could. I felt lucky to be here with Doug and Lyons. I still do.

Thinking back to them years in Cincinnati, though, I recollect what a strange and frightening place it was when I first got there.

As a child and later a young mother, I never expected to leave Eastern Kentucky. At the time, my world was confined to what I realize now was a right small plot of land, rimmed by dark hills on all sides—the Cumberland Mountains on the east and Pine Mountain and the Log Mountains on the west. I'd never been on the other side of them natural barriers, even though Cumberland Gap was just a handful of miles outside Middlesboro. That could've been the gateway to an enchanted kingdom, but I never saw no need to go through it.

At that time, I thought Middlesboro was a big city. The fact that it sits in a giant bowl more than three miles wide made it feel even bigger to those of us who come out of them hills surrounding it. We'd never seen that much open space.

But from any point within Middlesboro the mountains was still looming on the horizon. It just never occurred to me to go beyond em. Until Frank put us on the train and we headed north.

Moving to Cincinnati was quite a shock. I was plum miserable at first, but I tried my best not to show it. Particularly in front of Doug. He had his own adjustments to make. Frank was really kind about it and did everything he could to make it easier on us. Eventually, though, I had to learn to find my way among that tangle of streets and all the people who seemed so different from me. They talked different, they dressed different, and they looked different.

Back in the coal camps, we had gotten used to being around foreigners who had come looking for hard work: Italians, Russians, Poles, Hungarians. Negroes, too. I'll admit it: it was a little unsettling at first. But we was all union folk, and we all had the same dreams. In most of them camps, the housing for the coloreds and the immigrants was separate, and they was typically assigned the cruelest jobs, just like here at the Point. But I ain't never heard none of em complaining, at least no more than anybody else. They was happy to have the work, even if they wasn't always treated right.

In Cincinnati, though, I felt like the foreigner. I was the stranger. In fact, I sometimes felt like I was from one of them planets my daddy would point out when the sky was bright with stars. The simplest things overwhelmed me: managing real money instead of scrip; navigating the streetcars; making people understand what I was saying. Sometimes they just stared at me like I was speaking a foreign tongue, like in them churches in the mountains where folks get consumed by the spirit of the Lord. Yeah, I learned right quick how them Italians had felt when they come to work the mines.

While I was struggling, though, Doug seemed to take to it like a tick to a dog. He was curious and wide-eyed. He had a thousand questions for Frank every night. If he felt out of place in his classroom, he never let on. I was so proud of him. He was a real trouper.

Frank had found us a little house to rent not far from the B&O rail yards. We could hear the trains come in and out at night, and that helped me feel connected to Yellow Creek and Logmont and all the little coal towns they was heading to or coming from. Most of the men around us worked for the railroad or at the nearby mills or machine shops. I slowly got to know some of the womenfolk, and I eventually got enough confidence to wander out a bit.

Frank sometimes worked days, sometimes nights, so Doug and I was frequently on our own. On weekends, we might walk downtown and roam through the library or one of them department stores. I just couldn't get over how big everything was. And there was just so *much*.

We eventually fell into something like a routine and I started feeling more comfortable. When that happened, I was finally able to see just how good we had it. Frank's salary let me fix regular meals and put real food on the table every night. I could occasionally buy something to pretty up the house. When our shoes was wore out from walking the city, we could replace em rather than shoving cardboard or newspaper inside. Frank even had presents for us on our birthdays. If I paused to think about it, I couldn't believe my good fortune.

Sure, I missed everyone we had left behind. I kept thinking Eileen would change her mind and come live with us, but she never did. I tried to write once a week to let em know that I still loved em and I missed em. But they was getting on with their lives. Virgil and Lee seemed to have it all under control and evidently weren't bothered by me not being there to help. That hurt a little bit, I won't lie. But I reckon they did prove to me that they could take care of theirselves.

When we went back to visit just before Christmas, I was surprised at how tiny that house felt and how black everything was from the coal dust. I had already forgotten what it was like to fight that fight every day. After a light supper we all sat around the stove and Frank presented Lee with the old banjo he had found up in Cincinnati.

Lee didn't say a word. He held the instrument in his lap with reverence, running his callused hands up and down the neck and occasionally plucking a string, then holding the instrument up toward his ear and making an adjustment.

"Lee, do you remember any of them tunes your daddy tried to teach you back at Yellow Creek?" I asked.

I watched as he tucked the fingers of his right hand toward his palm and strummed the strings. He then alternated striking one string and then another with his thumb. His left hand eventually found its place along the frets and he started picking out a tune. In short order we all recognized "Shady Grove," and Valarie started singing, with her soft alto. Then Eileen dropped in the harmony. Virgil went into the bedroom and came back with his harmonica. He joined in quietly in the background, trying not to overwhelm the music Lee was pulling outta that banjo.

> Shady Grove, my little love
> Shady Grove, my darlin
> Shady Grove, my little love
> Goin back to Harlan
>
> Cheeks as red as a bloomin rose
> Eyes the prettiest brown
> She's the darlin of my heart
> Prettiest girl in town

At first, I just sat back as my eyes filled with tears. This was my family. Frank had given me and Doug everything we needed, but I could never really leave them others behind. I loved em all so much. They was safe. And they was together. After a minute or two, I joined in, messing up the beautiful harmony my two girls had going. Doug was clapping his hands and grinning ear to ear. Lee picked up the tempo once he got the hang of it, and when Eileen jumped up to dance I joined her, shuffling and stomping the best we could in that confined space.

As the train headed into Corbin on our way back to Cincinnati, I remember how sad I was to leave them mountains behind. The mountains soothed me somehow, protected me. I felt exposed when the landscape opened up. I hadn't noticed it too much them first months in Cincinnati. If we went downtown, the tall buildings created that closeness I had felt in the camps. But as the train chugged north through central Kentucky, I was a little panicky. It was beautiful and all, that rolling farmland, but there weren't no landmarks on the horizon, nothing to set your gaze on and get your bearings. The fence lines seemed to stretch forever. I felt like if I stepped off the train I would simply float away with nothing to ground me.

When we got back to our little house down near the tracks, I felt better. It didn't take me long to get adjusted again. In January Doug went back to school and we fell right back into our routine. Frank made us feel loved and cared for. I think we provided a constancy that contrasted to the unpredictability of his job. He never knew what he would face when he went to work. Sometimes he would have to be gone for a few days. It seemed to calm him to know we would be here when he got home. He was a man who enjoyed a quiet evening with his family even though, or perhaps because, the work he had chosen pitted him and his wits against brutes and scoundrels. On the job, he had to be as tightly wound as a panther stalking a rabbit.

When the police officer showed up at our door with Frank's boss one rainy night in late March, I knew our bliss was about to become a distant memory. I calmly held the door open for em, but I felt my heart twist into a knot. I somehow found my way to a seat on the sofa. Mr. Wallingford, Frank's boss, sat down next to me. By that point, the only thing I didn't know was the details.

I stared at the officer in front of me and tried to listen to what he was saying, but everything was muffled. My sight narrowed until all I could see was his mouth moving.

"Can I get you a glass of water, Mrs. Foster?" I finally heard Mr. Wallingford say. I must have nodded, because I felt him get up and walk toward the kitchen.

Doug was already in bed, thank goodness, and he didn't wake up. Eventually I pieced together that Frank had been investigating a report of some men breaking into the rail cars down at the switch station. As he was peering in the door of one of them boxcars, sweeping his flashlight from side to side, someone hit him from behind with a two-by-four. He went down on his face, and the suspected thief was able to get to Frank's gun and put one of his own slugs right in the back of his head. Another detective heard the commotion and got there in time to see the guy running off, but I don't think they ever tracked him down.

I was thankful that it sounded like it was all pretty quick, like he really hadn't suffered too much. He was too good a man for that sort of end. He had hoped to retire in just a few years and find a quieter line of work, and we was both looking forward to that.

After the men left, I lay down on the sofa and invited the tears to come. But I guess I wasn't ready yet. The choking cries would surprise me later, it turned out. But I had no trouble that night, as I listened to the rain splatter against the window pane, thinking about what a fine man Frank was and how lucky I'd been—for however short a spell. I already knew that happiness never outstayed its welcome, that it was one of them visitors you wish would stay another week. But, eventually, it always takes its leave.

As I saw it, this was just another of them gut-punches you absorb cause you have no choice. As we stumbled through the next several days, I think Doug was even more devastated than I was. He'd never knowed a real daddy, and suddenly the one who had gladly stepped in to fill that role was gone.

He came to me one night after supper, a big ol ten-year-old boy looking for his mommy. I was sitting in the shabby armchair with the newspaper spread out in my lap. He crawled right up in the chair with me. We sat quietly at first, as he snuggled up against me, and I ran my fingers through his light hair.

After a bit he spoke. "What are we gonna do, Mama? Where are we gonna go now?"

I hadn't realized he was feeling that burden. It had only been a coupla weeks, and our landlord had been kindly enough to give us another month to sort out what we was going to do. Making that decision was my responsibility, and I didn't have Virgil to lean on this time. Sure, we could've gone back to Logmont, holed up with family, wrapped ourselves in that familiar terrain. But going backwards at that point just didn't make no sense. There was a much bigger world for us there in Cincinnati.

"I don't know yet, honey," I finally said. "But we're gonna figger it out. I reckon I can find some sort of work up here. You just keep focusing on your schoolwork. Frank would want you to soak up everything you can. He was so proud of you. You know he really loved you. I expect he'll be keeping an eye on you from up there in heaven. We'll just keep doing what we've always done."

I pulled him closer as I heard the first soft sobs. I hadn't seen him cry since Frank had died.

Nearly fifteen years later, sitting in that little kitchen waiting for Lyons to get home, I rubbed the back of my hand across my face to wipe the moisture from my eyes. My life had had a lot of twists and turns. A lot of heartbreak. I had to suspect that Lyons' had, too. I was more amazed, I think, that I'd never dug harder to expose them cracks in his own story. Maybe it was time.

I got up from the table and went into the living room, where I turned on the radio. The news announcer was once again talking about the war in Europe and whatever island nation Japan was threatening this time. He was also sharing more details about that 70-ton flying boat that done caught fire in Baltimore harbor the day before, but I didn't have no patience for any of it. I turned the dial until I found Bing Crosby singing "Silent Night," and then I sat in the rocker with my eyes closed and hummed along as I thought about the Christmas tree lights twinkling down the street.

Lyons
Thursday, October 27, 1921

Mother took my right arm as we walked up Vine Street from the depot. It occurred to me that we presented a perfect tableau for one of Norman Rockwell's disturbingly ironic covers on *The Saturday Evening Post*. All we needed was the wicker baby carriage I had seen waiting for us at the Marrs home.

Mother interrupted my artful reverie.

"So, how does it feel to be a father?" she asked.

Terrified didn't sound like an acceptable answer. So I went with a rather ordinary evasion.

"I don't know," I replied. "I've hardly spent any time with her yet, Mother. But I am beginning to feel the awful weight of responsibility."

I wanted to lasso those words right back in as soon as they were out of my mouth.

"Raising a child is a big job," she said. "But you and Nell will figure it out. You just take it one step at a time."

"Are you excited about being a grandmother?" I asked to shift the conversation.

"Of course. Although it's still hard for me to believe." She looked at me somewhat quizzically. "I sometimes regret that I made the move to Louisville, now that you've settled here in Hopewell and started a family. But moving to Louisville to be near you and Belle felt like the right thing to do after your father died. And now I have my own responsibilities there."

Mother's cousin Belle Clay had transported herself inconveniently to Louisville when she married William Lee Lyons. I had always assumed my name, William Lyons Board, was a nod to my mother's affection for this family, as well as respect for my father, of course. But after finding the note from my mother's former suitor, I wasn't completely sure how I had gotten my name, or what it signified for her.

Next to Belle, Mother's closest friend was Mrs. Swift Champ, whose husband published the *Bedford County News* here in Hopewell. I was secretly hoping that Mother planned to stay with her this visit, but I hadn't yet broached the question.

"With Nell and Mary Rose still in Lawrenceburg, will you be keeping me company at my home while you're in town?"

"No, no. I expect to stay with the Champs, as usual. They told me the invitation is always open. And I don't want to inconvenience you."

I tried to tamp down a giddy sense of relief. Hosting my mother while sorting through all that had happened over the last couple of days would be like battling the Minotaur while trying to navigate Daedalus' maze.

However, I was glad I had captured her for the trip back to Lawrenceburg. She got along well with Nell and her family, plus she could help me negotiate this new situation. I still wasn't sure what to expect or what I was supposed to do, as a father. I felt a bit like the ingénue who's just landed in the big city.

By early afternoon, we were on the road. My stomach roiled as we approached the scene of the accident, so I was relieved to see that Glenn had already been out with his tow truck and hauled away the remains. I felt an eerie sense of unease, as if the Oakland's disembodied spirit remained behind to pass censure on my crimes. I decided it might be a good thing that I was heading out of town. Word would travel fast, and I hadn't yet had a chance to choreograph the fancy footwork I might need to successfully land one jeté after another.

It was a glorious day, and Mother confidently shared terse reports on the irreproachable beauty or the ignominious disrepair of one farm after another as we drove west. The air was filled with the enchanting smell of putrescent leaves, and bright pockets of red and yellow identified those trees already donning the funeral pall. The Maxwell behaved properly and we chugged along, thoroughly enjoying meaningless conversation. Behind the wheel of my own vehicle this time, I eventually began to sense the old bravado stealing back into my veins. I pulled in front of the Marrs home with a renewed sense of calm.

Things appeared a little quieter around the house. The men were still at work. Rosalie welcomed us at the door as usual and immediately insisted we stay for dinner. I was pleased to find Nell sitting in an armchair in the parlor, with Mary Rose asleep in her lap. Nell still looked tired, but she smiled as we made our way into the room.

"Why, Mary Rose, there's your other grandmother," Nell said, gesturing to Mother to have a seat on the sofa.

The baby stirred but did not wake up. I kissed Nell on the forehead, careful to keep the left side of my face away from her line of sight, and reached down to gently caress the baby's face. She was tiny, even smaller than I had realized the night before. My hand nearly covered her, from head to toe.

"My goodness, Nell," said Mother. "She is an itty-bitty thing, just like you. But isn't she beautiful. How are you feeling, dear?"

"I'm a little worn out, but my strength is coming back. It was good to get out of bed today, although moving around is a bit harder than I expected. She's already keeping me busy. Would you like to hold her?"

I watched as Nell carefully handed Mary Rose over to my mother. I could see the joy radiate from her face as she took the sleeping child and laid her against her shoulder. In that single motion, all of the weariness and the grief that had long settled there seemed to dissolve.

Nell turned to me. "How did you get off work today?"

"I simply told them I had to bring Mother over here to see you and the baby. After I worked yesterday, I figured they owed me one. Harlan didn't give me any trouble."

"I hope to get home over the weekend," said Nell, "if I can figure out how to escape my mother's watchful eye. I've been here long enough, and I think I'll be up to making the trip. Maybe we can get J. P. to take us over there in that big, comfortable Hudson of his. That might make the trip a little easier."

"That's a good idea. I'll talk to him."

"I think Lydia and George and J. P. and Katie will all be at dinner tonight. We can ask him then."

"It'll be good to get you both home," I said, trying to imagine what that would be like. "Is there anything else I need to do before then?" I was thinking about the dripping kitchen faucet I had promised to address while she was away. I knew her homecoming could be fraught if I didn't get that taken care of.

"I think we're well stocked with everything we need, at least for a week or so. I'll take an inventory when I get home. You just get some rest while you can. This baby has good lungs, and we may not be sleeping much for the next few weeks."

I looked over at my mother. She was gently bouncing Mary Rose on her shoulder. I had never seen her look so at peace.

As soon as J. P. McWilliams came in the front door, I could tell something was up. I had gone into the hallway to greet the newcomers, and the look he gave me chilled me to the core. I swallowed hard and tried to maintain my equanimity as I greeted Katie and then Lydia and George, who were right behind them. The two women took their warm dishes to the kitchen as the men headed to the parlor. Nell was in the bedroom putting Mary Rose to bed. Mother was in the kitchen helping Rosalie.

J. P. didn't waste any time.

"There's a rumor going around that you wrecked a fella's car last night, Lyons. Is that true? That would explain your condition when you got here, I suppose."

My heart nearly stopped. If J. P. had already heard that in Lawrenceburg, word must have spread fast among all the nearby garages. I was not prepared to respond.

J. P. was glaring at me. I recalled that around town everyone referred to him as "The Boss."

"Where did you hear that?" I asked, trying to stall as I figured out what to do.

"I had some business with Gibson Motors over there in Hopewell, and Raymond Crutcher told me about it. He said Johnny Childers is beside himself. He's threatening to sue you. You could be in big trouble, Lyons. What the hell were you doing with his car, anyway?"

I looked over at George, who was pouring himself a glass of bourbon. Before I could respond, Robert Marrs came in the room. Sensing the tension, he asked, "What's going on, boys? Did I miss something?"

"Lyons here stole a car last night and wrecked it," said J. P. without missing a beat. "It was a brand new Oakland. The owner's pretty fired up."

Robert looked at me. "Surely that's not true, son. There must be some mistake." He paused a moment. "Lyons, what's going on?"

I looked at my father-in-law and tried to remember to breathe. "I told Johnny I was going to borrow his car," I started. "I didn't steal it." I could see no way out of owning up to the wreck. The car was incontrovertible evidence, and my aching jaw was proof that I had already confessed the crime to Johnny. "Some lunatic ran me off the road as I was heading over here last night. He came right at me without his lights on. Must have been a Model T. Those fools are always trying to preserve their batteries. I had no choice but to swerve to miss him. I ended up tossed out of the car and the car ended up head-on in a tree."

I couldn't believe the whole story had just spilled out. But what else was I going to say? I had no other defense, really.

George had joined the other two men. "Did Johnny take a swing at you? Either that or you're hiding a pretty big plug of tobacco in your jaw."

In my panic, I had forgotten to keep my left side facing the wall. I automatically lifted my hand to my jaw.

"Yeah, when I talked to Johnny this morning, he reacted pretty badly. But I deserved it, I guess."

"Well, you'd better get this straightened out," said J. P. "You have big responsibilities now and a reputation to uphold. Have you told Nell?"

"No. She doesn't need to hear this right now. And no one here is going to tell her." I looked each man in the eye, one after the other.

"Harrumph," muttered J. P.

"Son, you're going to have to tell her sometime," said Robert. "Did you offer to pay for the repairs?"

"Our conversation this morning didn't get that far," I said. "When Johnny cools off, we'll talk about that. There has to be some way to make amends."

I had not yet allowed myself to think about how I was going to make this right. Nell and I were still in the throes of feathering our nest, and we didn't have the cash to pay for the repairs—or replace the car, if that was necessary. We were barely getting by as it was. If Johnny was patient with me, maybe we could make an arrangement that we could both honor. If he didn't unleash the firing squad on me first.

Johnny had bailed me out before. We were just west of the Argonne Forest, pressing toward the Aisne River. Part of our recently skeletonized unit had been assigned to support the French Fourth Army and our Second and Thirty-sixth Divisions at Sommepy. I was part of a crew that had set up a telephone switchboard and radio station in a stone culvert under a railroad embankment.

"Fuck," I heard Allen mutter over the ceaseless gunfire coming from the east. "The radio's not working,"

The rain had let up momentarily, but the darkness wrapped around us like a waiting shroud. It was early October. I hardly mourned the diminishing daylight that, even with the nearly impenetrable smoke and mist, cruelly revealed the human and animal wreckage around us. Even the trees had been splintered, stripped of bark and leaves— woody corpses left leaning into the wind. It hadn't taken long for me to learn to embrace the blindness of night.

I scooted next to Allen and pulled on a headset to see if I could do anything more to diagnose the problem. My expertise was Morse code, but my days around the garage made me feel dangerously proficient with complicated equipment. Allen was undoubtedly our best technician, so I expected my frantic tugging of wires and flipping of switches would be futile. The mysteries of the whole contraption still eluded me.

"Nothing," I said. "Can we get word back to the boys behind us? We got anybody who could work some magic?"

"Johnny's still back there, I think," Allen said. "If somebody can wake him. Hard to tell how many miles of line they repaired today. But I still don't think they got the phones up and running. The artillery wagons and mortar shells just tear right through it again."

"Wonder if he salvaged any insulated wire. Or at least something the Germans left behind. This French shit is gonna get us all killed."

"Well, if we don't get this radio working, we'll be wishing we had a few pigeons to send out an SOS."

The rain had picked up again, and the cold was beginning to squeeze like a tourniquet. The mules shuffled restlessly behind me. I felt the familiar numbing of my fingers as I wrestled with the radio. I looked out from under our temporary hideaway. I could see the flares from the shells. Thankfully the thundering on the stone overhead muffled any screams.

"I got word to Johnny using the buzzer," Reggie yelled from behind me. "He's gonna try to make a run for it."

I felt the blood slow in my veins. What chance did he have to get through the fire? What other options did we have? The Third Brigade had pushed forward. They were depending on us to get them instructions, warn them what was ahead. It was one man risking his life, or the potential slaughter of dozens. Johnny had no decision to make.

I hadn't known Johnny at Camp Taylor, but he'd trained there before I'd arrived. He'd been plucked from another small Kentucky town and conscripted into heeding Uncle Sam's call. Our paths hadn't crossed until my unit got divided up in France. Like me, he was an "elder statesman" in a crowd of teenagers recruited from their mother's breast. I had turned twenty-six the day before I set sail for France. Johnny was pushing thirty.

I knew he had a wife, Elizabeth, who was staying with family in Campbellsville. I wondered who would contact her if he didn't make it to our position. What would that person say? *I'm sorry ma'am. He died trying to get to a broken radio.*

Allen, Reggie, and I sat silent, occasionally catching the look of helplessness in each other's eyes. We were all toy soldiers being shuffled around a playroom at the whim of our dangerously unprepared superiors.

I had no sense of how much time had passed, but I heard the gunfire pick up. I peered into the smoky darkness. It was impossible to see beyond a couple of feet. The rain was coming straight down.

Then I heard a grunt. I caught sight of Johnny just as he launched himself in one final lurch toward our position. His burly body landed in a ball, tucking and rolling as if he'd jumped from an overhead blimp. A spray of water and mud washed across our faces. I heard him let out a short moan. That was a good sign.

We were operational in an hour. An intrepid lineman had outgunned our best engineer.

My throbbing jaw refocused my attention. I looked around the room. J. P. seemed to be holding forth on a new topic, having dropped the harangue on me. The ache in my jaw slowly transformed into a more baleful affliction. It was impossible to keep track of all the ways I felt my life unraveling.

But Johnny seemed to hold the key to my escape from at least one of my self-imposed crises. I wondered if I could rely on him to come through for me one more time.

DINNER WAS AWKWARD. I hardly looked up from my plate. The women chatted amiably, but the men were largely silent. After a while, Rosalie couldn't take it anymore.

"OK. What's going on? J. P., you've hardly said a word. Robert, look at me. Is there something we need to know?"

Lydia looked at George—Nell and Mother at me—searching for clues. No one answered her.

"Well, it's not very often that family gets together like this to celebrate such a happy event," said Rosalie, "and I expect everyone to be mannerly and participate in the conversation. I don't know what's bothering all of you, but we've worked hard to put a good meal on the table and you'd better enjoy it. Here, Lyons, have some more corn pudding. Katie, pass those yeast rolls to J. P. If nothing's wrong, then let's get back to visiting. And wipe those glum looks off your faces."

I tried another bite of country ham, but chewing was not easy. I accepted a second serving of corn pudding, which I could manage a little better. I noticed that Nell seemed to have found her appetite. She had seconds of the French green beans and the ambrosia.

Things loosened up a bit after Rosalie's stern talking-to. Katie had everyone laughing at a story she told about a trip they had recently made to Natural Bridge. Mother talked about how impressed she was with the young nurses entrusted to her care at Norton Memorial Infirmary, where she had recently traded her status as a euchre-playing dowager for the juicy role of housemother and confidante. J. P. eventually took over the conversation with talk about local politics. I tried to relax.

"So, Lyons," J. P. thundered, as he got on a roll, "did you sign that petition asking Gov. Morrow to pardon old man Threlkeld?"

I felt my face redden once again at the mention of my old headmaster. Everyone in the state was following the sensational story. Professor Threlkeld's passion for football—perhaps combined with his infamous temper—had recently landed him in the state penitentiary, where he was to pay penance for shooting a prominent local businessman who had expressed little interest in purchasing season tickets to the school's football games. His first trial ended in a hung jury, but a second group of jurors imported from Mercer County decided rather indelicately that he had indeed committed murder. The judge thereby decreed he should spend his few remaining days in prison, a sentence that was not received well by the good professor's legions of loyal admirers. After all, the ailing scholar had devoted his life to sharpening the intellectual acuity and moral barometer of his young charges.

"Actually, I did," I said. "Logan Threlkeld and I have been friends for years, ever since we were classmates. I felt I owed it to him to do any small thing I could for his father. He's well into his 70s and he's unwell. He has cancer. He won't last long in prison."

"Do you think he deserves to be pardoned? He killed a man, didn't he?" J. P. glared at me once again. I had the feeling that his heart-shaped visage mocked the organ beating reassuringly in the breast of others.

"I don't think he denies that he shot him," I said. "But he claims it was self-defense. I wasn't there. None of us at this table was. I'm not really in a position to judge him. I just know the old man did a lot of good for a lot of young people all around this state. I owe him."

"Do you think the governor will pardon him?" Rosalie asked.

"I don't know," I said. "I hear they got almost three thousand signatures. A lot of his former students are judges and lawyers and ministers and men of some esteem. I have no idea if that will influence him. The governor has made it clear that he wants to put an end to the rogue violence that has plagued Kentucky for generations. He's campaigned against carrying concealed weapons. He signed that anti-lynching bill last year. He even took a couple of county jailers out of their positions when they couldn't stand up to local mobs intent on illegal acts." I felt my throat close up after those last words fell out of my mouth. "So he may not be inclined toward leniency."

"Did you say Logan was teaching up in Michigan now?" Nell asked, trying to lighten the mood.

"Yeah, after the incident he left Nicholasville and headed up there to teach science. He got his degree in biology and chemistry over at Georgetown, you know, before he served as an officer in the war. I suppose he'll follow in his father's footsteps." I decided not to mention that Logan had been party to the bruising assault of the dead man's brother after the shooting. That wasn't as widely reported, and it didn't help my case any to bring it up.

"I guess it's hard to know what will provoke a man to do the unthinkable," said Rosalie.

On the way home I was quiet, and Mother asked if there was something on my mind. I just shook my head. "Nothing more than trying to figure out this whole fatherhood thing," I said. "And worrying about Nell. But it looks like she's going to be just fine."

Effie Mae
Saturday, December 6, 1941

I must have dozed off. I claw away the mixed-up dream of snow-covered roads and my daddy carrying me on his shoulders as he talks to Mr. Fowler down by the harbor. The wind is blowing something awful and I can barely hear their conversation, but it has something to do with Doug and some girl.

I check my watch. It's eight thirty. I expect Lyons will be home within the hour.

What have I learned from an evening spent resurrecting the past? Did I find any clues about how to begin this conversation with my husband? Do I still have the will to confront him? Should I?

Doug is right. I ain't got much choice. While part of me wants to leave the past in the past, another part tells me I cain't be satisfied until I know what happened. There's a child involved, for god's sake. My stepdaughter. I have to know.

He'll be tired when he gets home, but I don't care. I'll just show him the clipping and ask him straight up to explain it. He knows that's how I am. If he feels cornered, tough. I won't be able to sleep until I have an answer, and I'll make dang sure he doesn't sleep until he fesses up.

I notice the radio is still playing Christmas music. I lean back in the rocker and try to focus on the words so I won't think about nothin else.

The sharp ring of the phone nearly catapults me outta the chair. I calm the rocker and hobble over to the table to take the call.

"Hello?"

"This is the operator. I have a call from Mr. Logan Threlkeld in Blacksburg, Virginia, for Mr. Lyons Board."

"This is Mrs. Board. Lyons ain't here."

I hear the operator on the other end. "Sir, would you like to speak to Mrs. Board?"

"Sure," I hear the male voice respond. "Connect me, please."

There are a few clicks and whirs. "Effie Mae? Can you hear me? It's Logan Threlkeld. I just thought I'd take a chance before the holidays got too busy to call and wish you all a merry Christmas. What's the old boy up to tonight?"

"How are ya, Logan? He's handling a Christmas party over at the Clubhouse. How are things there in Blacksburg? Are you planning a big Christmas?"

"It's hard to think much about it until exams are over. I think faculty are more eager for the holidays to arrive than the students. It'll be kind of hard not having my mother around this year, but we still have a houseful, I suppose. The two oldest are starting to lose interest, but Josie is trying hard to hold onto believing in Santa Claus. So Carrie and I will play along while we can."

"I reckon it's nice still having some young'uns around. You better enjoy that. I'll let Lyons know you called."

"Thanks, Effie. You all have a nice holiday."

And then the day's events lurched back into my consciousness. "Uh, Logan?"

"Yes?"

"What do you know about Lyons' first marriage?"

There was silence on the other end of the phone. "What do you mean?"

"Well, I just found a newspaper clipping announcing the birth of his daughter. Back in 1921, I think it was. It names a wife, Nell. You knew him back then, right? Do you know anything about that?"

I waited for a response. I could hear the clock ticking off the seconds in the kitchen.

"Um, are you saying that you didn't know about Nell?" he finally asked.

"No, and I had no idea he had a child."

Silence again. "Then I think Lyons better be the one you talk to about that. All I can tell you is that was a long time ago. Don't go too hard on the boy. We were all young once. I know I did some things I regret."

"What are you saying, Logan? Why would he regret having a family?" I was starting to lose patience. These goddamn no account men and their secrets.

"I'm not saying anything, really. I was thinking about my own youthful exploits, that's all. You ask Lyons about Nell. Meanwhile you all have to come down to Virginia sometime soon for a visit. Why don't you make some plans for the spring?"

"Logan?"

"I've got to run, Effie. Merry Christmas."

I stared at the receiver after he hung up.

It appears I'm the fool. Am I the only person who has no clue who I'm married to? Well, that ends tonight. Tonight I rip away that moldy tarp and uncover whatever blackness lies beneath it.

Lyons
Friday, October 28, 1921

When I came into work, they were all there waiting for me. Harlan, Jamie, and Charlie. They reminded me of Macbeth's three witches ominously predicting my ruin. Charlie took the lead, as he usually did.

"Lyons, we've got a real mess here. Johnny Childers has already talked to a lawyer, and his lawyer has contacted us. I sure hope you're able to cover the expenses from that wreck, because we sure as hell don't want to be in the middle of this."

My head was spinning. I couldn't believe Johnny hadn't at least waited to have a conversation with me.

"Who's his lawyer? Maybe I can talk to him," I said.

"I'm not sure that's the wisest move at the moment. What the hell were you thinking, taking a man's car like that?"

I have no idea, I thought. What was I thinking? What could possibly have made that seem like a sensible thing to do?

"I certainly didn't plan to do any harm," I finally said. "I don't know what I was thinking."

"Well, we've got to get this straightened out. And fast. You know we're already facing increased competition from every garage and dealership in town. Ruggles Ford just slashed their prices again. They're selling that little runabout for $325. Hell, their sedan is only

$660. Even the Buicks over at Ball Garage are down to $1495. And we're still struggling to pay for this $25,000 building. Then here you go bringing us bad publicity—and that's even if we don't end up having to cover your debts. How are you going to fix this?"

I had no answer.

"Let me go talk to Johnny and see if I can get him to slow this thing down," I finally said. "Surely we can work something out. There's no reason any of you or Big Four Motors needs to be involved. Talk will die down once we get this settled and everyone finds something else to gossip about."

"Well, that had better be quick. This business is hanging by a thread as it is. Every weekend people are auctioning their cars over at the courthouse just to get a little cash to pay their bills. No one's buying. People don't even have the money for new tires or basic maintenance. We're really hurting, and we won't survive another big hit caused by your asinine recklessness. I want this straightened out by next week, Lyons."

"Yes, sir."

"Oh, by the way . . . Congratulations on your new daughter. And stay away from any more fistfights."

Charlie turned and headed to the back bay. The other two looked at me, perhaps a little sympathetically, and then followed him. No one else said a word.

I hadn't even had a chance to take off my hat and overcoat, so I wheeled around and headed back out the door and over to Johnny's garage.

He wasn't there when I arrived. The young man helping him told me he had gone out and he didn't know when he'd be back.

I wasn't sure what my next step should be. With no answers, I didn't see any point in going back to work. Mother was comfortably ensconced with the Champs. I was in no mood to drive back to Lawrenceburg and face more incoming there.

I headed down the street to the pool hall and took a table in a dark corner. No one was around at nine in the morning, so I had the place to myself.

I could hear some of the fellas in the kitchen starting preparations for lunch, yelling over the sounds of water running and pans banging. I looked through the pass-through window behind the counter and could make out black faces and white faces amid the rising steam. It seemed like a convivial atmosphere, the dishwasher teasing the fry cook, someone whistling, Sam barking orders above the din.

I slouched in my chair, aware that the faint ache in my jaw now seemed to have joined a rumba in my head. The smell of sour beer wafted up from the floor, further spicing the rhythmic dance. I wondered if the beer marinating in the scuffed wood planks was an artifact of pre-Prohibition days or more recent carelessness with some back-room brew.

As I sat in the semi-gloom, I felt my shoulders slump under a wearying burden, until breathing became difficult. I imagined my former friends and allies lining up to take a shot at a target square on my chest, each one landing near center. A runner in my unit once said there were times when he thought he could see his serial number on an artillery shell. I almost wished one would find its mark.

How had everything gotten so complicated? How would I ever extricate myself from this mess? Even if I got Johnny to settle down and work things out, what was on the other side of that? Bankruptcy? A failed business enterprise? Continued pressure to sustain a standard of living I couldn't possibly deliver? More recriminations from successful family and in-laws? Where would it end? What was the reward?

I heard the kitchen door swing open and looked up to see Sam heading my way. I wasn't sure I was up for a conversation, but I smiled at him. He was a good sort. He seemed to understand what his customers needed, offering a cozy, relatively safe hideaway from wives and girlfriends as well as some of the best food in town. Prohibition had made his job tougher but business hadn't appeared to wane too much, so he must have found a way to manage that little impediment, too.

He walked toward me, wiping his hands on a towel, leaving the perspiration to bead on his temples near what was left of his short-cropped hair.

"How are ya, Lyons? Can I get you anything? It's a little early for food, but I could bring you a cup of coffee."

"No, thanks, Sam. I just needed to duck into a neutral corner for a minute."

"Yeah, heard you got yourself in a little fight yesterday. You OK?"

"Oh, yeah, I'll be fine. Johnny laid one on me pretty good, and I'm feeling it this morning. But I deserved it, I guess. I just want to get this all straightened out."

"Well, it's none of my business, of course, but that Johnny can be a mean bastard. You better watch yourself."

"Johnny and I go way back. We'll figure this out."

"You let me know if you need anything. Come on over later and shoot a few rounds of pool. Get this off your mind. Hey, did I hear your wife had the baby?"

"Yeah, everyone's doing well. I was over there last night. Hope to get them home this weekend."

"Well, congratulations. Again, let me know if there's anything I can do. We'll put you to work washing dishes if you need a few extra dollars—or just a place to hide out for a while." He grinned at me. "People know better than to bring their battles in here."

"Thanks, Sam. It's good to know I have a safe haven nearby." I forced the best grin I could. "Well, guess I'd better go see what new trouble I'm in."

I got up from the table and headed back outside. The clouds were beginning to thicken and the smell of rain hung in the air. I decided a walk might do me some good, so I headed out Second Street toward my old neighborhood for a change of pace. As I walked, I tried to peel away each layer of the oppression I was feeling so I could see it more clearly, strip it of its magnetic hold, and eventually lock it away in an airtight chamber.

First, how could I resolve this situation with Johnny? Was there someone I could go to for advice? For money? My in-laws were already biased against me. My family had called in all our chips around town when we sorted through my mother's and father's complex financial entanglements a couple of years ago. From the perspective of the local banks and lenders, that was now all settled. I didn't think I could hit them up again right now, when everyone was suffering. I had no collateral, no assets to back up a loan of that size.

And we were probably talking about a large sum of money. I hadn't heard a figure yet, but I knew cars well enough to know it was going to be a lot more than I could come up with. Jesse James popped back in my mind, but I was fairly certain robbing a bank wasn't my best option.

Perhaps I should just go straight to a lawyer. Maybe one of my cousins could take up my case. Or at least give me some advice. Of course, I knew a couple of lawyers there in Hopewell, but I didn't yet know who Johnny had solicited and who might have already sided with whom.

Which reminded me that I also needed to address the rumors running rampant around town. I had to patch up my rapidly depreciating reputation, for my sake, for Nell's sake, and for the sake of Big Four Motors. But where do you start with something like that?

I looked up just as I came to the bridge crossing Houston Creek. A wave of memories overwhelmed me.

"Stop dawdling, Lyons," I heard my mother say as we approached the covered bridge. "I need to get home and get supper started."

She was gripping my hand tightly, trying to hurry me along

as winter darkness swallowed up the town. I had just turned eight and thought I was too old for her to be holding my hand. I glanced around, trying to make sure none of my friends were out and about. We had been Christmas shopping, looking forward to the holidays that would bring a merry end to the first year in a new century.

We stepped purposefully onto the bridge. Tiny slivers of the last light slipped between the side slats of the bridge, preventing total darkness from engulfing us. My eyes struggled to adjust. I looked down as our footsteps landed flatly on the wood floor.

Without warning I felt my mother's hand pull roughly out of my own and I heard her let out a very unladylike grunt. I looked up to see her trying to hold on to her purse with both hands as a tall colored man I recognized from town worked furiously to free it from her grasp. The smell of sweat assaulted my senses as he pumped his arms.

It took me a second to recognize that this was not a friendly encounter. When I tried to cry out, my voice appeared to be cowering somewhere deep in my throat, shirking its duties. I eventually coaxed it back to work.

"Stop it! Leave her alone!" I yelled as loud as I could.

I began pounding his lower back with my fists. The man whipped his head around and said something to me that I didn't understand, but I was overpowered by the smell of whiskey.

During the violent tug of war that was taking place just above my head, my mother lost her balance and fell backward onto the wooden floorboards of the bridge with a small cry. I watched as the man fell to the floor with her, refusing to let go of the bag. I'll never forget the look of horror on my mother's face as he lay on top of her, his contorted face an inch or two from hers, still wrestling for the purse that was now wedged between them. I grabbed one of his legs and tried to drag him off her, screaming at the top of my lungs. He kicked me away just as I heard men's voices coming toward us from Houston Avenue. As the sound grew louder, the man suspended his battle with my mother and looked in their direction. Then, without further hesitation, he pushed himself off her and ran toward the other end of the bridge in the direction of town.

Two of our neighbors, Mr. Thompson and Mr. Higgins, were kneeling next to my mother. "Mrs. Board, are you all right? Are you hurt?" I heard Mr. Thompson ask her. I couldn't hear her response, if there was any. The third man had run after the would-be thief. I stood back a little distance, uncertain about the role of a dutiful son in this unfamiliar situation.

My mother seemed dazed. I could see that her coat had been ripped in the scuffle, and I managed to scoop up two of the big silver buttons that had popped off and been kicked to the edge of the bridge floorboards. Feeling a little queasy and disoriented, I bent over to gather the wrapping paper and ornaments that had spilled from the shopping bag Mother had dropped.

"Lyons, I sure am glad you started yelling," Mr. Thompson said. "We were on my porch and heard your screams. Your mother could have been badly hurt. Yes, sir, this could have been much worse."

Mr. Higgins stood up and put his arm around my shoulders, pulling me close to his leg. He had the sweet smell of tobacco. I wanted to believe what Mr. Thompson was saying, but I secretly thought I should have been able to prevent the whole thing from happening if I had just been paying attention. If I hadn't been daydreaming. If I had been more of a man.

I was so confused. I knew George Carter. He was a fixture around town. He stood out from many of the other Negroes because he was always dressed nice, unlike a lot of the colored farmers and laborers. Someone told me he was educated, that he had gone all the way through the colored school. I was aware he'd been in and out of trouble, but he never seemed dangerous to me. I couldn't understand why he would attack my mother.

Twenty years later, I stood trembling in front of the bridge, the recollections turning me to a pillar of salt.

After that night back in 1900, there was a lot of whispering among the adults whenever I was around, as if Hopewell's Greek chorus had gathered excitedly to comment on the recent events. My mother, who had fought so fiercely during the attack, took to her bed for three days. My father appeared more attentive to my mother, at least temporarily. No one talked to me about what had happened. When Christmas finally arrived, it seemed a little less joyous, as if a pall had fallen over the whole season. By the new year, however, the incident seemed to be largely forgotten.

Then in February, rumors began circulating that the man who had assaulted my mother was in the local jail for another crime. A bad crime. An attempted rape of his sister-in-law. I didn't fully understand what that meant at the time, but I could tell from the adults that the whole situation appeared to have gotten much more serious. Then one day after school, the jailer came to our house and asked my mother to look at a photograph of a man he was holding at the jail to see if he was the man who had attacked her. I was peering in the room from the hallway.

"Yes, that's the man. I'll never forget that face," I heard my mother say.

"Now, Mary Lake, I know you didn't want to press charges at the time. You just wanted to put this ugly episode behind you, and I respect that. But now that we're holding him for another crime, would you be willing to come down to the jail and identify him in person?"

My mother hesitated a moment, looking down at her lap. "Oh, Warren, do I have to? Isn't this enough? I really don't want to see him again."

"Well, it would sure help us seal this case."

"Isn't there some other way? Did one of the men who came to my rescue see him?"

"No, I've already spoken with them. None of them got a good look. Sure, they had their suspicions who it was. But we can't hold a man on suspicions."

My mother was silent, frowning at Mr. Kiser.

"This is a little hard to ask," he started, "but wasn't your son there with you? Do you think he got a good look at him? Do you think he might be able to identify him?"

"Goodness, Warren. I am not going to ask my eight-year-old son to go down to the jail with you to identify some dangerous criminal you're holding down there. What are you thinking?"

"Well, I'm thinking about the other women who might suffer a similar fate. Like this fella's sister-in-law. I'm trying to prevent him from hurting someone else. But if we can't pin him to this crime, we may have to let him go. The lawyers won't have much of a case."

I could see my mother reconsidering. Lurking in the hallway, I thought, *Here's my chance to make this right. I couldn't do much the day of the attack, but I could go down to the jail and see if the man they're holding is the one I remember. That seems like a simple way for me to help.*

I stepped into the room. "Mr. Kiser?" I said.

"Lyons, you go back outside and play," my mother said. "This is none of your business."

"But I heard Mr. Kiser say he needed someone to identify the man who attacked you. I think I can do it. Will you let me go down there with him?"

My mother looked at me. Then she looked at Mr. Kiser. "Are you sure this is necessary, Warren?"

"Yes ma'am. It would help us close the door on this whole thing."

My mother sighed. "Lyons, are you sure you want to do this? I am not asking you, but you were there, too, so perhaps it will help you put this behind you."

"I can do this, Mother. I want to."

Eventually, my mother reluctantly acquiesced. Mr. Kiser and I took Second Street back toward Main, but instead of turning right toward the Courthouse we turned left and went under the iron railroad bridge toward Stoner Creek, near where it joined up with Houston Creek. I looked up at Mr. Kiser—Charon ferrying me across the rivers Styx and Acheron. His two-story brick home faced the tracks. Butted right up to the side of his residence was the three-story stone jail with its many narrow vertical barred windows. There was a basement that opened into the walled yard sitting on the banks of the creek. We all called it "the dungeon." I imagined Mr. Carter in leg irons somewhere inside.

But as it turned out I didn't have to go back there. We entered the brick building from the wooden front porch, and Mr. Kiser took me into his orderly office. He parked me in the corner and arranged for his deputy to walk Mr. Carter by the door so I could see him but he couldn't see me. As soon as I saw his face, I knew it was him. What I didn't know then was that my good neighbors, in their zeal to defend my mother's virtue, had already tried and convicted him, at least in their own poisoned minds.

"Yes sir," I said quietly. "That's the man who attacked my mother."

A few days afterwards, according to news reports, late on Sunday night when the recently installed electric streetlights were mysteriously unlit along a gloomy Main Street, about thirty men formed two lines and walked silently through the middle of town.

When they got to the jail, they stepped up on that front porch and demanded entrance, which Mr. Kiser steadfastly denied them. Several of the men then surrounded the jail, and someone on the front porch smashed the glass and unlocked the door from the inside. Mr. Kiser raised his Colt to defend the prisoners in his care, but quickly realized he was outnumbered. As the men stormed the jail, a frightened employee standing at the top of the stairs tossed them the jailhouse key ring.

The iron door to the cellblock breached, the men found George

Carter and dragged him to the street as the other colored prisoners howled. The mob marched him in total darkness back up Main Street to the front of the massive brick and granite courthouse with its looming 110-foot tower. Surrounding the courthouse lawn was a stout stone and iron fence with an ornate arched gate. According to the prominent plate affixed to one of the stone posts, all of the iron structures had been custom made by Atlas Metal Works in Philadelphia, the City of Brotherly Love.

The newspaperman reporting the night's events wrote that a man in the mob demanded that the accused man confess, but he refused to speak. The men then bound Mr. Carter's arms and legs and slipped a noose over his head, tightened it, and tossed the other end of the rope over the tallest arch in the gate. With the first strong tug, the rope snapped, and Mr. Carter fell to the ground. The men quickly prepared a second rope, tightened it around the man's neck, and tried again. This time the rope held.

When they were certain he was dead, someone in the mob stepped forward and pinned a handwritten sign to his chest: "There's no place on earth for a man like this." Within minutes, the streets were again deserted.

The body was still hanging in front of the courthouse early on Monday morning when the janitor arrived to build the fires that would warm the building. The next day the local newspaper headline screamed that "Judge Lynch" had prevailed. My mother's name appeared in large print just below. One line from the article will be etched in my memory forever: "The crime for which George Carter suffered the penalty of his life was one which causes a shudder to creep over everyone who possesses a wife, mother or sister when he hears of it."

I tried to recall if I had had any clues about what was going on that Sunday night. I seemed to remember our collie, Lady, barking in the wee hours of the morning and hearing the front door close. But I couldn't be sure.

By Wednesday, the boys at school could talk about nothing else. Few knew the role I had played in getting this man lynched, but everyone knew it was my mother he had attacked. I could feel the sideways glances when I walked in the classroom. "You really showed that nigger!" one boy yelled at me with a stupid grin on his face. I looked down at my desk. I was horrified. I could not understand why George Carter had to die. Later that afternoon, although my mother had tried to hide the newspaper from me, I was able to find a copy and slowly work my way through the story.

As far as I know, no member of the mob ever came forward or was ever charged with a crime. The case was closed for the citizens of Hopewell. My mother and father never spoke of it again. Justice had been served.

I realized I had been standing at the entrance to the bridge for several minutes. I reached for my handkerchief to wipe the perspiration from my face. My hands were clammy. It had been a long time since I had allowed myself to recall the details of that incident. As I was growing up, suppressing those memories let me peaceably coexist with my Hopewell neighbors whose sense of right and wrong continued to confound me. After that night, my own parents' actions and judgments seemed open to suspicion, or at least questioning. I had witnessed a criminal act, and I had told the truth about it. If being truthful can lead to such an inexplicable outcome, is it better to conceal the truth in innocent lies? Or to deny the truth altogether? Is living a life cloaked in deceit more virtuous? As a youngster, as best as I could unscramble it, that sure seemed to be the choice of many of the adults I was expected to look up to. How had everything gotten so twisted?

As I got older, of course, I began to understand what had happened: that fear and shame and a distorted sense of superiority had led to a man having his life taken from him for no just reason; that we are all pathetic wretches—all of us, whatever the circumstances of our birth—imprisoned in our narrow minds if not within those cold stone walls.

I read newspaper reports of similar incidents in nearby Shelbyville, in Nicholasville where I had gone to school, and all over the western part of the state. I learned that it was customary in my town to mete out justice for the supposed rape of a white woman by a colored man in this way. There were no trials, no verification of the facts. Mobs of upstanding Hopewell citizens simply stormed the jail and took care of business.

When I was an adult, I dared ask my mother one time about the incident on the bridge.

"That's in the past, Lyons," she told me. "There's no use thinking about it. Things are different now, at least I hope they are. But back when your father and I were first married, the next year in fact, a delicate young woman from our church, Mrs. Peter Crow, was raped by a colored man, a frightening man more than twice her size. After she identified him, the situation was taken care of the same way as mine was. I imagine some of the same people were involved. And over in Nicholas County, there had been two similar incidents that same year. This was just how we handled these things. It was the right thing to do with the least amount of fuss."

I dared not point out that she hadn't been raped. Perhaps she didn't recall that I had witnessed the entire scene.

But, sadly, things really weren't any different. The year Nell and I married, a mob pulled a colored man off the train just outside Hopewell and hung him on a nearby telephone pole. He was accused of raping the 14-year-old daughter of the landowner he worked for up in Maysville. After they lynched him, though, we all learned that he and the girl, who was actually a young woman, were simply seeing each other. I guess her daddy didn't like it, so he took care of it the best way he knew how. Doesn't seem to me like we've learned very much.

I tried to tell myself that my involvement hadn't really mattered, that George Carter's fate was sealed at the first rumor. At least I hadn't helped lay the twigs and dried grass for the pyre they built in Maysville for another man suspected of similar crimes, as it was reported many children did. I hadn't understood the consequences of my actions. I just thought I was being helpful.

Perhaps my mother was right; perhaps all of this was past and not worth dredging up. But it was somehow all tied to my growing discomfort with the life I had settled for here in Hopewell.

I had been strangely buoyed, however, by one incident in Shelbyville, which took place right before I went to work at the pharmacy in nearby LaGrange. A mob broke into the jail and pulled three men out to hang them. Two had been accused of detaining a fourteen-year-old white girl. When they strung them up on a nearby railroad bridge, which was the customary site of such events in that town, one of the ropes broke and the accused man swam away, only to be caught by some of the mob and peppered with bullets. A second man was successfully hanged. The third man evidently played dead long enough for the crowd to get caught up in the chase for the first. He somehow then untied the rope from his hands, extracted himself from the noose, dropped into the water and disappeared. His family eventually let it be known that he had escaped, and I've since seen reports that he served in the Great War with the rest of us reluctant patriots. Whatever he saw over there, it must have felt like a cake walk compared to what he had been through right here in central Kentucky.

The summer I returned home after the war, race riots broke out all across the country. Colored veterans, having grown accustomed to being treated with respect by the French, woke up to the realization that the democratic ideals they had fought for still didn't apply to them. When angry white mobs attacked Negro citizens that summer, they fought back. They were ready to work, to take their rightful place in a growing economy, but they were no longer willing to be shoved around. Or murdered for minor transgressions.

At Camp Taylor, before we were shipped off to fight, city slickers, farm boys, immigrants, Negroes, the educated, and the illiterate all donned the same uniform and executed the same drills. It was hard to assign status or separate into cliques when everyone looked the same. And in France, no one cared who your family was or where you came from as long as you followed your brothers over the top.

But here in Hopewell, I felt a responsibility to reclaim my station, to sustain a certain artifice, to present that unflinchingly brave face my mother had perfected. Generations of ancestors demanded it, but I couldn't see the point. And I wasn't sure I had the right. How was I any better than that working stiff next to me? The pretense exhausted me. I hated the falseness, the posturing, the immense effort it took to pretend the world was other than it was.

Why couldn't we just embrace the facts? My family had been financially ruined. My father's illness had disgraced us. My mother had retreated to the embrace of relatives in Louisville. I had watched this unfold. This was the reality I knew. These were the facts, for those who were willing to trade in such things.

And now the fact was that I had brought yet more ignominy upon my family.

The image of the beautiful blue Oakland Sedan, its front end crushed, flashed through my mind. With that fateful jerk of the wheel, it seemed my life had spun irretrievably out of control.

Or perhaps, I mused, the accident had freed me to pursue a life on my own terms. But what would that look like?

I allowed that fantasy to fill my thoughts, as I turned around and headed back toward town in a light drizzle. The prospect of shrinking into obscurity, fading into the gray underworld inhabited by all the invisible laborers—much as I had blended inconspicuously among the recruits at Camp Taylor and the doughboys in the French countryside—was vaguely comforting. That had come so easily. Could I disappear in civilian camouflage among thousands of others living on the fringes of society? Could I erase all memory, sever all ties to this life that had begun to torment me?

AT BIG FOUR MOTORS that afternoon, I was huddled in the office going through some paperwork when a courier came looking for me. He handed me an envelope stamped with the Talbott & Whitley firm's return address. I felt my face blanch. I dismissed the youngster and tore open the envelope.

So that's where Johnny had been earlier that morning. In my hands was the petition he had filed claiming I took possession of his Oakland sedan "against his express orders and wrongly started on a journey with said machine and tore it up and destroyed it to plaintiff's damage in the sum of at least $1,000."

One thousand dollars. How would I ever repay that sum? That was like asking Teddy Roosevelt to stay away from horses. It just couldn't be done. But what other options did I have?

I recalled a local news article I had read the previous summer about a traveling shoe salesman who put his wife and four-year-old daughter on a train in Hopewell and then simply vanished. According to the reports, the family had recently sold a home in Knoxville and were boarding a connecting train to Lexington, where they planned to live. The salesman handed his wife ten dollars as she and their daughter boarded the rail car, while he trailed behind with the family's luggage (and the remaining $4,000 from the sale of the home). Neither he nor the bags ever made it on the train.

In follow-up news articles, the wife had said she was at a loss as to what happened to him. By all accounts, they had a happy marriage.

Finally, she had told the reporters, "I guess he just left because he wanted to."

I wondered what had been going through that man's mind when he abandoned his family. Had he planned it? Or had he simply acted impulsively, as the opportunity arose? Did he regret his actions later? Did the family ever reunite? I had to smile when I remembered that the woman had been the daughter of a respected physician in Nashville. That poor schmuck, I thought. He must have known he would never live up to her family's expectations.

Effie Mae
Saturday, December 6, 1941

I heard his weary footfalls on the steps about quarter to ten. I was ready.

He turned his key and pushed the door open. As he stepped into the living room, I could see he was wore out. For just a second I felt bad about deciding to confront him directly. But I quickly shoved that aside. I needed to know.

He looked up and saw me sitting in the rocker.

"I'm surprised to see you still up," he said. "Isn't it cold over there by the window?"

"I like the view. I've been looking at the Christmas lights."

"Yeah, it's getting kind of festive out there. Two of the servers set up a little Christmas tree at the Clubhouse this afternoon. I guess that's one more thing you'll have to clean around."

"Hmmm…"

He hung up his hat and coat and looked at me.

"Is something going on? Where's Doug? I thought he might be here this evening."

"Down at the tavern. He's giving us a little space."

"What for?"

"So we can talk about this." I extended my arm, holding the newspaper clipping out for him to see.

He walked over and took it from me. His face reddened.

"Where did you find this?"

"In one of your books. I was dusting and accidentally dropped it. This fell out."

Lyons was quiet a moment.

"So I guess you want to talk about this tonight. Can it wait?"

"No, sir, it cain't," I said.

He took a seat on the sofa opposite me. All his weight seemed to sink into the cushions. His eyes was glazed.

"Do you wanna beer?" I asked.

"Do we have any bourbon?"

"I'll check." I went into the kitchen and grabbed myself a beer out of the icebox. I opened the cabinet and pulled out the Old Forester. Bethlehem Steel didn't allow no liquor sales there at Sparrows Point—technically they didn't allow consumption of alcohol neither—but I was glad we had made a run to Dundalk last week. I dropped some ice into a glass and poured a little bourbon over it. I hoped the beer would keep me calm. I hoped the bourbon would loosen his lips.

I handed him the glass and sat back down. "OK, cuddlebug. You wanna start at the beginning?" I asked.

He took a sip and laid his head against the back of the sofa, his eyes closed. "What is it exactly that you want to know?" he asked.

"Everything. Everything you ain't yet told me. Anything you ain't shared with me. Me, your wife. Or at least your current wife. How many have there been?"

He didn't answer.

"Well, let's start with Nell and this child. What happened to them?"

Lyons hesitated. "I don't know."

"What do you mean you don't know?"

"I suppose they're still living in Kentucky."

"You 'suppose'? You really don't know where your daughter is?"

I watched him struggle to answer. "No."

I was already getting angry, and exasperated. I tried to control the waver in my voice. "OK. Walk me through this. I thought maybe they had died, in an accident or somethin. Is that what happened?"

Lyons was quiet. "Not as far as I know."

"Then you divorced your wife and just left? And didn't stay in touch with her or your daughter?"

Lyons slowly wiped his hand along the length of his face, as if trying to squeeze together the memories. He dropped his head, staring into his lap.

"Not exactly."

"What do you mean, Lyons? Dammit, tell me what happened." I got up from my chair and started pacing back and forth. I couldn't sit still.

"It's complicated."

"How complicated can it be?" I yelled. "Just tell me the story, for god's sake."

His voice rose, and he leaned forward on the sofa, elbows on his knees. "Dammit, Effie, I was suffocating there. It's hard to explain. I was dying inside. I just couldn't do it any longer. I could not live in that world another minute. Play those games. Pretend everything was just fine. Well, it wasn't fine. It wasn't fine at all. And I hated everything about it."

I felt the heat rise in my face. "You hated your wife and daughter?"

"No," he said. I watched him deflate, sink back into the cushions again. "No. I didn't hate Nell. I felt bad for her. I still do. But I had gone numb. I knew I wasn't feeling what I was supposed to be feeling. I don't know if the Army had succeeded in stripping me of all human sympathy so I could get through what we had to endure over in France. Or if I was just a wrecked human being from mishandling all that had been thrown my way. I felt like I couldn't find my soul."

He stopped for a moment. "And that scared the hell out of me."

I backed off, let him keep sorting through all that he'd done buried for so long.

"Nell and I had a different view of the world, of what was important," Lyons started again. "I knew that. I never should have married her. But I thought I was doing the right thing when I proposed. I thought I could settle down in my hometown and live like my parents had. But I just couldn't. I'd already been gone too long. I'd seen too much. I couldn't go back to that world. And it was all so—so confining. So phony."

"Phony?"

"You know, everyone was trying so hard to be something they weren't. A big shot. A model citizen. But it was all a masquerade. All posturing. And to tell the truth, I was the worst of the lot. I tried, but I just couldn't do it. I knew I had flaws. I made mistakes. A lot of them. Some bad ones. But I got so tired of trying to fix everything and make everything right."

I was quiet a minute. I let Lyons catch his breath. He looked for a moment like he might start sobbing, but then he composed hisself again.

"Lyons, what did you do?"

I could hear the clock in the kitchen as it continued its relentless journey.

Lyons' head was still hanging low. When he finally spoke, I could barely hear him.

"I left."

"You left? What, you just took a powder?"

"Yeah, I ran off."

I stopped right in front of him and stared. "You abandoned your wife and daughter? How old was your daughter when you left?"

His voice was lifeless. "About a week."

My eyes widened and my ears started ringing. I couldn't believe what I was hearing. My husband had walked away from the people he had pledged to care for. People who depended on him utterly, for everything. He had just cut his losses and walked out.

And then I exploded. "You filthy sonofabitch. You've been living a lie your whole life? Talk about pretending to be someone you're not. I thought you was a man of some integrity. I've picked up and moved all over this country with you. I've watched you work hard to take care of us. And all the while you had a wife and daughter back in Kentucky? And you ain't never told me?"

He had no response.

"Is our marriage even legal?" I squeaked. I couldn't even get my head around that. I decided to back away from that cliff.

"Ain't you never even tried to get in touch with your daughter?" I asked. "The daughter your wife done raised all alone? Don't you want to know about her? About how she turned out? About her dreams? About the things you might have in common?"

He couldn't even look at me.

"What's her name?"

He was slow to answer. "Mary Rose."

I felt my throat tighten. "That's beautiful, cuddlebug. Do you know how old she is now?"

"She turned twenty on October 26," he said quietly. "I've never forgotten her birthday."

"But you've never called her? Never sent her a card or a gift? Written her a letter?"

He barely shook his head.

"What kind of man are you, Lyons? Are you a monster? Who could do that? If you don't love your own daughter, why would I think you could love me? I cain't believe how you had me fooled. Do you know how to love anyone?"

I could see I had beaten him down, and he wasn't even trying to fight back. It was pitiful, really. But I didn't feel sorry for him. Nary a bit. He disgusted me.

"Did you plan to keep this little secret your whole life?" I asked. "Hell, I reckon you might have succeeded if I hadn't chanced upon that clipping. Why did you hang onto that if you cared so little for your family?"

He looked up at me then, his eyes pleading with me to stop. But I couldn't.

"You are a despicable human being, you know that? It's shameful, what you done. How can you even live with yourself?"

And then I was plum exhausted, too. I dropped back into the rocker. The room was way too small for both of us, but I didn't know where to go. I had no idea what I was going to do.

Seeing me flag seemed to breathe a little life back into him. "Effie, I didn't see how any good would come of your knowing about this. I've loved you since I saw you bounce into that drugstore in Middlesboro. I knew you even then. You represented everything true and joyous in this world. I recognized immediately that you were exactly who you appeared to be. I didn't understand it then, but that was what I was looking for. You couldn't hide a feeling or an emotion or an opinion. And I loved that about you. I could not believe my luck when I ran into you again in Cincinnati. And I may not be very good at expressing it, but I have been very happy these last years with you."

I almost believed him. I wanted to believe him. Damn, he always had the right words. He was always a charmer.

"I don't know how I can ever again believe a word that comes out of that mouth of yours, Lyons Board. Is that even your name? How much of the rest of your story is made up? What else have you left out?"

He looked at me and tried to smile. I think I understood then. That's what he was trying to tell me. He relied on me to reset him back to true. Whatever his past, whatever his transgressions, whatever lies he had told, he needed me to bring him back to center.

At that moment, though, I didn't know if I could continue to play that role, to keep him on the straight and narrow. Or if I wanted to. I still needed to figger out who he was, and I had a sense that that was going to take a lot more work. What else was he hiding? Did I want to put forth that much effort? Was it worth it?

"So, what do we do now, Mrs. Board?" he asked.

The emotions of the day had finally sapped me of all energy. My head was just as muddled as it had been when I found the clipping, maybe more so. But I had no fight left in me.

"Let's go to bed and take this up again in the morning," I said. "You're not off the hook yet, you bastard. This conversation is just starting. But maybe we can sort through things more clearly tomorrow. You'll have eight hours to think up more lies."

He didn't look at me, but I caught just a glimpse of his lopsided grin. Then it was gone.

I picked up his glass and my bottle and headed into the kitchen. I heard him walk in the bathroom and turn on the water.

Lyons
Tuesday, February 24, 1925

*I*t was a relatively routine lunch shift at the Sinton Hotel, and I had gotten into the groove of preparing rather fetching shrimp cocktails for the typical lunch crowd: overbearing businessmen, harried secretaries, flibbertigibbety tourists. The unusually sunny day seemed to have prompted more orders for the chilled seafood dish that was a bewildering specialty for a Midwest destination on the banks of the muddy Ohio. With zealous concentration, I would scoop some shaved ice into the bottom of a hollow-stemmed, wide-mouthed crystal goblet, drop in the glass insert for the cocktail sauce, fill it, and then alternately hook shrimp and lemon and lime wedges around the rim. Finally, I'd add a sprig of parsley, and move on to the next one. Voilà—an evocative dish that would transport mollycoddled Midwesterners to piquant New Orleans. Nothing like a slimy crustacean appearing to slurp congealed blood from grandmother's finest champagne glasses. Was there a better use for all that cherished stemware during Prohibition?

However captivating for the landlocked diner, the dish's preparation demanded precision and quick hands. I had found the repetitiveness of the work surprisingly soothing. At the fringes of my consciousness, the mélange of smells in the wider kitchen, from garlic to brewing coffee to fried potatoes, comforted me like a familiar quilt.

When I was able to tune out the surrounding din, I could at times feel almost at peace amid the hurly-burly. And, after innumerable hours of practice, I would frequently allow my thoughts to wander as I handled the task in front of me.

I had started working at the Sinton not long after the lavish Cincinnati hotel had opened its handsome new coffee shop, which quickly became a popular lunch spot. With its labyrinthine counter snaking its way amid the heavy columns supporting interconnecting Romanesque arches, it felt more like dining in a medieval monastery than a modern city. The counter was edged in dark mahogany and the stained-glass windows diffused the natural light. The space was a cozier derivative of the hotel's Grand Banquet Room, where the ceiling soared to more than twice the height and the ornate columns and arches framed enormous Romantic murals. It all perfectly complemented the grandiose Second Empire style of the hotel, with its brick and stone exterior and mansard roofs—eerily similar to the old county courthouse in Hopewell before it burned in 1901, just a few short months after its arched gate was defiled.

When I first landed in Cincinnati, I suspected any sense of tranquility would depend on lying low. Johnny's lawsuit had stirred up big trouble, and, even some months later, officials of the court were still looking for me. I could never figure out what they thought they would get from me if they found me. I didn't have the money to pay Johnny for the car. They had already taken the little bit of real property Nell and I had, as well as my share of the Big Four business. There wasn't anything else for them to garnish. I heard that Nell and the baby had moved back in with her family in Lawrenceburg. I felt bad about everything—horrible, really—but, at the time, I couldn't see any other path forward. And, quite frankly, they were better off without me.

After I had settled Nell and Mary Rose into our little house on Vine Street the weekend after the birth, I tried my damnedest to carry on as if everything would eventually work out. I watched in awe as Nell soothed the crying baby, managed the middle-of-the-night feedings, fell asleep on the sofa with Mary Rose crooked in her arm. I did what I could, helping with the errands, the meals. But mostly I just stayed out of the way.

When I went back to work on Monday, the situation had only gotten worse. A little after lunch, Charlie pulled me aside as I was talking with a customer.

"I've had another call from Johnny's lawyer," he told me. "He said he has every intention of listing both Big Four Motors and North Middletown Garage as garnishees for the $1,000 you owe for that wrecked car. You had better come up with a way to pay that debt, Lyons. We are not interested in covering for your stupidity."

I just nodded.

On Tuesday morning, I got up as usual, dressed, and left the house. It was a raw November day. I pulled my muffler tighter around my neck and tucked my chin to my chest. I started the short walk to work, but something made me turn and head toward the train depot instead.

I opened the door to the passenger waiting area and felt a blast of warm air hit my face. I looked around and noted only one other gentleman, whom I did not recognize, half dozing on a bench. I stood there for what felt like a long time, asking myself what the hell I was doing.

When I could finally prod my feet into some sort of motion, I bought a newspaper and took a seat away from the ticket window, perhaps understanding the temptation it presented. I thumbed through the pages without really seeing anything printed there. After staring fixedly, blindly at a page of local news, something made me bring the words into focus: *"Mr. and Mrs. Lyons Board, of Hopewell, are the happy parents of a fine daughter . . . "*

I felt a convulsion of shame and grief. I must have known then that I had already turned my back on them. Why could I not feel any of the conventional happiness of others at this moment?

I tore out the birth announcement, folded it, and tucked it in the soft leather band inside my gray fedora, just under my monogrammed initials. I stared out the window at the gray November sky.

At some point, I felt myself stand up and walk over to the ticket counter. It was almost as if I watched myself take the steps necessary to purchase a ticket and get on the proper train, powerless to stop the unfolding drama. And then the curtain dropped, putting an end to Act I.

I wandered for a few months, picking up work as needed, corresponding with Logan intermittently—knowing that he understood the urge to disappear and put all vestiges of the past behind him—and hoping that anyone else looking for me had long lost my scent. I did not feel liberated, really. I felt sad. I had abandoned everything I had ever cared about. And I knew I could never return. Up to that point, my life had been consumed with trying to do the right thing, trying to please my family, trying to build a respectable name for myself. And then I had walked away. And I had no idea where I was going.

Eventually I got tired of moving around every few weeks, and I decided a big city—even one commonly frequented by friends and relatives—would be a pretty good place to hide. But what would I do? There was no way I could get back in the automobile business, or any related enterprise, so I had to find a new line of work. When I got off the train in Cincinnati, I learned quickly that there was a YMCA nearby, largely populated with railroad workers. That seemed like an excellent place to disappear into anonymity. Once settled there, I did what I could to blend in with the other laborers. I wasn't sure my pampered upbringing had forged a constitution fit for railroad work, however, so I started looking around for other employment.

When I picked up a newspaper a couple of days later, I saw that the Sinton Hotel was looking for kitchen staff to support its expanding lunch business. Working behind the scenes in the soupy air of a crowded kitchen seemed like the perfect way to achieve near invisibility. I knew nothing about the business, of course, but I was able to convince the hiring manager that I was willing to start at the bottom and learn the ropes. He seemed a little suspicious that someone of my bearing wanted the job he had advertised, but I told him I was new to the area and was looking for a fresh start in a new industry. He acquiesced after I promised I would show up for work every day and stay with them at least six months.

I started out lugging bags of onions up from the cellar, peeling potatoes, chopping lettuce, and keeping stacks of clean plates in front of the cooks. It was certainly different from the type of work I was accustomed to. Rather than trying to persuade well-heeled businessmen to spoil themselves and their families with an expensive purchase, I was back to doing manual labor and listening to the hard-luck stories of my co-workers, who were all within a day's pay of being out on the street. In a lot of ways, it reminded me of my time working at the Gulf station in Louisville, and it didn't take me too long to adapt to that milieu. I probably came across a little aloof at first, but, thankfully, the other kitchen staff poked fun at me, and I eventually became comfortable bantering with them. This was the life I had chosen, and I knew I had to adopt their habits, their language, and, at least while I was at work, their view of the world. It was a crash course in how the vast denizens of the underworld survive. I realized almost immediately that our shared financial desperation made us more similar than different.

I tried to pay attention to what the others around me were doing and how all the pieces fit together. It was a complex operation, fast-paced and sometimes high-stress. I made a nuisance of myself, asking questions and having them show me their tricks. Evidently those years studying logic and higher mathematics made me a quick study and I soon reassured my supervisors—after my début as a bungling novice—that I was ready for a higher profile role.

The work became more satisfying as I recognized that many of the tasks were similar to those I had mastered at the pharmacies years earlier. Preparing an intricate dish has a lot in common with medicinal compounding. In both cases the blending of ingredients creates something better than the sum of its parts. I learned about subtle flavorings and the importance of presentation. Eventually I achieved the venerable position of line cook, moving from one station to the next learning to assemble all the standard menu items. Recently I had frequently been asked to work the evening shift in one of the other hotel kitchens that supported the more formal Café or Grand Banquet Room. I was learning a different set of skills there, preparing more sophisticated dishes for the guests of the hotel and others who could afford fine dining. The very guests who might be driving the Chalmers I used to sell.

All along, I was intentionally living a fairly solitary life, a monastic life, if you will. That seemed appropriate for someone paying penance for past sins. In that cloister-like refectory, I sometimes saw myself as seeking indulgence through service to the more deserving guests. I interacted with few others outside of the job. I was fairly happy with the simple life I had carved out for myself. But as I wrapped up the lunch shift that day and headed out the rear of the kitchen into the startling sunshine, I sensed the seductive possibilities the world offered for the first time in a long while.

I lit a cigarette and headed around the building to start my trek home. I had recently moved to the new YMCA at the corner of Elm and Central Parkway to be closer to the hotel. The amenities there felt tantalizingly wicked for a reprobate and self-styled penitent like me: an expansive cafeteria, a barber shop, and even a bowling alley, where I whiled away a good bit of my free time.

As I came around the front of the hotel, I passed the entrance to the coffee shop. I could see through the single plate glass window into the nearly empty interior, and something made me stop. I looked closer and saw a young woman sitting on a corner stool by herself. She didn't have the air of the busy secretaries and other office workers who usually frequented the coffee shop. She was plainly dressed, sitting quietly with a cup and saucer in front of her, gazing around, apparently taking in the unusual architecture of the room. Amid the Romanesque arches and polished counters, she seemed a little out of place. The long suppressed desire to engage and conquer shook free from its constraints. I watched her a moment longer, then put out my cigarette and walked inside.

Without thinking or divining my intentions, I approached her. "Excuse me, but you caught my eye as I ended my shift, and I felt compelled to come introduce myself. I'm Lyons Board. What brings you to the Sinton?"

The young lady appeared a little befuddled yet perhaps pleased that I had approached her. Her cheeks flushed.

"Well I'm not sure I should be talking to just any man who walks up and introduces himself." She looked at me a moment and, having taken my measure, decided to reward my impudence. "I was just curious about this fancy lunchroom and thought I would stop in and put on some airs like I belonged here."

I grinned, entranced by her spunk. "May I join you for a moment?"

"It's a public place. I guess there ain't no harm in that." I could see that she couldn't help smiling. In my incipient state of infatuation, her careless grammar seemed more charming than off-putting.

I sat on the stool next to her. "Do you work near here?"

"No. I was just taking a little walk downtown in the fresh air. Taking a break from the family."

"Do you live nearby?"

"Not really. I live on the west end, near the railroad tracks, with my son and my parents."

The mention of a child momentarily set me back on my still well-shod heels. I permitted myself the briefest reassessment of the situation, but one more glance at her puckish smile restored my courage and revived my interest.

"Oh, you have a son? You look mighty young to be raising one yourself."

"James is three. His dad and me, we divorced a while ago. But that may be more than I should be sharing with you."

"Would you be willing to share your name?"

She smiled again, looking directly at me. "What the heck. I'm Louise Collier. How do you do?"

"Well, I'm doing a little better now that I know your name, Louise. Would you like another cup of tea?"

"No, thank you. I need to be heading back."

"May I escort you as far as Elm Street then? That's where I'll turn north to head to my place for a short break—before I have to come back for the dinner shift."

"You work here at the hotel?"

"Yes." I hesitated just a moment. "In the kitchen."

"And you have to come back to work again tonight?"

"I do. Most days I work a split shift. Shall we head out?"

I felt my heart begin to race like a roadster, and I had to keep reminding myself to slow my pace to match hers. We chatted easily about her family and where she had grown up. She was nearly as tall as I was and had that fresh-faced girl-next-door look. Her heavy blond hair was pulled back in a simple clasp.

At the corner of Elm, I drummed up the courage to ask if I might call on her at her home. She hesitated, but then decided that would probably be all right. She gave me her address, and I turned north with a decided spring in my step.

Effie Mae
Sunday, December 7, 1941

When I woke up, Lyons had done left the apartment. The corners of my mouth pulled back into a sorry grin as I wondered whether he'd up and left me, too. Let him go, I thought. I've done lost two before. Me and Doug can get along just fine without him.

I turned toward his empty side of the bed and pulled the covers tight around my shoulders. I had slept mighty soundly considering the drama the day before. So when I caught a whiff of bacon frying, that was enough to rouse me. I figgered then that Lyons was down in the kitchen making breakfast for the boarders. He usually had help on Sundays and could more or less just supervise the goings on.

I dressed and made coffee. As I put some bread in the toaster, I heard the front door close. Lyons came into the kitchen with a bag from the bakery and a bottle of eggnog, the newspaper tucked under his arm. His first peace offering, I thought. Well, I wasn't that easy.

"Thought maybe you'd done run off and left me," I said.

He looked at me and smiled. "You didn't hear a word I said last night, did you? I have no intention of walking away from you. You can run if you want. I know I've disappointed you. Like I said, I have flaws. Big ones. I've made mistakes. But none of that changes that I want to be right here with you."

That sounded kind of rehearsed to me. I wondered if he had been repeating it to hisself all the way to the bakery and back.

"Your pretty words ain't gonna cut it this time, fella. You ain't begun to tell me the whole story. I can tell. I hope you've been rehearsing how you're gonna fill in all them giant holes you opened up last night. I need to hear it all before I decide whether I'm going or staying. Or shoving you out the door."

"Can I pour you a glass of eggnog?"

I sighed. He knew that was my holiday weakness. "I suppose. There's coffee if you want it."

"I have an idea, if you're willing to listen," he said. "Why don't we call a truce this morning, catch the early show at the Lyceum, and then get a bite to eat over at the Beth-Mary or somewhere. Then we can talk. I'll do my best to answer your questions. What do you think?"

It sounded like a trap to me. Lull me into a nice quiet day together around town, sap me of all my fight. Well, it wasn't gonna work. This was too important.

"I'm not sure I wanna be seen in public with you, now that I know what kind of man you are. How are we gonna fix that?"

He kept his back to me as he poured his coffee. I saw his shoulders sag just a bit. He came to the table and sat down.

"Well, we need to fix this, Effie. I want to fix it. What's it going to take?"

"The truth. Plain and simple. Is that so hard?"

He didn't answer.

"Maybe it is," he finally said. "As you learned last night, I've been hiding from it for a long time. I realize now that perhaps that wasn't fair to you. And maybe it wasn't so good for me either. But any other option just seemed too difficult. And too complicated."

"Why didn't you tell me before we married that you had had another wife? And a child? Did you think that would scare me off?"

"Maybe. I was desperate to hang on to you. I wasn't sure why at the time. But I just felt like I had finally found someone who understood me. You were willing to pick up and go with me, to chase the next job or the next adventure. You seemed as excited by the prospect of hitting the road and heading to Florida as I was. I felt like you were ready to start over, too. I was getting old, Effie. I think I was ready for a steady companion."

"Is that what I am? Your 'steady companion'? I wanna be your wife, Lyons. I *am* your wife. You're supposed to let me in on your secrets. We're supposed to help each other out, work through the hard stuff together."

I heard my voice rising. I lit a cigarette and tried to calm down.

"You're right," he said. "But maybe I just don't know how to do that."

"Why don't you start by telling me about Nell."

"Are you sure you want to go there? It was such a long time ago. What does it matter now?"

"Because I need to know. That's all."

He sighed. "She was a teacher. She had come to Hopewell while I was in France, during the war. I never planned to settle in my hometown after I got home, but the place had some sort of magnetic hold on me when I went back with my mother to take care of some business. Someone offered me a job, and I decided to stay. Next thing I knew, Nell and I were engaged. Then we were married. Mary Rose arrived the next year."

"Did you have to marry her? Was she pregnant?"

"No, no. That wasn't it at all. Nell was a little older than I was, and she was ready to start a family, so we did. I don't think I even stopped to think about it. It was just the natural order of things. I fell in line. I took the same orders as nearly every other young man my age. For most everyone else, I suppose, that worked out just fine. But I felt trapped. Cornered. I could barely breathe at times as I began to fully grasp all of my responsibilities. Maybe I just wasn't ready to be a husband and father. Maybe I needed more time to adjust to being out of the service. Maybe I just wasn't cut out for that conventional life. I don't know. I didn't plan to abandon them. It just happened."

"What do you mean 'it just happened'? That's ridiculous. You made a decision, and you left em."

Lyons looked off in the distance. "I guess you're right. But it didn't seem that way at the time. It felt more like I was being carried away by something outside myself." He stopped, and then looked right at me. "You see? This is why I never tried to explain it to you. I can't explain it to myself."

I tried to sort through what he was struggling to tell me. "But you seem to have settled down just fine with me. And you and Doug have a good relationship from what I can tell."

"Sure. But remember, I was a dozen years older when I stumbled into you in Cincinnati on that frigid night. Maybe I had finally grown up. Or maybe it was fate. Maybe I was just always meant to be with you, and I had to break a few hearts to get here." He tried to force a grin.

"Oh, there's that bullshit again. Who knows how many women you've done snowed with that."

We was both quiet. I realized I had never taken the toast out of the toaster. I reached across the table and opened the bag he had brought home.

"What's in here?"

"A couple of croissants. And a half dozen donuts. Didn't know what you and Doug might want this morning."

"You and your fancy pastries. I'll take a jelly donut, if there's one in here."

"You know there is."

I got up to fetch a couple of plates.

"OK, I'll take you up on that movie. I really need to get out of this apartment. What's playing?"

"I think it's *A Yank in the R.A.F.*"

"It figgers. Everything's about the war these days. Ain't that the Tyrone Power movie about the lying, womanizing scoundrel?"

"All I know is it has Betty Grable in it."

"Well, I'm sure we'll have a lot to talk about afterwards. Maybe you can learn a lesson or two."

AT ABOUT ONE O'CLOCK we stepped off the front porch and walked down the sidewalk to B Street. The air felt more like early April than December but the sky was still a wintry gray. There was something oppressive about that warmth, like something was trying to hold us still so we couldn't feel the earth rumbling somewhere else.

We walked down B Street and turned north on Fifth toward the Lyceum Theatre, which sat on the corner of Fifth and D streets. Them steel mill execs who had laid out Sparrows Point named the east-west streets A through K, like in some nursery rhyme. I'd heard that A Street was originally set aside for one of the company owners, but he never bothered to move here. His brother, however, built the "Big House," with its grand lawn and private garden, on B Street— Bosses' Row. Eighteen rooms in that house, they tell me. B and C streets was lined with handsome single-family homes where the mill's general managers, superintendents, and engineers lived. Some of them had been turned into boardinghouses, like where me and Lyons had our little apartment, just two doors down from the "Big House." D Street—where the businesses and churches had collected—divided the grand residences of the big shots from the tidy row houses of the white laborers and merchants and teachers on E and F streets. Many of them houses, well-constructed of brick or stucco and company-maintained, had pretty gardens in the back, just visible through high plank fences. There was a real sense of pride along them streets.

Living conditions got worse as you went farther up the alphabet. The colored families congregated in shabby duplexes up on H through K streets, across Humphrey's Creek. I guess the bosses needed a physical barrier between them and the really poor folks. And beyond that, butted right up against the furnaces, was Shantytown, where they packed the single Negro and immigrant workers into bunks in barracks.

That's the way it always goes, it seems. Them people who work the hardest, who have to endure the dirtiest and most dangerous jobs to help the company make a buck, they're the ones who always get the short straw. But at least the company made sure they had their own schools over there on the North Side, even if they didn't get a high school until a coupla years ago. Folks who lived there opened their own restaurants and dance halls and small businesses to suit em. I just cain't for the life of me figger out why the people doing the same work cain't go to the same movie theater or bowling alley or grocery store. I remember Virgil saying, "It don't matter what color your skin is when you go down in the mine, you're all the same color at the end of the shift."

I took a deep breath. It felt good to be outta the apartment. Of course, no one else knew what I had discovered about my husband, but somehow I still felt different walking beside him. It was as if my pride in being his wife had been replaced by an uneasy suspicion, like a squirrel eyeing a nearby cur. What had been as comfortable as an old pair of house slippers now felt pinched. I tried to keep up my end of the conversation, but my mind kept wandering. Who was this man I had been sleeping next to for seven years?

"I forgot to tell you that Logan called last night to wish us a merry

Christmas," I said. "You might try to call him back when we get home."

"Huh. What did old Logan have to say?"

"Not much. We didn't talk for long. He's missing his mama this time of year, I think. And his children is growing up. He invited us to come visit em in Virginia sometime."

"That might be a trip worth making. Those Virginia mountains would remind you of home. Maybe we should plan to do that this summer."

"If I'm still talking to you by then."

"Oh, Effie, you know you don't want to live without me."

"That might just depend on who you are, buster. I ain't gotten to the bottom of that yet."

When we got to the Lyceum I dragged Lyons down toward the front of the theater where I like to sit. Once the movie started, we watched as Tyrone Power tried to schmooze his way back into Betty Grable's good graces. His arrogance wasn't scoring him no points though. Betty was probably wise to take up with that other R.A.F. officer.

Just as the British bombers was getting shot up by the big German ground guns in the obligatory fight scene, the screen went black. The theater got real quiet. People started shuffling in their seats, turning around to look up at the camera booth. The lights came up and the theater manager, Mr. Wheaton, appeared in the aisle to our left, striding with purpose toward the front, his head down, not looking at anyone.

All eyes turned toward him as he stepped up on the small stage in front of the screen. I was suddenly aware of the balls rolling down the duckpin lanes in the basement.

"Folks, can you hear me?" he asked. Heads nodded. A few people murmured something in response.

"I'm sorry to interrupt the movie, but I have an important

announcement to make. I want to read to you what has just been reported across the news wires. From NBC News in New York: *'President Roosevelt said in a statement today that the Japanese have attacked Pearl Harbor in Hawaii from the air.'"*

He then looked up. His face was blank, his lips tight. No one moved. It was if we had all been playing freeze tag and his words done froze us in place.

"That's all I have for now, folks. We'll continue showing the movie for those of you who want to stay."

Mr. Wheaton stepped off the stage, head still down and shoulders hunched, and walked slowly toward the back of the theater.

We continued to sit dumbly in our seats, awaiting a tag from someone who could release us from our suspension. Eventually people around us started talking; some even started crying, dabbing their eyes with handkerchiefs. The noise level slowly rose. A few people made their way toward the exit. I looked at Lyons, still trying to comprehend what we had just heard.

"What does this mean, Lyons?"

He was grim-faced. "It means we're going to war. Again."

Ever now and then Lyons would bring up his time in France during the last war. He didn't say much. I know there was a lot of waiting around, a lot of boredom. But I always got the sense there was a lot more he wasn't telling me. Just like he hadn't told me about Nell. And Mary Rose. His head must be full of tiny compartments where he done locked away all them things he's determined to never think about again. I think I'd rather have my head explode.

Sometimes in the middle of the night he'd sit bolt upright in bed, eyes wide open, something like terror leaking out of them pale blue eyes. He might even cry out. I always figgered them memories musta come unchained somehow, rattling around in his mind just when he was trying to rest hisself from that never-ending sentry duty.

"Do you want to see the end of the movie?" I asked.

"Nah. Even Betty Grable's not going to pull me out of this funk. Let's go see what else we can find out about what happened."

We pushed ourselves out of our seats and joined the others filing outta the theater. Out on the street, at first, it didn't seem like much had changed in our little world. People clustered on the sidewalk, talking in low voices. Someone turned up a car radio tuned to the news, and I noticed a handful of young men leaning on the side of a dark red Plymouth Coupe parked along the curb. I touched Lyons on the elbow, pointed in their direction, and we wandered over to join em.

I recognized Tommy Smith, a clerk at Gaver's Drug Store just down the street. The others appeared to be about the same age.

"What have you heard?" Lyons asked as we approached.

Tommy turned away from the window and nodded when he saw us.

"Hello, Mr. Board. Mrs. Board. Sounds like the Japs have bombed us. Out in Hawaii. Some place called Pearl Harbor. Could be pretty bad, but we haven't really been able to pick up any details yet.

"Looks like I may get called up after all," Tommy continued. "My mother didn't want me to enlist, even though they've been recruiting hard around here. Might not be up to me now. But I hear recruits can make up to $105 a month, plus uniforms and grub. Maybe that's not too bad a deal."

"You'll make a good soldier, if it comes to that," Lyons said to Tommy.

I couldn't tell if he believed that or not. Was a good soldier one who didn't get kilt? Or one who did something heroic that got him kilt? War never made no sense to me. I wish someone could tell me how killing young boys solves any of the world's problems.

I thought about Doug. Seemed like he just got home from patrolling the China Seas yesterday. Surely they wouldn't pull him back into this war. I told myself I was too old to live through that kind of worry.

"Lyons, let's just go on home and turn on the radio there. We'll fix some sandwiches. I want to catch up with Doug and see what he knows."

When we walked in the boardinghouse, about half the boarders was gathered around the big Philco in the sitting room. Several nodded as we came in, tired limbs draped across the oddly out-of-place Victorian furniture. The news announcer crackled from the set, but it was otherwise an eerily quiet gathering. I figgered the young ones was wondering how much time they had left with their sweethearts, and the old ones was recalling the horrors they'd been lucky enough to live through once before.

Doug wasn't among em. I couldn't recall if it was his Sunday to work. I headed up the stairs, slowly lifting one weary leg after the other. Lyons called out that he was going to check in with the kitchen staff before he came up.

I knocked on Doug's door first, but he didn't answer. When I got back to our apartment, I hung my coat on the rack and went to the fridge for a beer. I walked back in the living room and turned on the radio, then sat on the sofa with the morning newspaper.

Glancing at the headlines, printed the night before, I couldn't find no sign of anyone expecting the U.S. to get bombed. Was we completely taken by surprise? All anyone had been talking about for two years was the war in Europe and the Japanese threat in the Pacific. We'd been stockpiling razor blades and tin foil for the Brits and sending them our oil. The gas scarcity had hit us hard here at the Point last summer. Felt like we'd been sending half of what our farmers grew to England or Russia to feed their soldiers. Wasn't that enough? Did they have to drag us into the killing?

I saw articles about the football game being played that afternoon between the miserable Washington Redskins and the Philadelphia

Eagles and about the death of a 97-year-old man who never figgered out who he was after getting separated from his parents during a parade in New York in 1852. The only stories about Japan talked about how they was mad that Russia was siding with us. Right here in Baltimore harbor, we had rounded up Finnish ships earlier in the week when Britain declared war on Finland for joining up with Hitler. Meanwhile the Germans was marching on Moscow. It seemed like the whole world was bruising for a fight.

Lyons came in, with Doug right behind him. Doug's face was pale.

"What have you heard?" I asked.

Doug sat down on the sofa next to me, put his arm around my shoulders and hugged me awkwardly. Lyons appeared too restless to sit.

"What?" I asked again.

"Initial reports of the casualties sound pretty bad," said Lyons. "Several of our big battleships took direct hits. The news is sketchy, and it's hard to tell what's fact and what's rumor. Both the Army and the Navy have a significant presence out there. From all I can tell, we were totally unprepared for an attack."

Doug pulled his arm from my shoulders and clasped his hands together leaning forward, elbows on his thighs, face now red. "Them Jap bastards have been itching to get us into a fight for a long time," he said. "Ever since they bombed the USS Panay while it was anchored on the Yangtze in '37, it's been clear what they wanted. They just didn't have the balls to take us on. We was over there protecting our oil tankers, minding our own business. The Japs was supposed to be at war with China, but they never seemed to hesitate to take out some collateral damage on their bombing runs. I watched their shenanigans up close for three years. Now with all our allies embroiled in this mess in Europe, I reckon they figured they finally had a shot at us. Well, they're gonna find out they was dead wrong."

I looked at Doug. That was the most I'd heard him talk about his patrols around China. And I couldn't recollect if I'd ever seen him that angry.

"The fellas on the Panay couldn't even defend themselves," he continued, unable to stop hisself. "Their heavy guns was positioned to fight pirates along the shore. They couldn't do a thing about an aerial attack. Those men was sitting ducks. Just like the men on our ships in Pearl Harbor. It's amazing more on the Panay wasn't killed.

"I guess the Japs thought that attack would make us pull out of the China Seas. But they learned different. We weren't going nowhere. The Brits and the Americans, we just dug in our heels. But no one's protecting Shanghai now. Hasn't been any commercial shipping around there in months. The city's essentially abandoned. It was one heckuva place for us river rats to visit when I was there. Anything you could possibly want you could get."

He was silent a moment. No one said a thing.

"The Japs are brutes," he said finally. "You know what they did to them people in Nanking."

I didn't know nothin about Nanking. Didn't know what he was talking about. But I didn't want to ask.

Lyons turned up the volume on the radio as the news announcer broke in with another update.

"Admiral Claude C. Bloch, commandant in Hawaii, has reported 'heavy damage' to the islands, with 'heavy loss of life.'"

We sat in silence, just like the men down in the sitting room.

"I'm going down to the newsstand to see if there's an Extra yet," said Lyons, and he picked up his hat and headed back out the door.

Lyons
Wednesday, December 22, 1926

I hesitated momentarily before responding to the clerk. The courthouse felt surprisingly stuffy for a December day, and I hoped Louise wouldn't notice the bead of perspiration that was slowly rolling down my temple. My starched collar seemed to tighten like a constrictor teasing its prey. I glanced at Louise, her blond hair pulled back in a loose chignon, her burgundy coat buttoned tightly at her throat and a matching felt hat perched on her head. I felt myself exhale.

Louise nudged a little closer, her hand tucked just inside my left elbow as I balanced myself against the polished wood counter. Then, quickly, I responded to the clerk's question.

"No, I haven't been married before."

The image of Nell and Mary Rose flashed through my mind, but I shoved it away. That was then. That was a long time ago.

I barely heard the clerk's next question, as he continued to read in a basso monotone from the document before him. "...and you have no wife living and you are not nearer of kin to Louise Collier than second cousin and there is no legal impediment to your being married, and you are not an habitual drunkard, epileptic, imbecile, or insane person and you are not now under the influence of any intoxicating liquor or narcotic drug."

I smiled and shook my head.

Recovering my composure, I took the pen the clerk handed to me and signed the application for a marriage license. This desperado was ready to ride again.

I looked again at Louise, snuggled next to me.

"Are you sure you want to hitch your future to this old man?" I squeezed her gloved hand gently. Although I was only nine years older, at the moment that felt like the geological years represented in the colors of the Grand Canyon. As I expected, she responded playfully. Sometimes her childlike demeanor startled me. It revealed a naiveté that a less besotted man might have found annoying.

"Aw, now, I imagine I've seen nearly as much of the world as you have, Lyons Board. After all, I'm the one who married that huckster from New York City when I was only 18. You're the one I should have waited for."

Louise smiled, almost conspiratorially I thought, as she listened to the clerk repeat the same questions. When it was her turn, she did not hesitate to take the pen and sign her name.

"Come on, old man. Let's do a little Christmas shopping before we pick up James and meet with the judge."

We left the office, arm in arm, and headed down the cavernous hallway, Louise's heels clip-clopping on the marble floor, drawing attention with every step. I wasn't sure I deserved this attractive embellishment striding confidently beside me, but my vanity swelled as I nodded at the other Cincinnati residents we passed, all eager to handle official matters before the holidays. Once out the door, staring across the city from the steps of the imposing limestone and granite court building, I took a big gulp of the cold, damp air.

It's done. I'm going through with this, I thought. I screwed up before, but I'm going to get it right this time. I'm more comfortable in this new life I've carved out for myself, and I'm ready to get on with it. Louise's expectations are modest, and I think I can make her happy.

I know I can. Now I'm ready to take care of a family. This time I'm sure of it.

I put on my hat and lit a cigarette before we headed west toward Louise's parents' house, where her five-year-old son awaited us. Louise chattered, but I hardly heard her. I found myself studying the cars as they chugged by. A brand new 1927 Oakland Greater Six caught my eye as it purred to a stop beside us, a haunting reminder of the life I had just denied.

It had been raining off and on, and I flicked my cigarette into the street to help Louise raise an umbrella. I mildly dreaded the interaction with her parents. They had also moved north from Kentucky a few years back, with their two youngest children, but claiming Kentucky as our home state was about the only commonality in our backgrounds. Louise's family had been farmers for generations in a wild part of north-central Kentucky where the land was hilly, rugged, and unforgiving. Eking out a living with a few cows, some chickens, a couple of hogs, and a small plot of corn was a far cry from shuffling people's money around at the bank. Cynics called the Neal family's enterprise "rock farming." Her parents were solid, well-meaning people, but Mrs. Annette Threlkeld's intensive training in poise and decorum hadn't prepared me adequately for their refreshingly gruff manner.

When Louise was still young, her dad, then in his sixties, had finally waved a white flag after the devastating tornado and flooding of 1915 and headed to Ohio to look for work in a factory. As war rumbled in Europe, some U.S. industries were already expanding in preparation for U.S. involvement. He got a job at the Bullock Electric Company in Norwood, just north of Cincinnati. The plant was owned by Allis-Chalmers, a company familiar to all farmers in those parts, and Mr. Neal was able to transfer decades of experience coaxing old farm equipment into grudging compliance to his job inspecting motors for defects.

Louise's first husband, Irwin, had been a machinist at the plant. When she filed for divorce after three years of limited bliss, her father, his hands and back beginning to balk after nearly seven decades of labor, quit work and moved the family to Cincinnati to put some distance between the warring parties.

Mr. Neal was a tough old bird, and I felt like a bit of a dandy around him. I was fairly certain that my employment as a hotel chef didn't quite live up to my soon-to-be father-in-law's definition of man's work. But we could talk about the intricacies of electrical motors or marvel at the new General Motors plant in Norwood, where workers from the farms and coalfields of Kentucky and West Virginia had joined the local boys to build Chevys.

As we stopped at a corner for the streetcar to pass, I tried to focus on what Louise was saying. "Let's stop by Pogue's and pick up a small gift for James. Whaddya think?"

I remembered how disconcerted I had been when I had realized that James was born the same month as Mary Rose. I occasionally allowed myself to wonder what she looked like, how she and her mother were getting along, what she was getting for Christmas. But there was nothing productive in going down that path. At times I would study James' delight when I read to him or when he learned how to do something new. I was interested in the boy, but I still wasn't quite sure what kind of parent I would be. After all, I had already abdicated that responsibility once.

We took a detour south on Vine Street to Fourth and turned right in front of the Sinton Hotel, my former place of employment. The hotel's soaring architecture always reminded me of the cities in France I had glimpsed during my brief tour of duty. I wondered how my old Sinton comrades were getting along, now that I had moved on to Springfield.

The H. & S. Pogue department store occupied the next corner, Fourth and Race, and stretched six stories into the gray Cincinnati sky. The lights from the store's Christmas display were visible a block away. We had brought James to the store the day before so he could participate in the comically absurd local childhood rite of sharing his Christmas wishes with the life-sized wooden deer standing in the elaborate enchanted forest that store employees erected each year. James had whispered into the microphone that he wanted a bicycle, but Louise and I had agreed that we couldn't afford that this year. To distract him from what we were sure would be a disappointment, we had taken him to the fourth floor, where he had been properly mesmerized by the miniature train winding its way through the toy department.

Today, after making our small purchase—a tin of Tinker Toys that I suspected might intrigue me more than it would James—I suggested we grab lunch in the snack bar in the store's basement. It was already after noon, and I was fairly certain Louise's family would have eaten by the time we made it to the house. Our appointment with the judge was at three o'clock, so we should have just enough time.

The restaurant was packed with Christmas shoppers, but we found a small table near the back. The voices of cheery diners and the clap-trap of dishes and silverware being cleared from tables ricocheted around the large room. The smell of cigarette smoke mixed with the aromas of grilled onions and fried chicken coming from the kitchen. Louise ordered a turkey sandwich and iced tea. I asked for a bowl of vegetable soup and a cup of coffee. When the waitress left, I reached across the table and took Louise's hand.

"I hope you're OK with our plans. I know it's not an ideal situation, but I have to be back at work tomorrow to prepare for two big Christmas parties tomorrow night and Christmas Eve. My boss was kind enough to give me Christmas day off, so I thought we could come back to Cincinnati that morning and spend the day with your family before heading back to Springfield with James that evening."

Louise was quiet for the first time since we had left the courthouse.

She bowed her head and bit her lip. "It's hard to imagine not being around on Christmas morning when James first wakes up. But I do want to go to Springfield with you tonight so we can have a couple days to ourselves. I know that sounds selfish, but my parents will be there for him Saturday morning. Then me and James can get settled into your apartment on Sunday and wander around Springfield."

Louise had never been away from her family for any extended period of time, and I knew this was going to be a major adjustment for her. Even when she was married to Irwin, they lived with her parents in their small house in Norwood. I worked long hours at the Bancroft Hotel, including a lot of evenings, and she and James would be on their own much of the time. And in the fall, James would start school. She was giving up the simmering hostilities of a crowded household of human wreckage for the quiet life of a bored housewife. I wasn't convinced she could make that transition successfully.

"You may find you like having a place all to yourself," I said. "You'll be right downtown, close to the market, the library, theaters, just about everything. The school is just a couple of blocks away. I think it will grow on you."

Louise nodded. She was uncharacteristically quiet. I ate silently, letting her mull over the changes that were about to occur. Despite her reticence, I felt optimistic about our future.

By the time Louise finished her sandwich she had perked up again. We left the store and headed west toward her parents' home. Louise had been the one who had suggested we walk to the courthouse that morning, so we could have a little more time with each other before the afternoon ceremony. As we approached the tangle of tracks at the expansive rail yard where thousands of passengers and tons of raw materials and consumer goods passed each day, we descended into the vast industrial plain filled with warehouses, junkyards, metalworking shops, small factories, and smelting furnaces. Louise's family lived in a little residential area amid this man-made Hades, served by a nearby kindergarten, a creamery, and a couple of gas stations. We walked up the short sidewalk to the tiny frame house. I could see James' nose pressed against the storm door, his hand waving furiously at us.

"Mommy!" he cried, as Louise opened the door. She bent down and hugged him and kissed him on the head. I noticed that James was already dressed in his best clothes. I gently tousled the boy's hair as I saw his eyes widen at the sight of the large shopping bag.

"Is that for me?" he asked.

"Maybe," said Louise, as her mother came into the front room from the kitchen. "Why don't you put it over there near the Christmas tree and we'll talk about it a little later."

Louise's mother, Letha, was twenty years younger than her husband, but I wouldn't have known that by looking at her. I could see the furrows plowed by years of intermittent drought and deluge in the lines of her face. She was fairly short and sturdy, although she walked with a rocking motion as she slowly shifted from one foot to the other, a gait that certainly manifested unspoken pain. She never complained, but she also never smiled. Today she wore the same unhappy look on her face that she always seemed to have, but she had put on a dress that I hadn't seen before.

She didn't start with any pleasantries. "So let me get this straight. We're all going to troop down to the courthouse to see you marry my baby girl, and then you're going to take my daughter and my grandson 100 miles away from here."

"Momma..." Louise began.

I wasn't surprised by her bluntness. "Well, it's not really that far away, Mrs. Neal. You know I've been making the trip down here to see Louise every couple of weeks or so. So there should be plenty of chances for you to see us. Your husband can put you in that old Dixie Flyer touring car and bring you up for a visit. I'll be able to get you a good rate on a place to stay. I happen to know a few people in the hotel business who might be able to help us out."

Letha snorted as she took the damp umbrella. She tried to take our overcoats, but I thought we had better be heading back to the courthouse. It might take a few minutes to round everyone up into her husband's car for the short drive.

"Is Mr. Neal ready to go?" I asked.

"Jimmy!" Letha called. Mr. Neal ambled into the front room fooling with a tie that I was surprised to see, along with the suit coat he was wearing. He looked mighty uncomfortable, but I appreciated the effort. In about fifteen minutes we had everyone in the car, and we trudged back downtown for our appointment with the judge just as it started to rain again.

I HELD LOUISE'S HAND as I led her up to my apartment at the hotel. I put the key into the door and shoved it open. Louise giggled as I scooped her up and carried her into the front room. I took a few strides into the bedroom and gently dropped her on the bed. After turning on the bedside lamp and removing my hat and coat, I placed one hand on either side of her shoulders and leaned over her as she lay on the bed grinning, my breath on her neck.

"Don't you dare go anywhere," I told her. "I'll get the suitcases from the hallway."

It had been a very long day. After the brief marriage ceremony, we had returned to the Neals' home, and then Louise and I had made the trip to Springfield in my Westcott coupe. The rain slowed us a bit, but I was thankful it wasn't snow. Louise had handled the separation from James better than I had expected, and we had had a gay time in the car on the way up, talking about what we could do with the apartment and how we could best accommodate James there. He would have to have a bed in the main room, since there was only one bedroom. But we thought we could partition a corner that he could make his own. And she hoped to have a small Christmas tree in place before we picked up James on Saturday. She had worked hard to convince her mother to part with a few ornaments from their family tree, including a couple that James had made. Louise thought she and James would string some popcorn and cranberries for the tree while I worked on Sunday. That way they could extend the trappings of the holiday until the New Year.

I had been working at the Bancroft in downtown Springfield for a year. The rapidly growing city lured Midwesterners year-round, their pockets heavy with lucre in a robust economy, and the Bancroft sat poised on the east side of a bustling commercial center to accommodate them. When visitors tired of the nearby specialty shops and department stores, seven theaters showing motion pictures beckoned. Those looking for other entertainment might find their way to a performance by the Springfield Symphony Orchestra, the Folding Theatre Players, or perhaps a vaudeville act at the Regent Theatre. A number of handsome Romanesque structures gave the city a stately, permanent feel that could almost make a vagabond want to settle down.

The summer after I met Louise, one of the other line cooks at the Sinton had told me about an opening for a sous-chef at the Bancroft. Although I liked the anonymity at the Sinton, I was becoming a little restless, and I was always eager to move on to new territory. I felt I was ready to parlay the wide experience I had gotten at the Sinton into a bigger role at a smaller establishment. The Bancroft sounded perfect. When I checked it out, I liked the city of Springfield, and the fellow doing the hiring liked me. I was still a little hesitant, however, because I wasn't sure if I was ready to walk away from whatever was developing with Louise. When I mentioned the new job to her, she was supportive, although her face had shown some trepidation. I promised I would come back to Cincinnati for a visit a couple of times a month, and I had been true to my word. After I moved, it was clear to me that I wanted her to join me in Springfield, and I had proposed to her the following fall.

I came back into the bedroom carrying the two small valises. Louise had packed a few things for her initial stay in Springfield, with the intention of picking up the rest of her and James' things when we returned to Cincinnati on Saturday. Before turning to Louise, who had removed her hat and coat and sat on the edge of the bed straightening her hair, I rummaged in my bag and pulled out a small wrapped box.

OK, buddy, I told myself. *This is your chance to get this right. You get one do-over, so you'd better make it good.*

I handed the box to Louise. "I wanted to get you something to mark the beginning of our new life together and the hope I feel about our future."

To my great relief, she brushed aside the absurdly mawkish statement that hung quivering in the close quarters. "Oh, Lyons," she said softly, taking the box. "Should I open it now?"

"Of course. We have a lot to celebrate."

She carefully tore off the paper, opened the box, and stared at the jewelry case. We had decided to forgo wedding bands because we didn't have the money to pay for them, so I'm sure the velvet box was a surprise to her. But cementing our conjugal relationship with an overt act of bribery seemed like a good plan when I succumbed to the rather extravagant purchase. She slid open the box and gasped at the pearl earrings inside.

"Oh my, Lyons. What were you thinking? I can't possibly keep these. Can I? They're so beautiful."

She took them out of the box and tried them on. With her hair pulled back, the dim light in the room illuminated the small iridescent pearls. I thought she looked regal.

I took her hands. "I'm so glad you're here. You look absolutely beautiful."

I pushed her back gently on the bed and lay down beside her. Her soft scent ricocheted around my brain, lighting up my senses.

I liked having her in the apartment. It felt right. I hadn't been sure before if I wanted to give up my solitude and all the monkish habits I had adopted, but I decided it was a good thing.

I kissed her softly, and then more vigorously. Despite Louise's spirited engagement, shadowy doubt once again threatened to darken the moment. Who was this creature I had in an embrace? Were my intentions truly genuine? Or had I been tricked once again by societal conventions and my own selfish compulsions?

I refocused on the matter at hand. My increasingly addled brain declined to parse the situation further.

Louise seemed eager to see what I might have planned for the evening. We hadn't had much privacy during our courting, and we had been separated for weeks at a stretch. Here there was no son, no parents in the next room.

I removed my lips from hers and smiled. "Let me see if I remember how this is supposed to go," I said. Her half-mocking eyes appeared to laugh at my unexpected lapse of confidence. I turned out the light and pulled her tightly against me.

Effie Mae

Monday, December 8, 1941

*A*round noon I was already plum wore out from running the sweeper all over the first two floors and decided to take a lunch break. I had heard that the president was gonna be on the radio in a half hour, so I thought I'd try to catch that before I got back to work. We all knew he was just gonna confirm we was now at war, but I figgered I should hear it from FDR hisself. There was so many rumors swirling around that I wasn't yet sure what to believe. Some said the Japs had bombed a bunch of other islands in the Pacific while they was at it. Mr. Fowler told me he'd heard that Germany had been in on the attack and we was already at war with them, too. And we still didn't know how bad Hawaii had been hit or how many people had been killed. Lord have mercy.

As I walked by the main kitchen, I could hear Lyons whistling as he prepared a meal for the night shift boarders who would soon come straggling into the dining room bleary-eyed and a-grousing after a few hours of sleep. They'd be looking for coffee and some grub to jump start another bone-wearying day. He had done fixed one breakfast for the first-shifters and handed them bagged lunches as they filed out the door. I don't know how he kept up that never-ending routine.

I stopped and peered through the door a minute to watch him at work.

"You got plenty of scrambled eggs over there, Aaron?" he called out to the towheaded young man stirring the contents of the big black skillet.

I could see Lyons at the butcher block, cutting thick slices of bread from the hefty loaves the local bakery delivered each morning.

"I've got it covered, Mr. Board," Aaron responded. "You want me to add a little cheese this morning, and maybe some onion?"

"Absolutely. Do we have some already grated? Let me check."

Lyons opened the refrigerator and pulled out a coupla glass bowls covered with wax paper held in place with rubber bands. As he turned to hand the bowls to Aaron, he caught sight of me standing at the door and winked at me.

"We've got an audience, Aaron. Let's put on a show!"

Without even casting me a glance, Aaron tossed his spatula in the air, turned around and caught it behind his back. He bowed deeply as I applauded—although I knew better than to encourage them.

"We always aim to please," said Lyons, as he looked my way.

"You boys better pay attention to what you're doing," I called out. "Big Al will flip you on your head if his eggs is dry or his toast is burnt." I turned away, smiling and shaking my head.

I took my time climbing the two flights of stairs to the apartment. All morning, when I wasn't getting interrupted with more talk of the damn war, I had thoughts of Nell and Mary Rose rumbling around inside my head. I was trying to tamp down an impulse to find Nell, to see if I could learn from her directly what Lyons couldn't or wouldn't tell me. On the one hand, it was none of my business. On the other, I felt I deserved to know the truth about my husband's life, and especially about my stepdaughter. The tug-a-war going on in my brain reminded me of an old hound dog trying to follow two scents.

I finally decided there was no harm in seeing if I could get her number. I picked up the phone and dialed the operator.

"Operator."

"Could you get me a number in Lawrenceburg, Kentucky?"

"The name of the party?"

"Nell Board."

"Could you spell that last name?"

"B-o-a-r-d."

"Hold, please."

A few moments passed. "I don't have a listing for a Nell Board in Lawrenceburg."

My spirits sank. She probably done remarried. Or moved. Or both. There's no way I would find her.

I was about to hang up, and then I had one more idea.

"Could you hold just a minute?" I asked the operator.

I reached in the pocket of my apron and pulled out the newspaper clipping.

"Do you have a listing for a Marrs family in Lawrenceburg? That's M-a-r-r-s."

"I have two Marrs households," she responded. "Do you have a first name?"

"No, I don't. Could you give me both?"

"I have a Mrs. Robert Marrs and an Edward Marrs."

I tried to think fast. I figgered there was a good chance that Nell's father would no longer be alive. If she had moved back in with her parents after Lyons took off, maybe the phone was now listed in her mother's name, Mrs. Robert Marrs. The other name might be a younger man, perhaps a brother or cousin, who would have a wife with the last name Marrs. Not Board.

"Gimme the number for Mrs. Robert Marrs," I said.

I scribbled the number on the pad of paper next to the phone, then I tore off the top sheet and stuffed it in my pocket.

"Would you like me to connect you?" she asked.

I hesitated. "No thanks." I hung up.

My heart was beating fast. What did I think I was doing? Was

I really gonna reopen this woman's twenty-year-old wound? Nose around in her business just to satisfy my curiosity? Upset her life because I wanted to know what my husband didn't?

I walked into the kitchen to fix a sandwich. What did I think I would learn? Why did it even matter, really?

I put a coupla slices of bread on a plate and found the peanut butter and grape jelly. I made a sandwich and poured myself a glass of milk. I sat down at the little table and stared out the window.

More questions rumbled through my brain. I was feeling flustered and determined, all at the same time. I finally convinced myself to sleep on it before trying to call. My tendency to rush into action had caused me grief before.

I finished my sandwich and put my dishes in the sink and then went into the living room to turn on the radio. Maybe war talk would distract me enough to keep me from doing something I would later regret.

WHEN LYONS SETTLED DOWN with the newspaper after supper, I decided to try one more assault. Maybe I could uncover some more information from him without upending someone else's life.

I sat down on the sofa next to him with some stitching I needed to do. I peered through my glasses as I tried to thread the needle.

"What's in the paper tonight?" I asked. "Guess we've done gone to war with Japan. I caught the president's address today. Sounds like they bombed everything in their way."

"Yeah. I guess Britain's glad that we're finally in this thing. Even the isolationists seem to be on board now."

"Anything else in the paper?"

"Well, the stock market plunged this morning, but it looks like steel is climbing. That should be good news for Sparrows Point. They may have to do some hiring here to meet the war-time demand."

"Huh."

"Did you hear about those boys in Baltimore who hung an effigy of a Jap?" he asked.

"Yeah. Mr. Fowler was telling me about it this morning. That don't seem right. I don't want to see people taking it out on the Japs who live here. They didn't do nothing to us. It's their government that decided to attack us."

"It says here that we're already starting to round them up and shut down their businesses," he said. "I bet they didn't have any more warning than we did that their government was getting ready to attack the U.S. But we've never been much for nuance when it comes to war.

"I think they're getting nervous around Washington that the Japanese might try to attack our capital somehow," he continued. "That's getting pretty close to us. I'm not sure how I feel about sitting out here on the coast like we do. Of course, I guess the west coast would be an easier target for them."

I let a coupla minutes pass. I thought it might be a little jarring to dive right in to the other battle I wanted to launch. Then I screwed up my courage and let it fly.

"You know you still owe me some explanations," I said.

I felt him tense up next to me. He didn't look up from the paper.

"For example," I said, jumping right in, "you know I've been married twice before. You know all about my former husbands and how them marriages turned out. Somehow, though, you never managed to find an opportunity to tell me about Nell."

He didn't say nothin. I felt him slowly turn and look at me. I decided it was finally time for the direct questions I somehow never got around to asking during our seven-year marriage.

I dropped the sewing into my lap and took off my glasses. "How many times you been married, Lyons?"

He lowered his head and stared at his knees. I could see the muscles in his jaw tighten. I could almost feel his graying hair stand on end.

He slowly folded the newspaper and placed it on the battered coffee table in front of us. Then he turned and looked at me again. "Effie, what good is getting into this with me? Will it change anything? I love you. I'm happy with our life just as it is. Can't we just appreciate what we have?"

But I had already waded in, and I wasn't going to retreat.

"Why cain't you answer that simple question? What are you hiding?"

"I'm trying to protect you, Effie. You don't need to know everything about my past."

"You're trying to protect me?" I said, my voice rising despite my best efforts to contain it. "Or are you trying to protect yourself? I'm your wife, Lyons. Don't I deserve to know? Who the hell are you? Why cain't we talk about this? What have you done?"

He didn't say a word.

I dug in my heels. "We're not leaving this sofa until you come clean."

He remained quiet. I could see he was tore up. I was torturing him, and I didn't care. I started to put my hand on his leg, but I thought better of it. I didn't want to give him no solace or refuge just yet.

"Lemme get you started," I said finally. "I now know you was married to Nell in the early '20s. We married in 1934. Should I expect to learn about any other wives in between? For example, was you married when you was in Toledo?"

Lyons rubbed his face with his hands. He looked at me, his eyes blank.

"Yes. I married a woman when I was in Toledo. Her name was Flossie. It was a short-lived situation. The Depression hit so damn hard up there. I lost my job and I didn't know what to do. That's when I came back to Cincinnati."

I didn't respond. I couldn't really say that I was surprised. Nothin was gonna surprise me at this point. But I still didn't fully expect to learn there had been yet another wife.

I started slowly, picking my words carefully. I didn't want him to clam up now that I had him talking.

"So Flossie was your second wife?"

He was quiet again. "Actually, Flossie was my third wife."

I looked at him. Now my head was reeling.

"Your third wife? Are you saying that makes me your fourth wife?" I felt the steam creating a halo around my head. "I cain't even count that high, Lyons. Which one are we missing? Who else was you married to?"

"Louise. I was married to Louise."

"Who the hell was Louise?" My temper was getting the best of me again.

He stopped to take a breath. I looked down and saw his hands was trembling.

"Louise was my second wife. I thought she would be 'the one.' I poured myself into that marriage. I intended for it to be my last, that she and I would spend the rest of our days together."

"What happened?"

He didn't answer right away. "I realized just how different we were. She was tied to her family in Cincinnati. I wanted to be free to follow new job opportunities, move around as things came up. You know, exactly as you and I have done. It took a little time, but I finally had to accept that she just couldn't do that. I wasn't proud that I couldn't make it work. I got pretty down on myself, pretty reckless. I think that's why I fell in with Flossie. That never should have happened. And then the loss of my job—my career, really—that was a blow. I hightailed it back to Cincinnati. And then I found you."

I couldn't process what he was saying. Granted, I had asked for it. I couldn't push back on him for telling me all this. I reckon I had gotten what I wanted.

"You're not making up stories just to shut me up, are you?" I asked. But I knew he wasn't. I could tell by the pain on his face.

I was feeling a little weak-kneed myself. But I had to keep going. I had to know.

"Do you have any other children? Other than Mary Rose?"

"No," he said quietly. "Louise had a son, James, when I married her. He was born the same year—the same month, in fact—as Mary Rose. I wanted to be a good father to him. I wanted to care for Louise. And I did, I think, until I realized her family—her parents—meant more to her than I did. So I moved on."

I tried to put all these pieces together. "So is that what you do? You just move on when the situation ain't no longer to your liking?"

He dropped his head again. I had never seen him look so defeated.

"Yeah, I guess that's exactly what I've done."

"How long was you married to Louise?"

"A couple of years."

"That's it? And then you was done with her?"

"And then I realized we had no future."

I was struggling to make sense of all this.

"So, do we have a future, Lyons?"

He shook his head. "That's what I keep trying to tell you, Effie. We've been together a long time. We've moved all over the country. Each time we've landed on our feet. You've been as willing as I have to strike out on a new adventure, to embrace whatever situation we found ourselves in. I love that about you. We're perfect together. We understand each other. I've never been happier."

I looked at him. We weren't two to talk about how we felt. We just moved through our days together, content to share the rhythms of our simple lives. Perhaps I had made it easy for him to hide all this from me.

"If you feel that way, why couldn't you be honest with me? What were you so scared of?"

He looked at me, tears beginning to well in his eyes. "Losing you, of course. I didn't want to confess to you what a compromised man I was. How I had failed. I didn't want to put all of my weaknesses on display for you. I wanted to do what I could to take care of you and to keep you close. Isn't that obvious?"

Bless his heart. I almost felt bad for him. I couldn't hide a smile and a little chuckle.

"So now you find this amusing?" he said, also breaking into a small grin.

"Yeah, I reckon I do," I said. "Just seeing you sitting there all pathetic, whining about all them women you talked into marrying you, only to leave em along the side of the road like used up old rag dolls. It's tragic, you know, what you did to them women, how you waltzed into their lives with a promise and a prayer and then ran off chasing some new dream. I don't know nothin about em, of course, but I know you. And I can just see you deciding things had to be better somewhere else."

Then I scooted a little closer and put my arm around his shoulders. I couldn't understand why I was feeling like comforting him. I should've been furious. But just the fact that he had finally shared a little bit of his past seemed somehow promising. Rather than making me want to run away from the lying, deceitful sonofabitch, I wanted to protect him. What the hell was that all about?

"So where does this leave us," he asked, "now that you know what a wretch I really am?"

Once again I couldn't suppress a little smile. "I don't know yet, cuddlebug. I cain't even sort through what you've told me. Or what it means for us. Or how to react, really. I feel like I have no idea who I've been married to all these years. That's pretty sorry. And it makes me feel like a fool. But I'm not a damned fool. At the moment, I ain't got no better option than to stick with you. But I need to do some thinking. That's a lot to throw at a girl all at once. Mostly, I guess I'm just hurt that you didn't feel you could be honest with me."

We was both quiet a moment.

"Can I get you a little bourbon?" I asked.

He looked at me. "Yeah. I could use that right now."

I shuffled into the kitchen. I had thought my life was pretty simple. Maybe it still was. What was knowing all this about my husband going to change? Did I feel any different about him? I couldn't tell yet. I needed to let it simmer a bit. Maybe tomorrow I'd have a clearer head.

Lyons
Friday, May 6, 1927

*I*t may have been early May, but it felt like Lucifer had gallantly thrown open the doors of hell and welcomed us into his oppressive parlor. The kitchen was sweltering, and our tempers had risen to the occasion. After a tense dinner shift memorable only because of several minor fracases among the staff, I sympathized with the wrung-out dish rag hanging lifelessly next to the steaming sink of wash water. I hated it when my job devolved into refereeing. As long as things were running smoothly, I could focus on the myriad tasks I juggled every day, from scheduling staff to managing stock to reviewing menus to overseeing plating to ensuring that dishes were properly prepared and customers were properly served.

During those times I felt great satisfaction. I sometimes imagined my job was like orchestrating a ballet. I was the artistic director nudging my talented staff into creating an applause-worthy experience for our guests. But when basic operations got the least bit out of sync, usually because of temperamental cooks or hurt feelings, I would lose patience. Why couldn't everyone just focus on the work to be done and leave petty gripes aside?

It was after ten o'clock when I got back to the apartment. I stepped stealthily through the darkened living room, trying not to awaken James sleeping soundly on his cot. I was surprised to see under the closed door that the light was on in the bedroom. Louise was usually asleep at that hour.

When I opened the door, I saw her sitting on the bed in her dressing gown darning socks. Even with the small fan humming on the dresser, the room was suffocatingly close. Louise's hair was down on her shoulders and she frowned as she pulled the wooden darning egg from the sock she had just finished and inserted it into another one. She didn't look up. I walked over and kissed her on the head.

"You're up late," I said. "That can wait until tomorrow, you know."

She didn't respond. In a less fatigued state, I might have paid more attention to the signs of impending battle. But as I undressed, all I could think about was lying in a tub of cool water and washing away the day's cooking smells.

She looked up. "As me and James was coming back from the library late this afternoon, we saw you standing near the back of the hotel with that colored man again, having a cold drink and a cigarette. I was able to hurry James along before he saw you, but I don't like it. People will talk, Lyons. You have a certain station to uphold here at the hotel."

I stared at her. "You know who that is. That's Willie. He's been working with me since I got here. He and I were just taking a break from the 100-degree kitchen."

"Well, it's unseemly. I don't know what you're thinking, standing there with that nigger like that."

I had little energy left to control my anger, but I tried to keep my voice down so I wouldn't wake James. "He's one of my best workers, Louise. He and I occasionally get to talking about the war. He had it a lot tougher than I did, being on the front lines and all, but it's probably good for both of us to unload sometimes. I don't know what your problem is."

Louise fell silent. She put her darning tools away and got up to turn back the covers on the bed.

"Where I come from, that's just not natural. You have plenty of other men around you can talk to. You can talk to me. You've hardly told me anything about what happened during the war."

"Well, that's partly because very little happened to me over there. And that's part of the problem. But I can't forget what I saw and what I heard and what I smelled. It's hard to explain... to you or anyone else who wasn't there. But I'm going to maintain cordial relations with all my staff, colored or white. So you'd better get used to it."

I headed toward the bath. My need to maintain a respectable calm amid heated emotions stopped me in my tracks. I turned back before leaving the bedroom.

"Listen, I don't have to go to work until four o'clock tomorrow. I hear they're replaying Charlie Chaplin's *The Kid* over at the Majestic. Let's take James to see it and then take a stroll through Fountain Square, if the weather holds, and maybe do some window shopping in the Arcade. I know this transition has been tough for you, and you've had to put up with a lot of change. Heck, you haven't even been back to Cincinnati to see your parents since Christmas. We can stop by the station and check the train schedule tomorrow and plan a little break for you two, now that spring is fully here."

Louise didn't respond, but I could sense she was softening. Perhaps my tactic had indeed defused the situation.

"Just think about it," I said before turning around again.

As I lay soaking in the tub, smoking a cigarette, I thought about Louise's reaction. Hell, I was from Kentucky, too, and I knew what could happen when the races mixed in ways the locals didn't like.

But surely things were improving. The Bancroft didn't permit colored customers, of course, but there were Negro businesses thriving in Springfield. Colored men held public positions in government and industry. I had heard there had been an ugly standoff between the races in town about five years back, when a staggering economy had pitted rural whites coming to the city looking for jobs against black laborers. As I understood it, a white mob—angry about rumors of a young white girl being harmed by a black man—met resistance from a large group of colored men, some armed and trained by Negro veterans. No one had been seriously hurt, and tensions seemed to have cooled a bit after that. I suddenly wondered if Willie had played any role.

I did remember a story Willie had shared about a gruesome murder in Springfield just over twenty years before, when a mob dragged a colored man from his jail cell after he was accused of shooting his common-law wife and a policeman. Someone in the mob shot him to death, and then they hung him at the corner of Fountain and Main. Afterwards, several in the crowd used the lifeless body for target practice. Their anger still unslaked, the mob had later burned down an unsavory section of town frequented by blacks.

I toweled off and went to bed. Louise appeared to be asleep. I tried to shove the images of dangling black limbs out of my mind as I stared at the ceiling. Occasional wisps of sultry air fought halfheartedly to dry the sweat threatening to bubble up on my skin.

THE NEXT DAY THE three of us slept a little later than usual. James was up first, tapping at our bedroom door, asking about breakfast. Louise slipped into the kitchen and made some cinnamon toast and coffee. I heard her pour him a glass of milk and help him settle into a chair at the little table in the living room near the window. I shaved and pulled on a pair of trousers and a shirt and joined them there.

Our apartment was on the top floor of the eight-story hotel, so we had a grand view of the town. From our window, facing High Street, we could look directly south and see the top of the Big Four Depot and the busy rail yard—where twenty-six passenger trains stopped every day—just on the other side of Washington Street. By peering southeast, we could see the turret on the handsome sandstone library building at the corner of Spring and High. And if we got close to the window and looked west, we could see the long building housing the Arcade Hotel and the trees from Fountain Park peeking above its roofline. Just beyond was the Romanesque clock tower of the massive city hall.

The Majestic Theatre was just around the corner from the hotel. Mid-morning we headed west on High and took a right on Limestone, passing the Bookwalter Hotel on the corner and then Woolworth's before reaching the theater. I knew Louise enjoyed the movies, and she liked to follow the real-life escapades of the stars. For me, it was a distraction from whatever troubles had bubbled up between us. It was also time to sit quietly in the darkness, away from the clatter of dishes and the chaos of the kitchen. I usually found the stories amusing, but the characters themselves leaned toward the ridiculous.

Charlie Chaplin didn't disappoint. Louise and I had seen *The Kid* before, and I was hoping the tale of a little boy abandoned by an unwed mother and taken in by the flimflamming Tramp wouldn't raise any hard-to-answer questions for James. But he was clearly focused more on Chaplin's physical antics and the fact that a boy his age was in the movies. Of course, the film had a happy ending, when the mother and the Tramp are both reunited with the youngster. I secretly sneered at that improbability.

When we left the theater, James was full of energy, imitating the Tramp as he marched down the sidewalk. Louise put on her sun bonnet and then we each took one of his hands. I stole a glance at her out of the corner of my eye. In her simple gingham dress—coral pink with a white collar and a small tie at the throat—she looked lovely. I felt a sense of pride escorting my family around town. In fact, I was a little surprised at how easy it felt. Perhaps I really could pull this off this time.

"Let's walk through Fountain Square," I suggested.

"Why do they call it Fountain Square?" asked James, peering up at us. "There ain't no fountain there."

I smiled. "*Isn't. There isn't a fountain there.* You're right. But I understand there used to be one, right in the middle of the park. It was about four stories tall, made of ornate black iron. Too bad they didn't replace it when it fell into disrepair. It's a nice shady park, but the sound of cascading water would have made it special."

The bright yellow-green leaves on the trees heralded spring, and the lilac bushes at the north end of the small park groaned with blooms. A light breeze carried their irresistible scent. The sun was high in the sky, portending another very warm day. The scene was almost magical enough to turn a skeptic into a believer.

Louise and I took a couple of turns around the park, keeping an eye on James as he ran toward a youngster close to his age. The nice weather had brought a number of people out, and we nodded at a few familiar faces. Louise had started attending the handsome gray stone Gothic-style Presbyterian Church recently built at the corner of Limestone and North streets—an adjustment for her after attending a Baptist church with her family—and she had become acquainted with a number of our neighbors there. We waved at Mrs. Hedger—an older woman Louise had met at church who had become an occasional babysitter for James—as she got in a car with her son, an attorney in town.

Most Sunday mornings, I was either recovering from a busy Saturday night at work or preparing to cook for the after-church crowd at the hotel. Louise didn't like that I couldn't, or as she suspected, wouldn't, accompany them, and it had become a sore spot between us. I liked the idea of James being exposed to Sunday school and church, but I didn't see much value in my spending time there. After all, I could surmise that my fate was already sealed.

I bought hot dogs and Coca-Colas for us at Myers Market on the west side of the square before joining Louise, who had found a bench in the sun. She called to James to join us.

"James," I said, "after we look around the Arcade, what do you think about walking down to the station to check the train schedules? I was talking to your mother last night about the two of you possibly making a trip to Cincinnati to see Mamaw and Granddad. Would you like to do that?"

James twirled around. "I'd get to ride on the train? Can we, Mommy? Please?"

Louise smiled at him. "We'll see."

When we entered the Arcade on the east side of the square, the sun was pouring through the glass ceiling. There were two dozen shops to explore, so we ambled from the north end of the Arcade to the south, chatting about things we saw in the windows. James was a little impatient, tugging at Louise's hand, trying to keep her moving.

When we reached the southern end of the Arcade, we cut through the old-fashioned hotel lobby and exited onto Washington Street, then headed east past Limestone toward Spring Street. The depot commanded that corner, with its enormous Romanesque window and red slate roof. We stepped inside and began to examine the timetables.

"It looks like you could get on the train Saturday morning at seven and be in Cincinnati in time for lunch with your family," I said. "What do you think?"

"Please, Mommy? Please?" James was tugging on her sleeve.

Louise didn't respond immediately.

"Do we need to check with your parents first?" I asked.

Louise looked at me. "They'll be delighted to have us any time. Why don't you come with us?"

I hesitated, irritated—perhaps unfairly—by her neediness. "You know I always work weekends. You two go by yourselves, and then you won't be limited by my schedule."

"You're making me think you just want to be rid of us." Louise paused a moment. "Can we afford it?"

"I think so. I've put a little aside for something like this. I think you should do it."

Louise gnawed her bottom lip. "But I thought we might use that money to go to Kentucky to see your family."

I froze. I'd been fairly successful at avoiding this conversation, but I felt trapped here in the train station, James staring up at me.

"I want to go to Kentucky!" cried James. He started twirling in circles, punching at some imaginary beast high above his head. I grabbed one of his hands, trying to get him to calm down before he spun into an unsuspecting traveler wrangling a suitcase.

I could see that Louise had set her jaw. It appeared she was determined to see where this went.

"Well, James," I began, "We should go to Kentucky sometime. It's beautiful, especially the area where I'm from. But I don't have much family around there anymore. And it wouldn't be much fun for you if you didn't have cousins to play with."

"I still haven't met your mother," Louise said firmly. "Why is that? Are you ashamed of me, Lyons? Are you afraid I won't meet her standards?"

I winced. I assumed my mother was still living in Louisville, but contacting her was out of the question. And I obviously couldn't bring home a new wife. And a son.

"Let's just focus on getting you two as far as Cincinnati for a visit. How long do you want to stay?"

Louise appeared annoyed and didn't immediately respond.

"A week!" exclaimed James.

Without waiting for a confirmation from Louise, I stepped up to the counter and requested two round-trip tickets to Cincinnati, departing on the following Saturday. I tucked them safely in my inside jacket pocket and turned to head out of the station.

"Come on. We'll have just enough time to stop for ice cream before I have to head to work. Who's with me?"

"Me! Me!" said James, as he broke free of my grasp. Louise still didn't respond as she steered James through the door I held open for them.

Effie Mae
Tuesday, December 9, 1941

*A*fter my second cup of coffee, I knew I had set my mind to it. I had crossed some invisible line and I wasn't going back. I had to try to call Nell and see what I could find out.

I checked the clock. It was eight thirty. Surely the Marrs household would be fixin to get going by now.

I dug in my apron pocket and pulled out the number I had scribbled for Mrs. Robert Marrs. Perhaps whoever answered would be able to tell me how to reach Nell. I just needed to know what happened to Mary Rose. I wasn't sure why. But she was Lyons' daughter, and I was ate up with finding out whether she was OK, even if my husband weren't a bit curious.

I realized other thoughts was crouching along the edges of my mind, too, thoughts I was trying to kick aside like an unwelcome dog. The whole situation made me think about the half-grown children I had left behind when me and Doug moved to Cincinnati with Frank. If I admitted it to myself, I still carried some guilt about walking away from em, even though they seemed to have done OK without their mama.

But when I peered in them darkest corners, what was lurking there was a more painful truth. Long before I took off for Cincinnati, I had done yanked them kids from their daddy. Like Mary Rose, my young'uns mostly grew up without their father around. That was my burden. I made that decision. I made that decision because I didn't like the man I was married to at that moment.

How was that fair to my babies? Did I even think about them when I dragged em off to Logmont? Sure, they had Virgil as a stand-in daddy, but how much damage had I done with barely a second thought? Maybe I was no better than Lyons after all.

I held the piece of paper tight. Was I doing the right thing? Or was my intentions now just as selfish as when I left Wilson more than twenty years ago?

Even if that was the case, I couldn't help myself.

I slowly walked over to the phone. I hesitated one last time and then I picked up the receiver and dialed.

"Long distance."

"Could you set me up a call to Lawrenceburg, Kentucky, please?

"The number?"

I gave her the number.

"The party's name?"

"Mrs. Robert Marrs."

"Thank you. I'll ring you back when I've patched the call through."

I hung up. The call would not be cheap. I'd have to keep an eye out for the phone bill next month. I'd rather not explain this to Lyons. It occurred to me that this might be the first secret I'd have to keep from him.

When the phone rang, I jumped as if Gabriel had done blowed his horn, calling us sinners home. I picked it up.

"This is the operator. I'm ringing through to Mrs. Robert Marrs. Your name, please?"

I hesitated. I decided to use my maiden name. "Effie Mae Brady."

"Thank you. The phone is ringing."

I heard an elderly woman answer on the other end.

"Hello?"

"Is this Mrs. Robert Marrs?" the operator asked.

"Yes, it is."

"I have a call for you from Effie Mae Brady of Sparrows Point, Maryland."

"Oh." There was a moment of silence. "I don't know anyone by that name, but I suppose you can put her through."

"Hello. Mrs. Marrs?" I asked.

"Yes?"

I gathered my courage. "I'm calling for Mrs. Nell Board. Is she available?"

Another brief hesitation.

"Just a moment, please."

I caught my breath. Nell was there. She either lived there, or she was visiting. I realized I was a little surprised her mother agreed to call her to the phone. Back in Kentucky, my kin would've stubbornly demanded, "Who is this? What d'you want?" Mrs. Marrs, however, chose to assume I was a friend rather than a foe. I guess generations of feeling secure in your place lets you choose politeness at times when other people would have slid into suspicion.

"Hello?"

A different voice. I nearly gasped. That must be Nell.

I fumbled for words. Why hadn't I thought this through before I called? I asked myself again, *Why the hell was I even doing this?* Then I remembered Mary Rose. I needed to know about her.

"Mrs. Board," I began. "My husband..." I stuttered. "Your husband..." No. Stop. Think. "My name is Effie Mae. I live near Baltimore. I'm calling because..." Because why? How could I possibly put this woman through this?

"Yes?" she asked. Again, all politeness, even if I did detect a cold reserve and perhaps a bit of impatience.

"I'm married to Lyons Board," I blurted out. Oh my god. What had I done?

There was silence. And then, "Who is this again?"

I relaxed just a bit. She could've hung up, but she didn't. "My name is Effie Mae Board. I've been married to Lyons Board for seven years, and I just learned that you had once been married to him. And that you and him had a child. A daughter." My courage was building. "I'm calling because I just had to know that his daughter, that Mary Rose, is doing OK." I hesitated again. "As a mother myself, I just had to know."

A longer silence. I let it just sit there. I didn't have nothin else to say. I had laid out all my cards.

"How did you find me?" she asked cautiously.

"I discovered an announcement of Mary Rose's birth in some of Lyons' things. I tried to get him to tell me what had happened to her, to you, but I couldn't get much outta him. For some reason, I just had to know that you're OK. That his daughter is doing OK."

"So the bastard married again, did he?" Twenty years of fury and grief seemed wrapped in them words.

"Yes, ma'am." I didn't dare tell her what I had learned. That I was his fourth wife. That he had tried this marriage thing many times. That might have soothed her in some way, to know that she wasn't the only one he had done wrong. But I didn't want to risk making things no worse for her. And I had a clear goal. I wanted to know about the daughter. I didn't want to muddy the waters with all the other details.

"What do you want from me? Why are you calling?"

"As I said, I just felt the need to know that Mary Rose is OK. I cain't explain why Lyons ain't tried to get in touch with her. I don't know what happened. I'm ashamed of him, at least in that respect."

"Shameful is as good a word as any for his behavior," she started. "And I've done my best to forget that man. But having raised his daughter without her father...I'll never forgive him for that. Most of the time I thought it was for the best that he ran off. He was no good. I'm appalled that I married him, that I had a child with him. But for twenty years I've seen the pain on my daughter's face that comes from not knowing her father. It broke my heart. It broke me."

She was silent a moment. There weren't nothin I could say.

Then she continued. "I don't know why I'm telling you all this." A few moments passed. "Do you have children with him?"

"No. I had my children with another man, a long time ago. Me and Lyons married pretty late in life."

Another silence. "Do you love him?"

I was startled. I wasn't even sure how to answer that question. "Yes, I do. Though right now I'm wondering why."

I waited just a bit. "Does Mary Rose live with you?" I asked.

She hesitated. "I don't know that I should tell you anything about her." Another pause. "But you seem sincere. So I will simply say that she is off at college and she is doing well. She's a beautiful, bright young lady. But she will always carry a sadness that comes from not knowing her father. And you can tell him that if you want. But I would prefer that I never again hear from you or from him. I have closed that chapter in my life, and I don't care to reopen those wounds."

There was another silence.

"Good day to you, Mrs. Board." And the phone went dead.

I slumped down into the straight-back chair near the phone. I was sweating. My heart pounded in my chest. I had just spoken to my husband's first wife. And his daughter was a college girl.

I wanted to beam with pride. But what did that have to do with me? Or with us? Lyons had done nothin to raise that girl. But she was a young woman with a bright future. She could find her way in the world. And, for some reason, I felt confident that she would.

An enormous weight seemed to be lifted off my shoulders, and the fog I had been in for days began to clear. As I sat quietly, I felt for the first time that I knew what I needed to do. What I wanted to do.

Lyons had made some mistakes. He had hurt a lot of people. But, at our core, we're all pretty tough. Whatever pain he done scattered behind him, life seemed to be ticking along, as it inevitably does. People had to go about their days, making decisions big and small, clinging to what brought em comfort and discarding the rest. We didn't all have a lot of choices, or good choices. But we all muddled along the best we could.

And my best choice was to stick with my husband and try to forgive him for a past I knew nothin about three days ago. I had to embrace the man I had known for seven years. The man who had befriended my son and worked hard for all the time I'd knowed him. I had poked my nose in where it didn't belong. Now I felt I could leave his mysteries be.

All in all, we had a good life. And I didn't want nothin to change.

Lyons
Sunday, September 23, 1928

The Sunday dinner shift at the Bancroft had tested the well-oiled machine I had assembled around me. Our bulwarks had held, however, despite the relentless onslaught of hungry diners. Must be a convention in town, I thought. I'd better check our stock and the staff schedule for the next few days.

As I was making mental notes, I happened to look up and saw a short, balding man approaching me with a purposeful waddle. He reminded me of the misfit duck trying desperately to hang with his noisy brethren as they race through the grass to the water's edge. The buttons on his silk vest strained to preserve his modesty, preventing unsuspecting onlookers from glimpsing the likely damp starched white shirt underneath. I wiped my hands on a dish towel and turned to the man as he drew near, trying to hide my bemusement.

"Are you Mr. Lyons Board?" the man asked.

"Yes, sir, I am," I said, puzzled and just a little uneasy. Auditor? Attorney? Coroner? Private investigator?

"I'm Sebastian Fineman, general manager at the Waldorf Hotel in Toledo," he said, extending his hand. "Is there someplace where we can have a brief conversation?"

I started breathing again. I was familiar with the Waldorf. It was one of the largest hotels in all of Ohio, built about the same time as the Bancroft. It had an excellent reputation as a classy operation. My brain quickly wiped the scenes from the detective movie it had started playing when the man first approached and replaced them with less threatening images of well-heeled travelers relaxing in the opulent Waldorf lobby.

I showed Mr. Fineman into my tiny windowless office and closed the door. There was just enough room for my desk, a file cabinet, and two chairs.

"I'll cut to the chase, Mr. Board. We're looking for a sous-chef to support our main dining room. An acquaintance of yours, Mr. Oliver Sparks, one of our stewards, recommended you for the job. He said the two of you worked at the Sinton in Cincinnati before you moved here to the Bancroft. Mr. Sparks felt that with the natural capacity you had demonstrated at that previous job, and the experience you have acquired here at the Bancroft, you would be an excellent choice for this position. I told him and Mr. Dupuy, our dining room chef, that I was headed down to Cincinnati for a meeting this week anyway, and I thought I would stop here in Springfield unannounced so I could observe your dining service under pressure. I must say, I just had a superb meal and everything flowed flawlessly from the kitchen. That leg of lamb was exquisite."

"I'm glad to hear that, sir," I said, trying to keep the rising excitement out of my voice. In my interior movie, two lines of chorus girls were entering the lobby from stage left and stage right.

"I checked with your manager before I arrived, and he said you would be working today. He wasn't eager for me to talk to you, but I convinced him we should both have your best interests at heart. I've already chatted with a few of your staff as they left for the day, and they all gave me excellent reports on your abilities and your management style.

"So, I'd like to know if you might be interested in joining our staff at the Waldorf. We're a much larger operation, as you probably know.

The hotel has 505 rooms and the main dining room seats 275. We also have two sizable banquet rooms and a cafeteria that seats more than 300. I think you'll like our kitchen, which is designed to serve all of the dining areas. It has abundant natural light and state-of-the-art equipment. You'd be managing a staff substantially larger than you have here and, of course, your pay would increase proportionally."

Mr. Fineman finally paused to take a breath. "So, what do you think, Mr. Board? Shall we continue this conversation?"

I was taken aback. I tried to shut down the dance scene that was building to a crescendo and focus on the proffer that had just been made—assuming I had heard the man correctly amid the rumpus in my head. I tried to corral my thoughts. Although I'd been at the Bancroft three years, I felt in some ways that I was still settling into my role. James had just started second grade and seemed to like his school. Louise seemed a little lonely, but she didn't complain too much. A bigger job might require my working even longer hours. But it sure sounded like a good opportunity.

I finally managed to speak. "Well, sir, I certainly appreciate your confidence in my abilities. Oliver Sparks is a good man, and I am indebted to him for mentioning me. I also must say that I'm relieved to hear you had a good meal today. As you saw, we were quite busy, and on days like that I don't feel that I'm always able to oversee every detail the way I'd like. But I have an excellent staff here, and I can generally rely on them completely.

"So I'm quite honored by your offer," I continued. "Of course, I would have to discuss this with my wife. When would you need an answer?"

The filmstrip playing in my head had snapped and the loose end was flapping repeatedly as the reel continued to turn. I tried to slow it down. I was comfortable in Springfield, but I could never deny that itch to take off for someplace new, to take on new challenges or a new job. I liked feeling a little off balance, having to rely on my wits and charm to find my way in a new situation. The desperado in me was always lurking just below the surface, watching for a ready escape. With just a moment's reflection, I recognized that I had started to feel a little stale in my current position. A little pent-up. And it was getting harder and harder for me to figure out what might make Louise happy. Maybe she needed a change of scenery, too.

"I'll write up a formal offer, with job responsibilities and salary specifics," said Mr. Fineman. "I'll have my office get that to you this week. That will give you a few days to talk with your family and think about your future. I hope you'll see that your future is in Toledo.

"Here's my card. If you have any questions in the meantime, I'll be back in Toledo by Thursday. You can call me."

I took the card and thanked him. I opened the office door and escorted Mr. Fineman back into the dining room and shook his hand again before he turned to leave. I was feeling a little wobbly on my feet. On the one hand, I was pleased to know that I had built a small reputation among the hotels in the state and that it was opening doors for me. But I was anxious about how Louise might respond to the offer. I'd never glimpsed any signs of a gypsy in her soul.

I went back into the kitchen and finished up the last of the cleanup that Mr. Fineman had interrupted. I removed my apron and put it and my chef's toque in the laundry hamper. I lit a cigarette and leaned against the prep table for a few minutes, imagining myself reigning over hundreds of scurrying staff in the expansive Waldorf kitchen— somewhat like a benevolent, and certainly taller, Emperor of Lilliput. I decided I should wait until I had the written offer in hand, with the salary specified, before I mentioned it to Louise. That would give me additional ammunition for making the move. I hadn't been to Toledo before, but I knew it was a busy commercial city with lots of industry and large numbers of businessmen needing a place to stay and a place to dine. I could see opportunities for more contacts and possibly a more exalted coronation—perhaps as a lionized hotelier à la Julius Manger.

WHEN I WALKED IN the apartment around three thirty, James sat at the table staring out the window. Crayons and a coloring book were laid out and I saw some scattered paper where Louise had evidently tried to work with him on his arithmetic. It appeared she had already discovered the limits of his very short attention span. A baseball game was on the radio. I knew the relative quiet wouldn't last. I smiled at Louise on the sofa reading a *Motion Picture* magazine as I closed the door behind me.

James jumped up from the table and ran to give me a hug. My mind was happily focused elsewhere, and I wasn't sure I was in the mood to countenance his unmitigated energy. I squeezed his shoulder and delicately pointed him back toward the table. He pressed his lips into a rather unconvincing pout.

"Aren't you supposed to be doing some schoolwork?" I asked, pointing to the numbers scribbled on the paper.

"We're listening to the baseball game," he said. "The Indians are playing the Yankees. But I ain't sure who's ahead."

"The Yankees," Louise said. "I think it's two-nothin. Babe Ruth and Lou Gehrig have both had hits. How was your day?"

"Busy. I'm beat. I'm looking forward to joining you on the sofa and looking through the Sunday paper. What's that I smell?"

"Bean soup. It just felt like a bean soup and cornbread day. Is that OK with you for supper?"

"Perfect."

"Are we having anything I like, Mommy?" James asked, with a hint of an oncoming whine.

"You'll eat what your mother puts in front of you," I said a little too curtly as I tried to prevent that whine from devolving into a full-blown tantrum. In an admittedly feeble attempt to temper my scolding, I added, "After supper, we'll take a look at that arithmetic you're working on. I have a bit of experience in that arena. Meanwhile, why don't you color something to show me before we eat?"

He grinned, turned on his heel, and sprinted the four steps back to the table. I slipped into the bedroom and changed my clothes and then collapsed on the sofa, resting my feet on the edge of the coffee table. The walnut furniture in the apartment was standard issue for the hotel: satisfactory for our needs but not overly comfortable. The sofa was a little more formal than I would choose, but perhaps that was something we could remedy when we moved to Toledo. I picked up the *Springfield News-Sun* and tried to read about the upcoming election, but my mind continued to wander. The more I thought about a possible move, the more excited I became. This would be good for all of us, I decided.

ON WEDNESDAY, I HAD the letter in hand. The salary was more than I had expected, a good twenty percent increase in my current pay. Of course, I understood that the cost of living in Toledo might be higher, but I hoped the salary would be enough for us to rent a small place of our own. It had been convenient living at the hotel, but I was ready to have my own space away from work. In my now unfettered fantasy, I saw a little clapboard as the first step toward that wood-paneled library in an understated mansion.

I arranged to have the dinner shift off the following evening and called Mrs. Hedger to see if she could stay with James for a couple of hours. I thought I would take Louise to dinner at the Shawnee Hotel over on Main Street and tell her about the offer. We almost never went anywhere by ourselves, and I was hoping to set up a special occasion to celebrate my good news.

I had a couple of hours between lunch and dinner, so I slipped up to the apartment and found Louise tidying the kitchen. James would be home from school soon, and I knew I didn't have much time alone with her. I frequently did paperwork or placed orders between shifts, so Louise didn't expect me. I managed to sneak up behind her and wrap my arms around her waist. She gasped and tried to turn around, but I held her snugly. I nuzzled my nose in her hair, which smelled faintly of apple, and kissed her neck.

"What are you up to, you old coot?"

I let her turn around and I kissed her, longer than I had in a while. She pulled back, surprised.

"Really, what is going on? I almost never see you mid-day. Did you get fired? Oh my gosh, you did, didn't you? No? Then what are you doing here? You're absolutely beaming."

"I want to take you out to dinner tomorrow night. Just the two of us. I've already made arrangements for Mrs. Hedger to come here and watch James for us. We'll go to the Shawnee and have a nice meal. I might even ask if they can find an old bottle of wine hidden somewhere."

"What has gotten into you? It's too early to celebrate my birthday. And your birthday was a couple of weeks ago. Are you going to tell me what's going on?"

I continued to smile. "I have to get back to work. But I just wanted to be sure you didn't make another date for tomorrow night. Who knows what goes on around here while I'm working."

"So you really have tomorrow evening off? You have to tell me what's up, you know. How can you keep me in suspense like this?"

"I like it when you want something from me," I said, pulling her close again. "You just hold onto that until tomorrow night."

I kissed her again and reached around and grabbed her on her behind for good measure. "We'll get back to this tomorrow."

I took the stairs back down to the kitchen, whistling the whole way.

ON THURSDAY, I WAS home by three o'clock. I bathed, shaved again, and put on my charcoal gray suit. I felt like a young man getting ready for a date, not a 36-year-old with a family and responsibilities. I checked the mirror. My hair was still dark, my eyes blue and clear, my father's aquiline nose untouched by the spread of age. I saw the dashing Charles Ferrell in *7th Heaven* as he rescues the fallen but adorable Janet Gaynor just before the war. I, too, was ready for a new adventure.

It was a clear fall day, and Louise had walked to the school on the other side of Spring Street to meet James so they could walk home together. When they came in, James stared at me.

"Where are you going?" he asked.

"I'm taking your beautiful mother out for dinner. Is that OK with you?"

James continued to stare. "I guess so. Is Mrs. Hedger coming over?"

"Yep. She'll be here in an hour. So, Mrs. Board, it's time for you to get dolled up for our date."

Louise shook her head. "I'll be glad to finally know what's going on here. But if nothing else, I plan to enjoy an evening out on the town. You and your secrets..."

She headed into the bedroom to get ready. James flipped through the stations on the radio. I settled down to the newspaper, scanning articles about the mayor of Flint, Michigan, being arrested on charges of conspiracy to commit voting fraud and Eleanor Roosevelt denying a rumor that Al Smith, my preferred presidential candidate, had appeared at a Boy Scout camp with the smell of alcohol on his breath.

When Louise appeared, she was wearing a narrow black skirt that came just below her knees and a white blouse opened at the neck. Her hair was piled on her head, and I saw she was wearing her pearl earrings. I looked appreciatively at her.

"Finally, a reason to wear my favorite earrings," she said. "Let's go, old man. I'm not getting any younger."

We went out the front of the hotel and turned north at the corner to head up Limestone. The modern eight-story brick Shawnee sat across Main from the Gotwald Building, a Springfield landmark with its 125-foot conical tower and limestone façade, now the home of the Merchants and Mechanics Savings and Loan. We crossed Main and entered the hotel's lobby. It was much like the Bancroft's, only on a grander scale. The square wood columns and dark wood trim of the first floor and the mezzanine gave it the feel of an English manor home. I thought the Bancroft lobby was more handsome, with its dominant two-story stained glass window and more intimate space. But it was good to be someplace not quite so familiar, even if it was just down the street.

We were welcomed into the dining room and seated at a spacious table near a window. We had arrived a little before the usual dinner crowd, and just a few other diners were already there. The tables were elegantly dressed in white linens, and the small lamp at each offered just enough light. I knew several of the staff at the Shawnee, since it was the Bancroft's chief competitor. I looked forward to having a meal and evaluating the service.

Dusk was approaching when the waiter appeared with menus. I pulled him aside and asked discreetly about the possibility of procuring a couple of glasses of wine. After a brief exchange, the waiter said he would see what he could do.

He came out shortly with a couple of tumblers filled with a light-colored liquid. I thanked him and slipped him a dollar bill.

Louise watched all of this without saying a word. This was the side of me she didn't see very often.

After we placed our dinner orders, Louise looked directly at me.

"OK, I've been a really good sport. This is nice and all, but now you have to tell me what's going on."

I took another moment for dramatic effect. "I've been offered another job."

Louise stared at me. "Where? Doing what?"

"As the sous-chef at the Waldorf Hotel in Toledo."

"Toledo!" cried Louise. "But that's, what, another two hours north of here? Why on earth would you want to go up there?"

I felt myself chafe at her reaction. "Because it's a much better job at a much larger hotel. And the pay is considerably better."

Louise continued to look at me. "How much better?"

"Enough that I'm hoping we could rent a place of our own."

Louise looked down at the table, and then back up at me. "I don't know that I want to go even farther away from my parents, Lyons. They're getting on in years, you know. I've only seen them twice in the last year as it is. And aren't the winters up there awful?"

She stopped for a moment when I didn't respond. "You've done accepted the job, haven't you?"

"No, not yet. I wanted to discuss it with you, of course. But I really think this is a good offer that we need to consider very carefully."

I felt the excitement and the romance of the evening slipping away as Louise resisted. Couldn't she see the possibilities of my taking a leading role in a bigger production? Wouldn't she want to play Diane to Ferrell's Chico as he struggles to elevate himself from his lowly position as a sewer worker? Wasn't I also a "very remarkable fellow"?

"I don't know, Lyons. James is doing pretty well in school. Do you want to disrupt him again? And I'm finally getting settled in Springfield. It hasn't been easy for me. I'm still a farm girl at heart, you know. I'm not sure I'm up to getting used to a new city."

I couldn't mask my disappointment. "I thought you'd be proud of me, Louise. This is what I've been so excited about for the last couple of days. The general manager of the Waldorf came to Springfield specifically to offer me the job. A fellow who used to work with me at the Sinton is now at the Waldorf, and he recommended me. This is a big deal. I need you to think about it."

"I don't know what else to say," Louise said flatly. "I just can't see me making that move. We're doing OK here, aren't we? I work really hard at making ends meet. I could look for a job here, if that would help, now that James is in school."

I waved my hand, brushing that idea away. "No, no, that's not it, Louise. I need the challenge of something new. I need the change. That's what keeps me going."

The waiter appeared and placed a bowl of French onion soup in front of each of us. We both stared at it blankly.

"I wanted this to be a celebratory dinner, Louise. I had planned on toasting our exciting new future. I had no intention of upsetting you, but I guess I didn't think this through. Let's see if we can at least enjoy the meal."

We had very little to say to each other as we nibbled at the beef tenderloin and roasted potatoes. Although I tried to make small talk, asking about her church activities and what James was enjoying most about school, our words were as clipped as the text in the silent film's subtitles. My passion was gone. I felt totally deflated.

After dinner, we walked straight home. Mrs. Hedger was surprised to see us so early, but James was happy to still be up. He wanted to hear all about what we had had to eat. Louise retired to the bedroom, and I settled up with Mrs. Hedger and offered to take her home. I called to Louise that I would be gone for a few minutes and told James to start getting ready for bed. Then I walked Mrs. Hedger to my car.

The next morning, after James had left for school, I asked Louise if she had had any more thoughts about the move.

She sighed. "I just don't want to move to Toledo, Lyons. You'll have to turn down that job. Maybe you can find something else here in Springfield, or back in Cincinnati. Have you asked about something back at the Sinton? Or maybe at the Palace Hotel down there? I just can't go no farther away from Momma and Daddy. And I think it's important for James to have some stability in his life."

I nodded without saying anything. I left for work shortly there-after. I went into my office, closed the door, and called Mr. Fineman. When he answered, I told him I would gladly accept his offer and asked when I needed to report to work.

I SPENT THE NEXT week quietly preparing for my escape. I let my boss know that I had accepted the offer from the Waldorf. If anyone in the kitchen asked what Louise thought about the new job, I ex-plained that she had decided to stay in Cincinnati with James while I found a place to live in Toledo and settled in there. Thankfully, Lou-ise hadn't interacted much with my co-workers, and I thought the chances were slim that anyone would ask her directly about the move.

At home, I kept to my same routine. I did everything I could not to let on to my plans. I had decided there was no reason to even dis-cuss it again with Louise. I had made up my mind, and she had made up hers.

Since I didn't bring up the subject again, Louise appeared to relax as the week wore on. I made arrangements for Louise and James to remain in the apartment another month, if needed. I trusted that her pride would keep her from trying to contact me.

On Sunday, after Louise and James left for church, I quickly packed my belongings and loaded them in the Westcott. Before leav-ing the apartment for the final time, I opened my wallet, pulled out a number of bills, and put them in an envelope. On the outside I wrote: "For your train trip to Cincinnati and any incidental expenses you may have. My best to you."

This time, I noticed I was surprisingly calm. I knew what I had to do. If I were honest with myself, I had to admit that I had known what I would have to do all along.

Jesse James was on the run again.

Effie Mae
Saturday, March 21, 1942

I was standing in the coffee aisle at the A&P, soaking in the aroma of yet another staple I had heard rationing might soon make scarce, when I looked up and saw Mr. Wallace Fowler heading my way. His face usually reminded me of a ripening tomato basking in whatever sun broke through the sooty haze here at the Point. But today the corners of his mouth seemed to point downward, like the plant's roots was searching the ground for soothing moisture. He was a sad clown, exaggerating his frown to get the biggest laugh.

At the boardinghouse, I usually heard him before I saw him. His friends and many of his boarders alike called him "Danny boy," or just "Danny," after one of his favorite songs. He always seemed to be singing or whistling an Irish tune, frequently a happy jig, which I tended to think masked the grief he was still feeling after his wife and daughter done left him and headed back to Ohio a few years back. Soon after that unhappy event he started taking in boarders to fill his empty house.

Sometimes I would recognize a song I had learned in the coal camps—my favorite was a quick-stepping version of "The Rambling Irishman"—and the two of us would launch into a rowdy duet full of feeling but probably hard for others to take. Occasionally I would see another boarder—frequently young Freddie Clymer from down in Tennessee—duck around the corner hoping to get outta earshot when he saw the two of us tuning up for an impromptu performance. But I loved those moments. They'd take me back to another time and another place and I felt free from any cares of the day. Music always did that for me.

"Effie Mae," he said with what seemed to me a mixture of happiness at bumping into his partner in crime and an unexpected sadness I didn't recognize. "I hear you'll soon be leaving us."

I stared at him. My childish excitement at running into him fell away, overpowered by a feeling of doom. I'm sure my face dropped as if the scaffolding holding up my cheekbones had been knocked down by an outta control bulldozer.

"Whaddya mean?" I demanded, in a voice I hardly recognized.

"I spoke to Lyons briefly this morning and he said he had accepted the job over at Aberdeen, at Camp Rodman. Sounds like he feels the need to be part of the war effort. I can certainly understand that. I've wondered the same thing myself. I have no desire to revisit the hell on the battlefield—I had enough of that, you know, driving that ambulance over in France—but I need to find some way to help our boys who are heading out to serve. I believe Lyons said he would be a cook in the officers' mess. Is that right? That sounds like the perfect job for him. We sure will miss you here at the Point, though."

I let him rattle on while my thoughts spun out of control. Lyons had mentioned this job to me a month or so back, but I'd made it clear to him that I wanted to stay in Sparrows Point, that I was comfortable here and didn't want to move again. Had he really ignored my wishes and taken that job? I couldn't believe what I was hearing.

Mr. Fowler must've seen the look on my face, and he came to an abrupt stop.

"Goodness, Effie, he has told you he accepted the job, hasn't he? I'm not interfering here, am I? You know I would never . . ."

"That's all right, Mr. Fowler," I said, cutting him off. "Me and

Lyons had discussed it, but I didn't know he'd made a decision. I'll get on home now and find out what's going on. I can tell you that I sure don't wanna leave the Point. We've made our home here, and I'm downright comfortable in your big ol house. I like taking care of you and the boys."

"I'm so sorry. Really, I didn't mean to..."

"No, no, it's fine. I'll go find Lyons and get it straight from him."

I couldn't get outta there fast enough. I was such a jumble of emotions. I couldn't decide which one to deal with first. My fury with Lyons for telling Mr. Fowler about his decision before he told me, or my outrage that he made the decision all by his lonesome? My terror at the thought of leaving the Point and starting over again someplace else? My sadness if I had to leave behind them people who'd become a part of my everyday life? My complete bewilderment at what was happening?

Once outside the supermarket, I found myself stumbling along, barely able to manage the two bags of groceries, so I decided to take the Red Rocket the coupla blocks back to the house. Sitting on the streetcar would give me a few minutes to compose myself before I tracked down that husband of mine.

I felt like things had been pretty smooth between us since I had decided to set aside my frantic digging into his previous life. I'd finally come to peace with just leaving that be. Sometimes when I thought on it, I could even imagine that he might be right. That was his history, his burden to bear. I couldn't do nothin about it. I couldn't change one thing. I did love him, and I wanted to be with him, however sketchy his past.

But right now I wanted to kill him.

I stepped up in the streetcar and smiled at Mrs. Greenlee as she got off. I supposed she was heading to work at Gaver's next to the grocery, where I'd see her whenever I stopped by the sody fountain for a Co-cola or a chocolate malt. She lived over on F Street with her husband and four young'uns. I always admired that somehow she still managed to win the annual garden contest on a regular basis. Soon I could walk by there and see what flowers she'd done planted for the spring.

I sat down and pulled my bags up on my lap. Why is it nothin could stay the same for no longer than a minute? Where did this pesky wanderlust come from? What made people want to pick up and go all the time, dissatisfied with the current situation, searching for something new?

When me and Lyons got married, I loved that we was free to go wherever we pleased, grabbing whatever work we could find and landing in a spot just long enough to get tired of a place and move on again. But now I was ready to stick somewhere. I didn't wanna pick up and go again. I was ready to settle in and draw comfort from the familiar.

If Lyons really had accepted that job, we'd be asked to leave the Point. We couldn't stay there if we didn't work there. But what about my job? I was still cleaning the Clubhouse in addition to keeping Mr. Fowler's boardinghouse. Would that be enough to argue they should let us stay while Lyons worked over in Aberdeen?

Knowing Lyons, though, I expected he done had this latest move all arranged. He wouldn't even understand why I'm upset. I could already see his eyes light up as he shared his "good" news. Dammit, why cain't we make these decisions together? This is my life, too.

The thought of Wilson coming home and announcing that he'd taken that job up at Benham flitted through my mind. Recently I'd wondered whether I'd responded the best way to that pronouncement, whether my children suffered because of my stubbornness. But when I took inventory, they all seemed to be doing OK. Lee finally left the mines and had been working at the Social Security office over in D.C., where he lives with his wife and four kids. It ain't that far, but I don't seem to get over there as often as I should. Valarie married a coupla times, but things seem to be settling down for her. And little Eileen, the independent one, she married that Pole and has been living in Michigan with him and her daughter.

I tried to take a deep breath. *This will all work out, Effie. It always does.*

I carefully stepped off the streetcar and fumbled up the sidewalk with my bags. As I approached the steps to the porch, Freddie came bounding out the front door, all arms and legs, his freckles marching steadfastly across his nose. The storm door slammed behind him. He come to a screeching halt when he seen me.

"Hi-de-ho, Mrs. Board. Let me help you." He took both the bags and held open the door for me.

"You're my savior, Freddie," I said. "These old knees are giving me fits. Any chance I can talk you into carrying them bags up the stairs to the apartment?"

"You betcha. Is Mr. Board still in the kitchen this late in the morning?"

"He was cleaning up after breakfast when I left. He might be up in the apartment with his feet up, or he might have launched right into lunch prep. You don't have to work today?"

"Going in for a night shift later. Slept in a bit this morning."

I glanced into the kitchen as we passed but didn't see Lyons.

"You heard anything yet from the draft board?" I asked as we headed up the stairs.

"No ma'am. But I expect it will come any day. Don't see much way I can avoid it. Unless they decide they need me here more."

My throat tightened. I didn't want none of my boys to go away to war. They was so young. Why do they have to learn about killing?

"We sure will miss you around here if you're called up," I stammered, grateful he was in front of me and couldn't see them tears welling in my eyes.

"I'll do my duty, whatever that is," he said. "But I suspect I won't have anyone as good as you and Mr. Board looking after me if that time comes. You sure have made me feel at home here. It hasn't been easy being so far from family."

I thought about his family, and what it would mean for them when he was shipped overseas. His mother. His father. Did he have brothers? Would they have to go, too? What would happen to them? I couldn't let my thoughts wander any farther than that.

"I can get them from here," I told him as we stopped in front of the apartment door and I reached for the bags. "You run on and enjoy the little bit of time you have before your shift."

"Thank you, ma'am. I'm meeting some of the fellas down at Gaver's. We might do a little bowling afterwards. So long." He bounded back down the stairs, taking them two at a time.

When I opened the door, Lyons was stretched out on the sofa reading the newspaper. He sat up and smiled when I came in.

"I was waiting for you. Put your bags down and come join me for a few minutes."

I'd nearly forgotten how angry I was with him. Somehow thinking about what Freddie might be facing made me ashamed of my little hurts. But just seeing Lyons all excited about his open secret made my blood begin to boil again. I knew that wasn't going to help the situation any.

I stepped into the kitchen and dropped the bags on the table. I came back in the living room and hung my coat on the rack by the door. Then I walked over and stood in front of him.

"I just ran into Mr. Fowler at the supermarket," I said.

I saw his face go white. His smile started to fade. He put the paper down on the coffee table.

"So you've already heard?"

"If you mean heard that you done took that job over in Aberdeen without telling me, yeah."

"Come sit down, Effie. Let's talk about this."

I didn't budge. "So now you wanna talk about it?"

"We have talked about this. You knew I was leaning toward taking that job. When they called and offered it to me first thing this morning, I said yes. I didn't want to hesitate and lose the opportunity. They're doing a lot of hiring right now, and I imagine they have a bunch of prospects lined up to take those jobs over there."

"And it didn't occur to you to talk to me first?"

"You were out. It's a Saturday morning. I never expected to hear from them today, but I didn't want to wait until Monday to get back to them. Anything could happen over a weekend."

"That's a lame excuse and you know it."

Lyons dropped his head and stared at his hands, folded in his lap.

"So how do you see this working out?" I asked.

"Well, I think I explained to you how the shifts work over there. It's three days on, one day off. They provide room and board in the dormitories they've built for all the contract workers. So I'd be there for three days and then come home to spend a day with you."

"And just where would 'home' be, Lyons?"

I saw his jaw tighten a bit.

"I have a lead on a house we could rent in Baltimore. It's in a neighborhood where a couple guys who work here at the Point live. In fact, it was George McGuire who told me about it. He stopped by to visit with Danny—I mean Mr. Fowler—one day last week. We got to talking and he told me that his supervisor in the machine shop had looked at the place but decided not to move away from the Point. I've called and it's still available. So I thought we might go over there this weekend and take a look."

I continued to stare at him.

"Unfortunately, the trains don't go all the way out to Aberdeen, so I'll have to drive to work. With the new 35 mph speed limit, I'm guessing it would take about an hour and a half, maybe two hours, to get from that little house on Ethelbert Avenue to Aberdeen—assuming

I can get the gas I need. Looks like we're heading toward rationing. Once I'm out there, I'll look for someone to ride with me. I think I can keep ol Bessie going. My tire maintenance skills may come in handy, now that we can't get tires either."

Yep, just as I thought. He done had it all planned out. He just took it for granted that I would follow along with his scheme. What made these men so certain they had all the answers and we might not have a different way of looking at things?

"What if I don't wanna leave here?" I asked.

Lyons looked at me. "You'd rather stay here than move into a house of your own, where you don't have to clean up after eight other men?"

"I like it here, Lyons. I'm used to it. I like the guys who live here, and I like looking after em. Besides, what about Doug? Would I ever see him way out there?"

"Of course you would. It's not like we'd be moving to the moon. We'd be in a nice neighborhood with different people who can talk about something other than steel markets and union fights and who got injured on the job. I'm ready for something different, Effie. You know I like to change things up every now and then."

"But what you're describing sounds awfully complicated, with all that driving and days on and days off and such. That just sounds like making life harder than it needs to be."

I tried to remain calm. I finally sat down next to him on the sofa and folded my dry, rough hands round one of his, surprised as always at his smooth skin. "OK, so what if we move way out there. What would I do while you was gone for three days? Sit around and twiddle my thumbs? I'd be lonesome, Lyons. And I'd need something to do."

"You could look around for a job if you wanted to, Effie. I'm sure there would be something you could do nearby. Someone would need help with cleaning or maybe child care. You'd like that. Or you could volunteer for the war effort. You wouldn't even have to work, at least for a while. We could see how it goes with my new salary and having most of my expenses covered. My pay's going to be pretty good—$100 a month to start, and that should go up. Of course, I'll have gas expenses for driving out there, but that's nearly double what we were making at the Commercial House in Charleston. Besides, maybe it's time for you to kick back a bit. It seems like we've both been working long hours forever. We're not getting any younger."

"You can say that again. Which is why I'm not keen on starting over somewhere else. There was a time when running all over the country was great fun, Lyons. But I'm just not sure I'm up to it this time."

"We wouldn't be going far, Effie. Doug would still be here. The No. 25 line runs right out to Reisterstown, so you could take the bus back here to the Point any time you wanted to. But we could get away from this grit and the perpetual orange haze and live in a real neighborhood. I haven't done that since Toledo. The war won't go on forever, and this job may only last a couple of years, but you know I can always find work. Baltimore's a big place. We could settle down there once and for all. I promise. That would be it. No more moving."

I had to admit that he did make it sound mighty appealing. Perhaps I could plant a few flowers or even grow some lettuce or some peppers. But I just wasn't sure I could leave Doug and start all over.

"Tell you what," he said. "Let's plan to drive over there tomorrow afternoon and take a look. Perhaps when you see the place you'll be able to imagine a future there."

I nodded. He got up from the sofa and gave me a kiss on the forehead. Then he pulled me up and wrapped me in his arms. I didn't wriggle away.

"It'll be fun, Effie. It'll be something new. And you'll have three days at a stretch without me. That may be the best part."

He looked down at me and smiled that devilish grin. I could tell that, in his mind, he was already off and running.

As he pulled away, I smacked him on the rear. "I don't know why I put up with you."

"Because I'm irresistible," he said, eyes twinkling. "And deep down you love a good adventure as much as I do."

Lyons
Saturday, April 6, 1929

I downed my third bourbon—precisely two more of the second-tier Canadian stuff than I needed—as the disembodied voice began to take shape. Smoky. Confident. Teasing the others it ensnared in conversation. It would rise and fall, battling the trumpet for the brightest notes, swinging with the sax when it got on a roll. Masculine laughter accompanied it. Somehow that voice managed to drag the spotlight away from the musicians. And its owner had no intention of relinquishing it.

I craned my neck to see around the dark-suited figures surrounding her at the bar. I caught a bob of wavy brown hair, a sleek pale-green sleeveless dress draping a figure with sharp corners and hardly a handful of flesh for the lascivious, tapered fingers theatrically waving a cigarette, an assured silhouette with a hint of harshness—was it just the light?—and a nose that seemed more than capable of sniffing out tommyrot. There was a sly smile—a sneer?—and an arched spine as she threw back her head and released a deep and throaty laugh.

She pulled me toward her without even knowing I was there. I found no way to resist.

It was crowded, as usual, at Chateau La France. The lushly furnished dining room felt comfortably overstuffed with men and women, most professing respectability in other aspects of their lives, who had nonetheless made the eight-mile drive out Dorr Street to the narrow dirt road that led to Toledo's poshest speakeasy, a three-story barn-shaped former mansion sitting next to the original family's bottled water plant. Just a couple of years before, Chet Marks had correctly identified the out-of-the-way location as an appropriate headquarters for his rum-running, high-stakes gambling, ladies-of-the-evening beseeching operation. The lavish dining experience was intended to camouflage the underworld business that kept it all propped up. It was the decent white man's den of iniquity.

On repeated visits, I had come to recognize newspapermen, ex-ballplayers, and gangsters among the patrons. Other faces soon became familiar—dissolute denizens of the night and the women who clung to them. And then there were the businessmen I had seen at the hotel but whom I scrupulously failed to acknowledge.

Initially, I kept my distance from most of the patrons, cautiously assessing the predictable dangers for someone trying to get a measure of the scene, someone who had casually tossed aside a rather conventional life to gamble on finding something better. Someone who had a lot at stake. I no longer feared the law was trying to track me down, but I was nonetheless acutely aware of the legal tightrope the establishment trod. I didn't need to get caught up in a raid and have officers of the law scrutinize my history. I had a good job, a good future. I had prospects.

In the beginning, I told myself, I came to check out the highly touted eight-course dinners—competition, I averred, to meals we served at the staid and stuffy Waldorf. Once I got past the Chateau's fortified front door and the peephole inspection by its gatekeeper, I discovered that the free-flowing hooch—whatever its caliber—heightened the allure. I occasionally checked out the gambling on the second floor, but I never allowed myself to visit the damsels on the third. Sir Knight William E. Board, Eminent Grand Warder, had taught me all I needed to know about that.

Soon, however, it became clear that I really made the pilgrimage west of town for the music. Rowdy, free-wheeling, soul-stirring, smile-inducing, get-up-and-shake-your-backside music. Whether it was Art Tatum at the piano or the "Toledo Terror" on the trombone, the bold, brassy, provocative sounds dragged you onto the dance floor in search of a partner. I was never so grateful for those adolescent co-tillions that had boosted my confidence as well as my ability to feign deference to the ladies.

At the Chateau La France, as at La Tabernilla on East Bay Shore Road, the crowd was white. The waistcoated waiters and the romp-stomping musicians were usually black. Propriety was para-mount. No mixing of the races here, not like at the Black and Tan Cafe, Chalky Red Yaranowsky's place over in the Tenderloin Dis-trict, where blacks and whites danced together, spurred by the Afri-can rhythms of Satan's music. That neighborhood was home to poor Negroes and poor immigrant Jews, with a weekend population of cu-rious whites hell-bent on selling their soul to the devil. I'd had some fun there on a few Friday nights. The good citizens of Toledo seemed willing to tolerate blacks rubbing elbows with whites when the out-come was a rollicking good time—such as when the Mud Hens let Moses Fleetwood Walker play catcher for them back in the 1880s, the first time a baseball team had dared to have two races on the field at the same time.

The Black and Tan was a marked step up from the other blind pigs, with their questionable booze and even more questionable women. When the cops weren't making a charade of raiding those places, they were blending in with the crowd, kicking back rot-gut and tapping their feet to the raucous music.

Tonight, however, one of the hottest jazz bands in the nation, McKinney's Cotton Pickers, had the crowd at Chateau La France in a frenzy. Some of the original band members hailed from Springfield, where they had studied music at Wilberforce. It pained me that I had never been able to get Louise to spend an evening at a club. The wise sages at her church had convinced her that jazz was a dangerous aphrodisiac, the ruination of civil society. I, of course, assumed that was one reason to go.

After I settled at my table, I had noted that Milt Senior was back on the sax, along with Don Redman and Coleman Hawkins. Todd Rhodes was at the piano. Dave Wilborn was there with his banjo. He and Redman were swapping out vocals. And Cuba Austin was savaging the drums. I recognized John Nesbitt on the trumpet and Claude Jones with his trombone. Their big brass sound swallowed up the room.

As the band let loose with "I Found a New Baby," I put out my cigarette and stood up. I edged closer to the pistol-packing bagmen than any fully cognizant human would consider wise. The siren in my sight caught me staring at her in mid-sentence, arm circling above her head to make her point. I have no idea what piqued her attention, but she abruptly excused herself, parted the fawning gunslingers, grabbed my arm near the elbow and led me, half pushing, toward the darkest corner of the room, farthest from the band. As I was shoved along, I glanced behind me and saw one of the men try to shake off the hand of another who was keeping him from following us. The whole room seemed to be watching. What vortex had I just been sucked in to?

I didn't resist, of course. I don't recall being concerned for my safety. Curiosity, fueled by libido, supplanted any other emotion.

When we ran out of real estate, I turned to face my kidnapper. Her lips were on mine before I could utter a word. She kissed me hard, pressing my shoulders into the wall behind me, sinking her body into mine. She earned the response I had to assume she was after. As her lips lingered—her initial aggressiveness relaxing into pleasure—I tasted smoke, some mildly fruity flavor from her lipstick, and, to my satisfaction, bourbon. Then, just as suddenly, she pulled back, daring me to react.

I fumbled for words. "That was quite an introduction."

"You looked like somebody I wanted to get to know," she said, the smile reappearing on her face.

"How do you do?" I asked, with all the sardonic politeness I could muster given the quiver in my loins.

There it was again—just a hint of a sneer. On her, however, it was seductive. A challenge I wanted to accept.

"I'm Flossie," she continued. "I'd noticed you staring at me tonight. I liked your look. I thought maybe you could use a friend."

"What's it going to cost me?" I asked, before I had considered all the implications.

She looked indignant, and then simply rolled her eyes. "Nothing more than your soul, big boy, if I do this right." She grabbed my hand. "Come on, let's dance."

We wound our way through the sweating, gyrating bodies, legs kicking and arms upraised, and carved out a little space for ourselves. I started to relax just a bit. The movement helped clear some of the alcohol from my head and gave my brain a chance to recover.

After a couple of numbers, I managed to lead her back to the table I had abandoned. I caught the waiter's eye and ordered drinks. While I was looking around, I checked to be sure her solicitous gangsters weren't still keeping an eye on me. It appeared they had decided Flossie could take care of herself. I didn't see any reason to argue with that.

When I turned back to her, she took my hand in hers and flipped it over, rubbing her thumb across my palm, studying it intently. "You weren't too bad out there on the dance floor. What are you, a music promoter? An agent for one of these boys?" She waved her arm desultorily toward the band, which had launched into "Shim-Me-Sha-Wabble." "Or are you some big-time financier in town to close a whopping deal?"

I smiled. "I'm afraid I'm not half as interesting as you have surmised."

Now it was her turn to laugh, that deep throaty laugh. "Oh, yeah, you are. It's clear as day. Behind those gentle-looking eyes there's something else. I can't tell yet whether it's heartache, or tragedy, or dumb meanness. But I'm going to find out. I sense a mystery, and I'm not one to let a mystery go unsolved. I hereby declare it my purpose in life to find out what you're hiding."

A small wave of surprise, followed by unease, washed through my consciousness. I carefully assumed a look of concern. "Don't you think that might be dangerous, given that you know nothing about me? What if I'm a truly unsavory character?" I studied her expression, making sure she was sufficiently bored with this inquisition and wasn't taking me seriously. "What if I'm a communist or a scab? Or, heaven forbid, a Catholic or a Jew? What if I'm a revenuer? Or maybe even a murderer?"

She waved her hand again, this time in the direction of the knot of men who had surrounded her earlier. "They're all murderers," she said. "And they don't scare me none. As long as you're not a member of the Temperance Union or some fundamentalist congregation, we'll get along just fine."

"Well, you're safe there." I grinned, thinking that I'd better keep my mother's activities with the Daughters of the American Revolution to myself. I'd recently read where that assembly of holier-than-thou harpies was campaigning to keep character-destroying jazz off the radio.

"So what do you do?" she asked. "You been around Toledo long?"

"About six months. I'm a chef over at the Waldorf. I'm here on an espionage mission, spying on the competition."

"Unless you're running gin off the wharf down there by the harbor or renting those eighth-floor rooms by the hour to lonely businessmen, I don't think you'll find any competition here."

"Actually, the cooks here put a fine meal on the table. I understand that may not be the lure for most of the patrons, but someone in the kitchen has some talent."

She looked at me quizzically. "So what's your name?"

"Lyons. Lyons Board."

She snickered. "What kind of name is that? Are you from some uppercrusty tycoon family or something?"

I smiled. "No. I'm just from the South."

"How far south? You mean like Mississippi or Louisiana? On a plantation or something?"

"No. I'm a small town boy from Kentucky. And since I can't enjoy fine Kentucky bourbon these days, I come to places like this to assault my stomach with this Canadian stuff."

"Oh, it's not so bad. I've acquired quite a taste for it. Why don't you buy us another round?"

WHEN I WOKE UP the next morning, it was close to eleven. I quickly squeezed my eyes shut to block out the early spring sunlight sneaking beneath my bedroom curtains. Good thing I didn't need to be at the hotel until four. Inside my head I could still hear Cuba Austin whaling on those drums. At times it felt like he was tap-dancing against my temples while his twirling sticks repeatedly nicked the backsides of my eyeballs.

Eventually I succeeded in muffling the noise, and my brain slowly made room for a hazy memory of the evening. What the hell had happened? I tried to pinpoint when everything went off the rails. Then I remembered Flossie pressing herself against me, her mouth on mine, my back against the wall.

I let myself replay the drama, editing and rearranging scenes as my senses cleared.

I could recall snippets, but I couldn't really construct a complete narrative. We'd danced. A lot. Turkey trot, Charleston, even a little Lindy hop. I imagine she led most of the time. We'd drank. A lot. I couldn't remember the last time I had drunk so much bourbon. At some point she suggested I drop her off at her apartment downtown on my way home. That seemed the gentlemanly thing to do, since I hadn't seen any sign of her mobster friends for an hour or more. When we got to her building on St. Clair Street, I figured I'd better walk her up to her apartment on the second floor. Once there, it seemed rude not to accept her offer of a drink. When she emerged from the bedroom wearing nothing but a flimsy black-lace corset-like confection and her sheer stockings, I knew I'd been snookered.

Afterwards, she seemed willing to offer up a little more information. If I remember correctly, she said her mother ran the dry cleaner on the building's first floor. Most of the profits went directly to the gang offering "protection" from others trying to move in on the territory. Their interest in the business did, however, ensure a lot of suits to clean. Not long after Flossie's husband had died during the war— right about the time Prohibition transformed the Detroit River into a highway for mahogany Dart boats ferrying liquor from Canada—the boys had taken special interest in protecting her. She seemed to both admire and chafe at their vigilance. But it had let her roam the night-clubs with abandon after working long hours in the sweatshop.

I recalled the involuntary shiver that had wracked my body when she casually mentioned the fate of her husband. Perhaps my timing could be questioned, but I pulled her a little tighter as we spooned in her narrow bed, and I asked if she knew what had happened to him. She laughed that husky laugh and said he never even got out of Ohio. He'd contracted the flu while training at Camp Sherman in Chillicothe—my second stop before shipping off—and she'd lost him before she'd grown accustomed to his absence. "The dumb bastard," she'd said. "He never even got a chance to make the world safe for democracy."

I had felt a vise grip my heart. What were the odds that I had escaped death in all its costumes? Even Nell had been forever altered by the Spanish flu—her hearing compromised by her bout with the illness—but I had kept company with thousands of men in close quarters at two different cantonments and never fallen ill. I had been on the edge of one of the bloodiest battles of the war and never suffered a scrape. I waltzed blithely through combat and through life, seemingly never harmed. Yet I felt as damaged as anyone who had returned.

All I knew to do was kiss the back of her head and rest my chin on her shoulder.

As my memory reconfigured the details of our tête-à-tête, I felt my hands exploring her angular body and her easy familiarity with mine. Before our talk, she had conducted every movement, controlled the tempo, indicated *pianissimo* or *forte*. She took us masterfully from *lento* to *allegro* to *presto*. From sighing to breathless. From anxious to exultant.

I suppose I had stumbled home shortly after that, but I hardly remembered how I had gotten here. It was still warm under the covers, and except for my brain's impatient demand for coffee, I might have rolled over and gone back to sleep.

I pulled on a robe and found my way to the kitchen. Nearly every day I had been in Toledo I had cursed the cold. Louise had been right about that. Down at the hotel, the brutal wind blowing off the Maumee River had made opening and closing the back door off the kitchen a real adventure. Even now, with the sunlight coming through the dirty window that looked out on the bare backyard, it felt like the cold had taken up residence in my bones. Summer couldn't get here fast enough.

I took my coffee into the front room so I could sit by the window looking out on Colburn Street. The shotgun house I rented was sandwiched between two similar frame houses with just enough room to walk between them. Since I largely worked nights, I didn't see much of my neighbors and, during the dead of winter, I hadn't made much effort to connect with them. I imagined a good number worked at the local auto plants—GM, Chrysler, and Willys-Overland all had operations in Toledo. General opinion seemed to be that Willys shouldered a lot of responsibility for growing bitterness between the races around the city. After the federal government sanctioned xenophobia and anti-Semitism with its post-war immigration acts, Willys brought in non-union black workers to replace the Eastern Europeans that the company foremen had smugly relieved of their jobs. I shook my head every time I thought about the auto manufacturers siding with the Negroes over uppity white Jews who dared to exert their power by organizing.

The Maumee River flowed east along the south side of my neighborhood and then took a 90-degree turn to the north as it made its way behind the Waldorf and eventually dumped into Maumee Bay. There, waters from Detroit, Ohio, New York, and Canada swirled together amicably in an international goulash to form Lake Erie. I frequently drove the two miles to the hotel, just a block from the city boat landing, since the new bus line wasn't always reliable for my uncivil work hours. With warmer weather coming, if I could swing an occasional day shift, I looked forward to walking up Maumee Avenue to Broadway and on to the hotel towering over the corner of Summit and Madison.

Flossie's apartment was just a few blocks south of the hotel, on St. Clair near the corner of Lafayette, not too far from Chicken Charlie's—just on the edge of "the Badlands," as the Temperance Union had dubbed the neighborhood. Evidently the night clubs and pool halls along Lafayette reeked of fun, something upright citizens were staunchly opposed to. I decided I'd shift my dry cleaning business to her mother's shop, just to do my bit to support the racketeers standing firm against the onslaught of piety.

I lit a cigarette and noticed that the previous day's newspaper was spread out on the coffee table, right where I had left it. I picked up a section and flipping through noticed an ad for an appearance of Bix Beiderbecke at the Armory on May 26. I made a mental note to get two tickets. I could just see Flossie swaying to his intoxicating cornet inside that medieval castle in one of the toughest parts of town. I remembered reading somewhere that Eddie Condon had once said that Bix's cornet playing sounded like "a girl saying yes." I hadn't had the opportunity to ask anything of Flossie just yet, but she seemed to have appeared before me fully formed with "yes" hanging perilously on her lips.

Effie Mae

Sunday, March 22, 1942

*A*fter Lyons checked that the boys had what they needed to get lunch for the working men, we loaded ourselves in Bessie and headed toward Baltimore. I was reminded once again how mad I was when I first seen the little '34 Ford coupe he'd bought when we was in Miami, right before we started that long trek up the east coast, the one that eventually landed us in Charleston. We'd been talking for weeks about trading in the old Westcott that was no more reliable than a stubborn old mule. I was preaching that we needed a bigger car—a sedan or a touring car—for the two of us and what few things we could pack into it if we ever hit the road agin. But he never listens. When he drove up in this sharp little number, the rumble seat open, grinning from ear to ear, I couldn't decide whether to giggle or give him what for.

I settled for my usual refrain. "Lyons Board, what the hell have you gone and done?"

He couldn't stop grinning. "You like it? When I found this honey at a price we could afford, with only 5,000 miles on it, I couldn't pass it up. And it's got the V-8 engine for quick getaways. I figured if it was good enough for Clyde Barrow, it's good enough for me."

I had to laugh. "What are you running away from this time, mister?"

"Not necessarily running away—unless it's from this god-awful heat and humidity, or another hurricane. Just thinking about our next adventure. You know. You and me. Bonnie and Clyde. Hitting the open road."

"I'm not getting into any shootouts with you, cuddlebug. Will this thing even get us all the way to Baltimore? You know I'm really hankering to see my boy."

"Yes ma'am. It sure will. Hop in and let me give you a ride. I think you'll stop all your complaining once you settle in here next to me."

And, although I still hate to admit it, he was right. I slid into that smooth, cool seat and right away felt a sense of possibility. A sense of joy. It don't make no sense, I know. But I was ready to go. It felt cozy, comfortable. It had everything you needed but nothing more. I had thought it was damn foolish to leave our good jobs at the Roney and go looking for trouble somewhere else smack in the middle of the Depression, even if it did get me closer to Doug. But there was something about that car that made me go all in with him and his crazy ideas.

I tried to recapture that feeling as we drove out Sparrows Point Boulevard and across the viaduct. It wasn't coming as easy this time. Maybe now I was too familiar with Bessie, who'd seen better days. Maybe the war had us all uneasy about everything. Maybe I was just getting old. It was hard to tell.

When we turned onto Ethelbert Avenue, I saw a few scattered white frame houses of varying sizes. Lyons checked the house number he had scribbled on a scrap of paper, and we rolled to a stop in front of a small house with a closed-in front porch and a single dormer window peeking up from the roof. There was a narrow sidewalk leading up to a handful of steps onto the porch. A few dandelions poked their heads along the edge of the walk.

It looked just a little sad, sitting between two slightly larger houses, all set pretty close to each other in what felt like one open yard.

But it looked solid. And I could sorta see the appeal for Lyons—it would be a place of our own, for $30 a month. I hadn't paid rent in all my life except for that one month after Frank died, so it made me feel a wee bit nervous to think about taking on that obligation.

As we got outta the car, I saw a man step off the porch of the house next door. He looked to be about our age, maybe a tad younger. He had a square jaw to match a solid body, wire-rimmed spectacles, and graying close-cropped hair. He threw his hand up in greeting and headed toward us. Me and Lyons waited on the sidewalk.

"You come to look at old man Cairns' house? His wife called and asked that I watch for you." He stuck out his hand to Lyons. "I'm Fritz Bodenheimer."

He had an accent. German, I thought. *"Vatch for you,"* he said. I felt my hackles get up. Why was he watching for us? We should be watching out for him.

About that time I noticed two towheaded young'uns, a boy and a girl seemingly both about ten years old, had plopped down on the top step in front of his porch, half curious, eyeing us.

"Pleased to meet you. I'm Lyons Board, and this is my wife, Effie Mae." They shook hands and I tried to smile. I didn't expect to be meeting people. I wished I'd put on my good coat and taken a little time to fix my hair. On second thought, why did I need to look nice for him?

"*Ja*, Mable decided to move close to her family after Walter died, oh, two months ago," Fritz continued. "He was, what, thirty years older than she is? Anyway, she wanted to rent the house and I told her I'd help out. I have the key if you want to look."

"Of course," said Lyons. "We'd appreciate it."

He looked at me out of the corner of his eye, surely suspecting I already wasn't feeling too good about this situation. I tried to give him a wink, but it felt half-hearted at best.

"It seems like a nice neighborhood," said Lyons as we stepped up on the porch. "We live out in Sparrows Point and are thinking about moving into the city."

"*Ja*, we have good neighbors."

"*Yah, vee have goot neighbors,*" I heard.

"Meyer Fishman has the grocery on the corner." Mr. Bodenheimer cocked his thumb in the general direction. "Young Morris Freedman helps him. Leon Schwartz, on the other side of this house, is a young man, too. He works with the horses at Pimlico. Let's see...John Wells is a lineman for the telephone company." He pointed in a vague direction. "Leonard Sterling has a seafood market. Raymond Wilson paints cars at the garage down the street. Oh, and Dr. Fleischman has his office in the house one street over. And you'll want to get a meal at Mr. Gianakos' restaurant. *Köstlich*. Interesting people. Good, solid people."

"What do you do, Mr. Bodenheimer?"

"I work as a clerk at the hospital. Walter (*"Valter"*), rest his soul, operated a little printing company. Mable's still trying to find someone to manage it for her."

He unlocked the front door and we stepped into the living room. It seemed a little worn, but roomy. We could see through to a smaller dining room and then the kitchen off to one side.

"The bedroom and bathroom are off to the left back there, and there's a narrow stairway up to the attic where the kids had their rooms. You look around. When you finish, lock the front door behind you and bring the key to my wife, Sofie, or me."

"Thank you. We'll just take a few minutes."

The German nodded and backed out the front door. I felt myself breathe for the first time.

Lyons looked at me. "What's up with you?"

I hesitated. "I just weren't expecting no Krauts next door."

He stared at me. "Why would that bother you, Effie? He seems like a nice man. Hell, I'm the one who fought the Germans. He could have been on those battlefields with me, for all we know. I assume he thought there might be more opportunities here for him and his family. I have no problem with that."

I felt myself grow sullen. I didn't like how I was feeling. I knew I knew better. I'd knowed lots of people who'd come acrost the waters to make a better life here. But maybe I'd never before had em inside what might be my home. And now that we was back at war with the Germans, that man felt like an intruder.

"Come on. Let's take a look," said Lyons, taking my hand.

It just took a few minutes to walk through the rooms. He could find something nice to say about each one. I could see everything that needed a good scrubbing. But I could tell it wouldn't take much work to keep it up once I had gotten everything to my liking. Then what would I do with myself all day?

Lyons was smiling. "It feels like a fresh start to me, Effie. It feels like we could create something just for us. I could look forward to coming home after three days away and settling down with you for a day."

He pulled me into a hug and kissed the top of my head. "What do you think?" he asked as he pushed my shoulders back so he could look me in the face.

I could hardly look at him. I couldn't shake my bad feeling. I tried a half smile, but I knew he could see right through that.

His smile faded. "Well, I hope you come around to this idea, sweetheart. I have to give Mrs. Cairns a call tomorrow and let her know whether we're interested. You know I want to do this. I start at Aberdeen on the first. I want us moved in here before then."

I nodded as we walked to the front door. I couldn't think of nothing to say. I watched as Lyons took the key next door. He spoke to the two young'uns as he stepped up on their porch and knocked. This time the woman came to the door. I caught a glimpse of a pretty blond who took the key from him. I don't know why I felt they was threatening.

It was a silent ride home. I wanted to break the ice, find something happy to talk about. But I just felt dead inside. I couldn't muster nary a bit of excitement about this move.

When we got back to B Street, Doug was in the big sitting room with a couple of others listening to the radio. He got up and walked with me up the stairs as Lyons stopped in the kitchen.

"So, whaddya think? You really moving into the city?" he asked.

I just kept plodding up the steps. When I opened the door to the apartment, I started to cry. Doug had no idea what to do. He finally wrapped me in his arms.

"What's the matter, Ma?"

"I don't know, honey. I don't know. I'm just all mixed up. Lyons is so excited about this move, but I don't wanna leave here. I like it. I have things to do, people I care about. It just felt so lonesome over there. And you're here. Why should we go way out there?"

He walked me over to the sofa and we sat down. I found a wrinkled handkerchief in my pocketbook and blew my nose.

"Do you hafta move cause Lyons took that job?" he asked. "Have you checked?"

"It don't matter. He's done made up his mind. He's my husband. I reckon I have to go."

Doug was quiet a moment. "I'm not trying to step in your business, Ma, but what if you stayed here while Lyons got settled in out there? I'm sure Mr. Fowler wouldn't say nothin. Heck, you'd still be working. Maybe Lyons will find he doesn't like this new arrangement either, and he'll want to come back here. Then you wouldn't have moved out there for nothin. Or maybe you'll get used to the idea and decide you want to go. I'd sure miss you, of course, but it might be a good thing to get away from this place. I'm sure you could find work out there. But this all came on so sudden. Maybe you can just wait a bit and see if it grows on you."

That made me feel a little better. Maybe I didn't have to rush into all this just because Lyons wanted to. Surely they wouldn't boot me out of the apartment as long as I was still cleaning the boardinghouse and working over at the Clubhouse. Maybe I just needed a little time to get used to the idea.

"Thanks, honey. I'll think about that." I looked at him. "You know, you're smarter than you look." I smiled and ruffled his hair.

"You didn't raise no fool, Mama. Let's just slow this down a bit and see what happens. I feel like it will all work out in the end."

Lyons
Thursday, September 3, 1931

I stepped out of the Green Lantern Diner, dazzled by the bright sunshine of a late summer day. Flossie had indeed proven to have all sorts of charms, but her cooking definitely wasn't one of them. Occasionally I tired of preparing food to keep the bills paid and our stomachs full, and I would sneak out of the house a little early for work and stop in the diner for a rib-sticking meal. Chicken and dumplings and southern-style green beans had hit the spot.

Today I was on foot, basking in the near perfect weather. As I headed up Broadway, I glanced over my right shoulder to catch a glimpse of the rebuilt Union Station. A little over a year before, Flossie and I had stood in a crowd of thousands and watched the rambling building with its Gothic towers and gables go up in flames. Everyone assumed it was the end of the outdated structure that many in the community considered an eyesore and an embarrassment. I was one of the few who had felt sentimental about the quirky Victorian architecture being swept away. It seemed the perfect complement to a train depot slowly acquiescing to the young upstarts—motor coaches and airplanes.

The *Toledo News-Bee* had described the burned-out station as eerily evocative of the scene that greeted American soldiers as they entered shell-torn Belgian towns. We were all surprised, therefore, when the

New York Central brass hats—soon after their vice president, R. D. Starbuck, visited the gutted site in his private car—decided in their indisputable wisdom that the damage was nothing a little elbow grease and some fresh lumber couldn't fix. Toledo, in the midst of Midwest industrial decay, evidently hadn't met the bar for the East Coast company's investment in a brand new station. As the Depression wore on, the building had become emblematic of the entire city crumbling into ruin—patched and bandaged rather than rising anew from the ashes.

As I looked around, Toledo's suffering seemed palpable. Well over half the city's industrial workers were already unemployed. If they were still working, it was for fewer hours a week at a pay rate their daddies would have been proud of at the turn of the century. Businesses closed nearly daily. New foreclosure and for sale signs decorated the windows. Families broke apart as desperate parents sought work elsewhere. Some of my neighbors moved back to the farming areas they had come from, hoping to have more luck wrenching food for their families from the unforgiving soil. For those who could find no way to escape, city workers offered a consolation prize: a meager cup of soup over at the Toledo Terminal Railroad Building on Cherry Street just north of the hotel. Rumor had it that others found a more direct route out, taking their own lives as they lost all hope of feeding their babies.

Amid all the hardship, one thing that didn't leave town was baseball. The marvelously monikered Mud Hens had been a fixture in Toledo for decades, and Flossie and I found our way to Swayne Field whenever my work schedule allowed. Unfortunately, after winning the league championship in 1927, the team seemed to be suffering from the same downturn as the economy, and they had sat at the bottom of their division two of the last three years, despite Casey Stengel's sometimes colorful management. But that hadn't dampened our enthusiasm. Somehow watching virile young men battle against the odds—and for a quarter less pay than they had made just a few years before—renewed the fight of everyone in the stands. This year attendance had dropped by more than half, but Flossie and I had done our best to remain loyal, huddled with the other stalwarts amid thousands of empty seats. I still had work, and we could indulge in a luxury or two. Baseball helped the faithful forget about our daily struggles for a few hours and gave us a reason to brandish our bedraggled local pride. After the game, we shuffled home and started scraping together the few dimes we would need to sit in the bleachers again the next week.

Meanwhile, the gangsters running the jazz clubs and casinos and brothels seemed to be the only ones still doing brisk business. After Flossie and I married, we delicately managed to extricate her from her underworld ties. She stopped working for her mother and we avoided her former protectors' favorite hangouts. Instead, we visited the smaller, sometimes rougher establishments where the musicians simply played louder to drown out the fights. There were a lot of options: Herman's, Chicken Charlie's, and the Green Mill, to name a few. Those places all had ties to gangsters, too, of course, but not the ones who had any interest in our well-being. Nearly every time I stopped by Chicken Charlie's I saw Big Clarence the bagman making collections. The local jazz musicians, who were as interested in putting food in their bellies as the rest of us, supported all the clubs no matter their connections and played regularly at neighborhood rent parties as well, helping struggling families ward off their creditors. We were all in this together.

For the most part, we, like everyone else, simply tried to keep on living. The previous year the optimists among us felt the suffering in Toledo might be short-lived. We simply had to gut through our troubles with a little pluck and determination. The Toledo banks appeared to be stable, and there were massive construction projects around the city that teased us into thinking things weren't that bad. Work had already begun on a flashy new suspension bridge over the Maumee, which was now expected to open next month amid a self-congratulatory orgy of city and state officials. Right after Union Station burned, new coal and iron ore loading docks raised Toledo's profile as a railroad and shipping terminal on the Great Lakes. A new Georgian-style hospital had opened back in May, possibly alleviating the crush of prostitutes appearing for their weekly inspections at the old hospital on Lafayette. Next week area students were expecting to get their first chance to bully each other or find young love in the hallways of the new Thomas A. DeVilbiss High School. We seemed as blind as the engineer on a midnight freight train to what lay just ahead on the tracks.

Then last month everything derailed. Four local banks closed and never re-opened. More area businesses filed for bankruptcy. Doctors and lawyers who had lost everything closed their offices. It's hard now to see where the cash for basic financial transactions will come from. Or how a hotel will have customers. How anything will survive. What the future will hold for any of us.

As I walked along Broadway, I couldn't ignore the vagrants and the hobos, eyes vacant, clothing filthy, digging halfheartedly through garbage cans. Their number seemed to increase every time I allowed myself to notice. I had to think that the majority of these wretches discovered there was little for them here and quickly hopped the next train out of town.

I crossed Swan Creek on Summit and tried to imagine the vibrant business area just two short years before. Now it seemed shabby. The last bit of hope appeared to be draining into the gutters. The city's splendor, such as it was, had faded into resignation.

Once at the hotel, rather than go in the service door at the rear, I entered through the lobby so I could pick up a newspaper. Even the *Toledo Blade* exemplified the times: scrawnier, with articles squeezed on each page as if they were desperately clinging to one another for warmth or succor, fearing the stingy printer would pluck them from the press to save ink and newsprint.

I glanced around the lobby as I headed to the newsstand. The Depression couldn't affect the fine marble floors and pillars or the solid marble front desk. The 30-foot ceiling and the bas-relief friezes still bestowed a feeling of grandeur. But the upholstery on the walnut neo-classical furniture appeared more worn than I remembered and the florist shop and haberdashery were now closed. The barbershop had managed to hang on, and I gave the proprietor my business as regularly as I could. Defiant tresses seemed to be the only thing that hadn't been cowed by the Depression, and I was thankful I still had some to cut.

Only the Hotel Secor on the corner of Jefferson and Superior could claim a more opulent lobby, with its multi-tiered marble ceiling. The oriental rugs and leather club chairs there seemed to attract a more discriminating customer. But the key attraction, at least in my mind, had to be the top-tier jazz performers the Secor had been willing to accommodate. Some prescient manager had understood that a certain clientele would embrace the novel sounds that seemed to outrage the more bourgeois clientele who chose the Waldorf. I had heard that after the Hotel Secor brought in the all-Negro Knights of Syncopation with Sammy Stewart back in '22, they never looked back. A teenaged Art Tatum honed his craft over there. They paid him in free meals, and I could just imagine his blistering version of "Tiger Rag" rendering the unsuspecting diners breathless.

As I turned down the hallway toward the kitchen, I saw Mr. Fineman, the general manager, come out of his office. His distinctive waddle always evoked a smile. Before I could extend a greeting, he spotted me, dropped his eyes a moment, and then called out my name.

"Mr. Board. How are you today? Do you have just a moment?"

I stopped as I felt a chill work its way up my spine. "Of course, Mr. Fineman." He indicated I should join him in his office. I couldn't recall exchanging anything other than polite pleasantries with him since the first day I had arrived at the Waldorf. I had had my hands full in the kitchen, and I assumed everything was going to his satisfaction. I reported directly to Mr. Dupuy, the main dining room chef, and I thought we had worked well together. It's true that I had my sights set on his job when he was promoted or decided to move on, so maybe that's what Mr. Fineman wanted to discuss. I convinced my heart to slow its histrionic beating.

He walked around to the chair behind his handsome walnut desk and indicated I should take the remaining chair on the other side. "Please," he said, "have a seat." I put my hat and newspaper in my lap and leaned forward, trying to mask my uneasiness.

He cleared his throat. "Obviously," he began, "you're aware of the challenges the hospitality industry is facing as this Depression deepens. We at the Waldorf have not been immune. Toledo has been hit hard, and the bank closings last month were a real wake-up call for all of us." He looked down a moment and pressed his lips together, before looking back at me. "I'm afraid we're having to trim our payroll. We had tried to keep the kitchen staff intact, as long as locals were still entertaining clients and eating out. But this latest business with the banks has hit us particularly hard, and we need to make some adjustments.

"We have been delighted with your work, Mr. Board, and Mr. Dupuy has given only glowing accounts of your management of the staff and your contributions in the kitchen. But we have to tighten our belts, and we can no longer afford to keep you. I'm sorry. Here's your final paycheck." He handed me an envelope across the desk. "Be sure to collect any personal items before you leave today."

I sat in stunned silence, unable to move or speak. The envelope felt like a live grenade in my hands. All the jobs I had held, in all the different industries, and I had never before been fired. And although I knew that my dismissal had nothing to do with my performance or my abilities, it still stung me to the core. Flossie and I had talked about the possibility of my losing my job. It had seemed inevitable, to be honest. But somehow I thought I would hang on, that I would magically escape the fate of so many others, that somehow I would not be affected by the grim reality around me. But it appeared now that I was no better, no different, than the others. I, too, might be reduced to delivering newspapers, selling apples on the street, or digging through garbage cans.

Mr. Fineman saw the look on my face and noted my uncharacteristic silence. He stood up, and I followed his lead. He extended his hand. "Mr. Board, it's been a pleasure having you here at the Waldorf. If I can be a reference for you as you seek other employment, I would be happy to do so. Again, I'm so sorry that circumstances have put us in this difficult situation."

I shook his hand. "Thank you, Mr. Fineman. I have enjoyed my work here at the Waldorf, and I will be sad to leave. It's quite a shock, as you can probably imagine."

"Yes, son, I know. Good luck to you." He opened the door of his office and escorted me out. He then closed the door behind me.

I stood in the hallway, not knowing which way to turn, what to do. My feet seemed cemented to the floor. What was I supposed to do now? Where should I go? How would I spend my days? I tried mightily to organize my thoughts, to bring some sort of rational order to the chaos in my brain. Finally I focused sufficiently to determine there was nothing in the kitchen that I couldn't leave behind. I had no interest in making an appearance there so the others could witness my ignominy. I did not want their pity. Nor did I want to see the fear in their eyes, as they wondered who would be next.

When I finally pried my feet from the floor, I marched to the rear exit, head down, picking up speed as I went. Once outside, I headed toward the boat landing on the river. I needed air. I felt myself gulping it greedily as I lurched forward. A few people stared at me as I passed, and I realized I must look feral in my state of anguish. I took a seat on a low concrete wall close to one of the piers and tried to catch my breath.

I told myself I had recovered from worse before. I would be fine. I just needed to think. I needed a plan.

Slowly I was able to organize my obstreperous thoughts. First, I realized I didn't want to tell Flossie right away. I needed time to sort through this. Then, I decided I could while away a few hours somewhere downtown that evening so as not to raise her suspicions by showing up at the house too early. After that, I would go to bed and see how things looked tomorrow.

I took a few more deep breaths, and then I pushed myself away from my seat. As I walked along the river, my senses awoke from their brief torpor and I noticed the dirty water lapping gently against the pier and felt the warmth of the sun on my face. I reached in my pocket for my cigarettes, then turned my back to the wind and cupped my hand around one as I fumbled to light it. I took a deep drag. Even these Lucky Strikes were better than the old Army Clubs they had provided us when we were overseas. Those had seemed heaven-sent at the time, helping us get through some tense situations. Maybe these "Luckies" would live up to their name.

I decided to hide out at Herman's for a few hours. The bathtub gin there was generally too bad to drink, so I hoped that would keep me from overindulging in my present state. And even on a Thursday the music should be loud enough and the crowd rowdy enough that one more bum in the room wouldn't draw much attention.

When I got home later that night and crawled into bed, Flossie turned toward me and smelled the rotgut on my breath.

"You been partying without me?" she mumbled.

"Stopped in Herman's with a couple of the others after work," I lied. She curled her body around me, draping one leg over my hips. "Don't you think about trying to take advantage of me in my compromised state," I teased. She snuggled her nose in my chest and promptly fell back asleep. I lay there for an eternity trying not to move.

"WHY DON'T WE HEAD up to the Lotus Beds this morning before I go to work?" I suggested as Flossie and I sat in the front window sipping coffee. "It's too perfect a morning to waste, and they probably won't be blooming much longer."

The fog had not completely lifted from my brain, and I had a dull headache from whatever I had drunk the night before. But I watched her face as she looked through the newspaper. Her hair was still a bit disheveled and her dressing gown was gaping so that one breast was nearly visible. I considered reaching over and starting something, but thought better of it.

She looked at me from the corner of her eye. "Really? You wanna drive all the way up there this morning?"

"Sure. Why not? Let's break out of our mold today. What d'you think?"

She shrugged her shoulders. "OK. Fine with me. At least I won't spend the whole day ironing."

She unfurled herself from the sofa, carelessly tightening her sash, and plodded off to the bedroom to change.

I thought if I could just get outside and get some air I would see clearly how to proceed. What my next step should be. How I would support the two of us. How we would muddle through this.

We took Summit Street north out of the city. As we passed the Waldorf, I tried not to look to my right. I couldn't reconcile that I no longer belonged there. That I was no longer wanted. It was another beautiful day, and with the top rolled back on the old Westcott I tried to focus on the sun and the air—the two things I seemed to need to keep going. We bounced over and around the potholes still left from the winter. As we passed the Yacht Club and its spectacular Spanish style clubhouse, I saw Flossie crane her neck to get a better look.

"It's like something from the Arabian Nights, isn't it?" she said, mostly to herself. "Just another world. I always think inside it must look like the Paramount Theatre, like Shangri-la. "

We parked and found the walkway around the Lotus Beds. The nearby beach, with its dance pavilion and dining hall, had closed the previous year as it changed ownership, and since it was a weekday late in the season, no one else was around. There weren't as many blooms as earlier in the summer, but there were still enough to offer quite a spectacle. Toledo claimed this was the only place in the U.S. where the Egyptian plant thrived in the wild. Evidently the marshes north of one of the country's grimiest cities were just dirty enough to please the exotic flower. The murkier the water, the deeper the mud, the happier the roots and the more beautiful the blooms. Each night the flowers would submerge themselves only to emerge the next day with nary a hint of the water's detritus on their brilliant white petals. Each day, a rebirth. Each day, new glory.

I couldn't help but think about the depths of my current despair. Could I find a way to emerge with new hope? Could I escape the blackness once again seeping into my soul?

I took Flossie's hand as we walked. I wondered whether I would be able to come back from this latest blow. My hopes of establishing myself in the industry here in Toledo appeared to have been dashed. The city was under siege. Opportunities were few. Those who could were leaving. Would Flossie be willing to pick up and go? Could she leave her mother and her ties to the area? I had heard things were a little better in Cincinnati. Maybe I needed to consider moving back there to see what work I might find.

We took a seat on a bench overlooking the marsh. We were both quiet. The beauty of the place had stilled our tongues. We watched the sun ricochet off the white blooms, dancing a gavotte. A number of American coots—our Mud Hens—skirted the lotus flowers in their stately black and gray suits, their white bills flashing in the light. I was reminded of Louise's favorite nickname for me.

Flossie broke our silence, jarring me from my reverie. She leaned against my shoulder. "It feels like we're on our honeymoon again. You remember being on the boat near the falls, with the spray completely soaking us? What a scene. What a roar. I never imagined the falls could be so loud. But it's so quiet here, so peaceful."

On a lark, Flossie and I had driven along Lake Erie to Niagara Falls to get married just a couple of months after we had met. We were buoyed by the exuberance of the times. Everything was moving fast, from the dances to the gin-swigging to the pacers over at Fort Miami Park. We just fell right in rhythm. We rushed to fall in love, rushed to marry, rushed to settle in on Colburn Street. Ecstatic about it all. There was little thought about what was happening, and none about what might happen down the road. Maybe that was a good thing. If we had paid attention in the spring of '29, we might have seen the ominous signs of the deprivation to come. My neighbors were already being laid off even then, but we thought we were untouchable. Surely the gay times would last forever.

"The *Maid of the Mist*," I said with a grin. "How could I forget that ramshackle old boat? I didn't think we had a chance of surviving that tour. I figured fate was already paying us back for our recklessness—running off and getting married like that. And now look at us, two years later. We've both turned forty. We're an old married couple." I kissed her on the cheek.

She laughed. "Now you're asking for trouble. Admit it. You've never had so much fun. Even after the crash, we've always found a way to enjoy the good times. It's getting a bit scarier, I have to say. But thank god you still have a job."

A punch to the gut. I nearly let out an audible *oof*.

"You know, I still can't believe nobody else had snared you before me," she went on. "How had you avoided getting married for so long? Of course, I didn't think I'd ever marry again, after Chester went off and died on me."

She took my hand and looked at it, much as she had that first night. I sat frozen, afraid my face or my words would betray me. When my silence began to feel like deceit, I felt I had to say something.

"What do you see there? Have you figured me out yet?"

"You're a tougher nut to crack than I thought you would be, I must confess. There's still something I don't know. Once I had you in my lair, I guess I quit working on uncovering the mysteries. Maybe that's something I need to recommit to."

Her sly grin creased her face, and she playfully knocked her shoulder against mine. I needed to put an end to this conversation.

"Come on. Let's walk a little farther and then head back. I don't want to be late for work."

I'm going to be found out for the liar and the charlatan I am. Those words hummed incessantly in my brain, on a continuous loop, as we drove home. The persona I had constructed appeared to be crumbling, just like the roads. I was no longer a chef. I was a two-timing—no, a three-timing—loser. I couldn't seem to hold together a family. My love was fickle. Truth be told, I seemed to care only about myself. The other people I dragged into my net were mere accoutrements. Baubles. Props for the charade I wanted to present. I didn't care about anything, really. Or anyone. And I never had.

I pummeled myself all the way home. I felt exhausted and battered when we walked in the house. It was two o'clock, and I told Flossie I needed to get into work a little early. When she went into the backyard to take the wash off the line, I ducked in the bedroom and put a few things in a bag. I was out the front door and on the highway south before she had carried her basket inside.

Effie Mae
Tuesday, April 28, 1942

I felt my hands shaking as I fumbled to open the envelope. Me and Lyons had been together every day of our married lives up until he done moved to Baltimore. I knew he weren't but about twenty miles away and, as he had pointed out to me, I could hop a Green bus or the Red Rocket most any time and be out there in a jiff. Still, he felt unreachable. We talked on the phone a coupla times. I know he figgered he'd be able to sweet talk me into joining him. And he came and picked me up once and took me out there for a night after he had the place fixed up a bit. But none of it ever felt right to me. I cain't explain why. I just wanted to come back to familiar surroundings. I liked the routine of my day. I liked feeling useful. I just couldn't peel myself away from this life I had grabbed on to.

I sat down at the kitchen table as I pulled out the thin onion-skin paper. I realized he'd never had to write me a letter before. He could always just snuggle up next to me and tell me about his day. Or he could take my hand without saying a thing. We communicated pretty good even without words.

But now we was reduced to this. I knew his signature and I'd seen him scrawl a note to hisself. But I'd never really studied his handwriting. It looked elegant, almost formal, on the page. It seemed to magnify the distance between us.

I smoothed the three-page letter out on the table. I lit myself a cigarette and pulled on my glasses before I started reading.

My dear Effie,

What have I done? Why aren't you here? This house is so empty without you. I dread my days off. This week I even tried to pick up an extra shift so I wouldn't have to come home. I don't know what to do with myself when I'm here alone. I miss you, darling, and I need you here.

I know I've made a lot of mistakes in my life. These last months have been hard. I've seen it on your face. I've seen it when you hesitated to take my hand or stroke my hair. Please know that I never wanted to hurt you, my dear. Honestly, I thought it would be best if you just didn't know about my previous wives. I realize I must look absolutely heartless to you, the way I ran off and left them. I'm still not sure I can explain it to myself. The one thing I do know is that all those times . . . I never looked back. I never once regretted leaving. It's indefensible, I know. I imagine it's impossible for you to understand. I guess I was trying to reinvent myself each time. That may sound silly, but it let me focus on the future, on settling into a new world, on releasing myself from what bound me to the past.

But this time is different. This time I'm terrified that I've made the biggest mistake of my life. I hope you can forgive my selfishness. I don't know how to overcome this overwhelming need of mine to change things up. To search for something new. What I know for certain, though, is that I want you with me every step of the way.

I remember our discussing not too long ago that you are what keeps me true. You keep me centered. I can fling out like a whirling dervish on one of my ridiculous escapades, but you are the only person who has been able to draw me back in. You are my gravity, my opposite pole in this crazy magnetic field.

Perhaps I just assumed that since you'd always come along with me before—leaving Cincinnati for Miami, landing in Charleston, coming to Sparrows Point—you wouldn't hesitate yet again. You told me you didn't want to move. You told me you were happy there at the Point. And I didn't listen to you. I'm just a self-centered sonofabitch. I can see it now. I didn't account for your feelings in this move and what it might mean to you. I saw how uncomfortable you were in this neighborhood, and I ignored it.

I sometimes wonder if my time in the war all those years ago—close enough to the front to fear whether I'd still be alive to see the sun set, wondering if this was the blaze of iron rations that would catch the back of my head if I wasn't paying attention, grappling with my gas mask as I felt the choking spasms begin, calculating how many of the men I had befriended wouldn't be around when the noise finally stopped—made me bury my emotions so deep that they had a hard time ever surfacing again.

Until you, Effie Mae. Until you showed me that it was safe to feel again. That I could trust someone with my life. With my heart. With my very soul.

I don't think I can go back to Sparrows Point. I understand Danny has hired a new cook. Do you like him? But I need you, Effie. I have a good job and I'm learning to like the routine. I'm getting accustomed to the drive. There are opportunities for advancement. We can have a good life together.

What can I say to convince you to come here and be with me? What can I do? What can I promise?

I love you, darling. I need you here. Forgive me for going on so, but I need you to know that you are everything to me.

Your loving husband,
Lyons

P.S. Fritz keeps asking when you're moving in. He's concerned about you being way out at the Point by yourself. Sofie has brought me food every night I've been home. I don't think she understands yet that I'm a chef, but I appreciate her kindness.

I took off my glasses and wiped a tear from the corner of my eye. I missed him, too, the dirty bastard. I was lonesome. Living apart didn't make no sense. But why did he treat me this way? Why did he ignore my pleas to stay here? It was as if my happiness, what I wanted, didn't matter at all. Everything was about him. He just packed up right under my nose, kissed me on the cheek, and told me he'd be waiting for me out in Baltimore. He seemed all matter-a-fact about it. I think he was confident I would follow him. Well, he shoulda knowed me better than that.

It hadn't been easy being here by myself. I was used to having him in and out all day. We might not spend a lotta time together, but we'd lay eyes on each other ever now and then. Maybe I hadn't realized how comforting that was. Just knowing he was nearby. And now I was able to sleep through the night without him jerking up all wild-eyed and sometimes swinging at some make-believe foe. Or whimpering like a child. I should be counting my blessings.

Once I knew how he had treated them other women, I should've knowed it was just a matter of time before he done me the same way. Why did I think I'd be any different?

Him and his pretty words. He always thinks that's gonna fix everything.

I folded up the letter and put it in my apron pocket. I'd look at it again later. I still had a coupla bathrooms to clean before I could call it a day.

AFTER I FINISHED UP my chores, I decided to take a walk down to the water before it got dark. I went up to the apartment and took off my apron and put on my old ratty blue cardigan. As I opened the door to head downstairs, I stopped and turned around and went back in the bedroom. I reached inside the apron pocket for the letter.

When I stepped out on the front porch I could hear the *clack, clackity, clack, rumble, clack* from the Clubhouse next door. I stood and smiled. The racket would grow to a deafening roar, drowning out even the familiar drone of the steel making, and then it would subside before it roared again. I looked over my right shoulder just as the first little girl came into view again, racing around the wooden floor of the Clubhouse porch on her skates. Right behind her came three more being chased by three little boys. I couldn't make out who they was—although I'd count on Mrs. Greenlee's little red-headed pixie, Sara, being a ringleader—but even from my distant perch I could sense the glee on their faces.

Any warm spring or summer night, if there weren't nothin going on at the Clubhouse, I'd growed to expect them skaters. Some of the muckety-mucks who lived nearby—the cigar-smoking company big-shots who was most likely to take advantage of the graceful parlors and the fine dining that Lyons offered there on special nights—got in the habit of calling the Sparrows Point police on them kids. I could never get over that. Calling the cops on young'uns having fun. They weren't hurting nothin, but I reckon them adults didn't like the noise or thought they might get into some other mischief. I just saw em letting off steam. I imagined their parents was grateful when they got out from under their feet and headed out the door of their homes over on E or F Street with their metal skates hung over their shoulders, their skate keys on strings round their necks.

I watched a few more minutes. The covered porch went all the way round the Clubhouse. The kids could get a good head a steam along one side before they had to maneuver one of them tight corners. But I never onct saw any of em slip off the porch and drop the foot or so onto the grass. Them kids was fearless. And the girls usually had the head start on the boys.

As I headed down the sidewalk to the street, I saw the black-and-white Ford pull up in front of the Clubhouse. I stopped to watch Officer Mulroney, looking heavy and weary, trudge toward the porch. The *clackity-clack* roar suddenly ceased as I supposed the kids jumped off the back side of the porch out of view. "Get goin or I'll throw you in the clink and your folks will tan your hides," he thundered. Then I saw a little smile soften his jowly face.

I couldn't hold back my own grin as I cut across the grass toward the harbor. I liked this little town, despite its obvious pitfalls. The orange haze hung low on that calm evening. I could see the flames flickering from the open hearths. As I headed toward the water, the briny smell of the harbor slowly overpowered the sulfur smell from the furnaces.

But I also loved my husband. Despite his obvious flaws. What was I gonna do? Had I let my stubbornness shove aside my better judgment? Was I trying to punish him for how he'd treated all them other women? Was I just trying to make a point, or did I really want to stay here by myself?

I walked along the water a bit, watching the last beams of sunlight glance across the murky water as it lapped gently along the shore. If I tried to shut out the noise, it could almost feel peaceful here. But I found myself longing to have Lyons' smooth hand in mine. I still wasn't ready to give up on him, though Lord knows why he deserved another chance.

I pulled the letter out of my pocket and opened it once again. The light was getting dim and I had a hard time reading it. I rubbed my fingers lightly across the handwriting. I felt my heart tighten like it was being wrenched from my chest with a pair of pliers. Something made me recollect the title of that book I'd dropped that day this whole mess started: *Tender Is the Night*. The words soothed me. I repeated them as I stood along the water's edge.

A gull went screeching overhead and woke me from my meditating. I stuffed the letter back in my pocket, then I cut up to B Street right before it got dark. I could just make out the tiny leaves beginning to emerge on the maples in front of the house. We'd had nearly two feet of snow on Easter, and the trees was still trying to catch up.

When I walked in the front door, Mr. Fowler was sitting by hisself in the big armchair near the reading light with a book. He looked up and gave me a big ol grin.

"My favorite gal. Have you been out carousing by yourself, Effie Mae? When are you going to give up on all of us worthless old men and go chase down that handsome husband of yours?"

I couldn't help but laugh. I went over to him and sat on the arm of his chair, put my arm around his shoulders and gave him a big hug. "I was just plotting my escape. Do you really think you all can get along without me?"

"No. But we'll do what we need to do to get you two back together. You're a perfect team, you and Lyons. You go on out there and set up house with him. We'll manage, one way or the other. I just wanna see some pink in your cheeks and a twinkle in your eye again."

I gave him another hug.

"You know," he started, "they'll be others leaving soon, too. It's not gonna be the same. Freddie already got his notice for his physical. I imagine there will be more. I just hope they leave us old veterans alone. I know I've had enough war. And I sure hate seeing these young ones go through it."

"You don't reckon they'll take Doug again, do ya, after he's already served onct?" I asked. I'd been fretting about that ever day. Doug didn't say much, but I imagine he had the same thing on his mind. "He's done his stint in the Navy. Surely they need him more here supporting the steel-making for all them guns and bullets and warships. We've been expanding here at the Point for months. From what I'm hearing, the U-boats are sinking them ships as fast as we can build em. It's hard to see how they can take any of these boys away."

"You know they'll find a way." His smile faded, and I sensed something bitter in his tone. "And now that they've frozen wages, even the ones who don't get called up will feel the sting. I hope they know how precious all these experienced workers here are. But I guess we'll hear more direct from FDR later tonight. You'll listen to his fireside chat, I suppose."

"Oh yeah. I try not to miss em."

We were silent a few moments, then I started singing, soft and low:

> Will the circle be unbroken
> By and by, Lord, by and by
> There's a better home a-waitin
> In the sky, Lord, in the sky

Mr. Fowler joined in, and we sat there singing our duet until Lonnie and Al—fresh from drankin and sworpin after a long shift over at the furnaces, still in their red neckerchiefs and dirty coveralls—interrupted our happy trance.

Lyons
Friday, October 5, 1934

*A*s we rolled into downtown Corbin, I could hear the train's whistle—a siren's call—as the rail cars trundled into the station on the east side of Main Street. Our feet felt the rumble through the floorboard of the old Westcott. Effie got quiet and strained to see around me.

"You thinking we should have taken the train down to Miami?" I asked with a grin. "Is your bum already tired of riding in this old jalopy?"

She waved me off. "You ain't gonna get me to cry uncle before you do, mister. Naw, I like taking our time and stopping when we want. I was just thinking about the first time I come through that station over there with Frank and Doug. I couldn't decide whether I was excited or terrified to be heading to Cincinnati."

"You wanna stop a minute, stretch our legs?"

"Ya mind? That might feel good."

I turned onto Depot Street and found a place to park next to the station. I was again surprised at how expansive the rail yard was in this small town. We watched for a minute as several passengers stepped cautiously off the train, many struggling with bulky packages or handbags. My memory roamed from the indignities of a troop train jam-packed with rabble-rousing raw recruits—some still believing

we'd been handpicked for an honorable fraternity rather than desig-
nated as expendable by vainglorious politicians—to the empty train
station in Hopewell where I'd abandoned everything I'd thought I'd
fought for. I'd escaped one fate on the battlefield only to stumble
headlong into a more infamous lot. I was spared when others weren't,
but for what? To wander aimlessly around the country, cobbling together a living, unable to commit to anything or anyone? I wiped my
hand across my face.

I'd been a little unnerved as we'd crossed the Ohio into Kentucky
the day before. By driving, we could take Route 25 straight through
Lexington and on south to the Tennessee border. If we'd taken the
train, we couldn't have avoided stopping in Hopewell. I wasn't sure
I was up for that. I couldn't tell you what ghosts I thought might be
floating around there all these years later, but I didn't want to chance
an encounter with them. So I was relieved that Effie had bought into
my romantic idea of driving all the way to Florida so we could lei-
surely see the country along the way.

We'd rolled through the Bluegrass on a sparkling fall day, admiring the farmland and the familiar towns that looked a little worse
for wear after the ravages of the recent economy. That night we'd
stopped at a roadside tourist camp near Berea south of Lexington,
trying to keep the long days manageable. The tiny cabin at the camp
offered shelter, if not much more. We nibbled on some sandwiches
we had packed and got up early the next morning to get back on the
road.

Berea bumped up against the foothills of the mountains, and I
could tell the change in terrain had caught Effie's imagination. She
could barely sit still as we got back on the Dixie Highway heading
south. She'd lean out of the car and sniff the air, or gaze fixedly at the
deepening forests and the rising hills.

After Doug had graduated from high school and enlisted in the
Navy back in the summer, we'd started talking about taking to the

road and landing someplace new. Cincinnati's charms were starting to wear thin, and we were both thinking a change of scenery might do us good. Word had it that the hotel industry in Miami was booming, despite the Depression, as Eastern Air Lines and Pan Am catered to well-heeled—and intrepid—tourists from New York, Europe, and South America. Several spectacular hotels had been built along the beach in the last decade, and the local population had soared to support them. I had plenty of experience to offer and Effie thought it might be a good time for her to leave the employ of Mr. King out on the east side of the city. Thinking that the change of season would offer cooler travel, we had gutted through one final oppressive summer along the Ohio River before giving notice and joining the legions of itinerant workers looking for a more promising life elsewhere.

Over the previous months, Effie and I had fallen into some sort of unspoken understanding that we belonged together, but we hadn't directly addressed what that meant. I had remained at the boardinghouse on Pine Street while she continued to work on the other side of town. There was no real courting to speak of. Whether that was because we were too old to imagine putting ourselves through that ritual or because there appeared to be no need to convince each other of the inevitability of our relationship, it's hard to tell. Everything was simple with her. Somehow she seemed to know who I was without my having to explain anything to her. She didn't ask questions. She didn't pry. She just accepted. She accepted that I loved her, that I wanted to be with her. It was comfortable, and easy. We made each other laugh. We were happy when we were together. My demons seemed soothed by her mere presence. I felt calmer, more relaxed. I almost felt whole.

When we got out of the car in Corbin, I noticed some clouds moving in from the west. I offered Effie a cigarette as we walked around outside the depot watching the people. After a few minutes we ducked inside so Effie could find a bathroom. Travelers from the coal towns east and south of Corbin moved with varying degrees of haste through the station. It was fairly easy to separate the operators heading to Louisville or Knoxville for business from the workers there to visit family, or like us, clinging to some hope of finding the next job in the next town.

Train stations all felt the same to me, with their alluring aroma of promise, adventure, and the unfamiliar. It was like the desire you feel for a woman you've just met: heady, insistent, reckless. It beckons you to act, to do something unexpected, unrestrained. To take a chance. To run headlong into the unknown.

I pulled out a handkerchief and wiped a little perspiration from my forehead. Then I went back outside and lit another cigarette.

Effie Mae came out of the station and stopped to take a deep breath. "I can just smell them mountains," she said, giddy. "It smells like home. I saw people in there who look like me. Who talk like me. You'd better get me back in that car before I buy me a ticket back to Middlesboro."

I pulled her into a tight hug. "You're not running off anywhere, my dear. I left you back there in Middlesboro once. I'm not doing that again. We're in this together now, you know." I gave her a kiss and tucked a curl behind her ear, and then turned her toward the car. "Let's go see what Miami has to offer. If it doesn't suit us, we'll head back up here. Nothing's holding us anywhere."

I looked around carefully as we drove back through town. "You know, I lived here in Corbin for a short while. Worked right there, at that pharmacy on the corner, soon after I got out of school. Guess I shouldn't have been surprised back in '19 when I heard that the townspeople had run off all the coloreds, just a few months after I got home from the war. There weren't many around when I lived here, but I think the railroad had brought in a couple hundred to work for them. That always puts the local white laborers on edge, thinking their jobs might be at risk. The story was that after some little fracas they just rounded them up and put them on the next train out of town. The Kentucky National Guard came in afterwards to restore the peace. That was a bad time for Negroes all across the country. A lot of unnecessary violence. Some of those boys were veterans, too."

I must have had a look on my face that revealed more than I wanted about my brush with Judge Lynch. Effie reached over and put her hand on my arm and gave it a little squeeze.

After a few minutes, she asked, "Whaddya think Miami will be like?"

I looked over at her, trying to gauge whether she was having second thoughts about running off with me or whether she was merely curious. "Probably like nothing we've ever seen," I said. "For starters, it's a brand new city, with skyscrapers perched on the beach. Most everything's been built in the last twenty years or so. And I think it draws a lot of people from Cuba and Central and South America. Those rum-runners needed a place to land during Prohibition, you know. Then there are the tourists from Europe and the Northeast. I imagine it'll feel very different from an industrial Midwest city like Cincinnati. Let's just hope there are still some jobs left when we get there."

"You said you talked to someone at a coupla the hotels earlier this week?"

"Yeah. I was able to reach managers at the Biltmore and the Roney. The Roney sounded a little more promising. They're both playgrounds for the rich and famous. No telling who we might see down there. I know Bing Crosby stops there frequently, and the big jazz bands get gigs at the Miami hotels whenever they can. And I saw a brochure for the Biltmore touting its aquatic shows, with everything from synchronized swimmers to alligator wrestling. After the shows there's dancing in the gardens. It's going to feel like a tropical bacchanalia."

I heard Effie let out a snort. "There you go using them big words again. You gotta recollect who you're talking to, cuddlebug. A tropical what?"

I smiled. "A big party. On a scale we're not likely to see again. In the middle of this goddamn Depression. Just imagine."

She settled back in her seat again. "Didn't someone try to kill the president down there in Miami last year?" she asked. "Do I have that right?"

"Yeah, I had almost forgotten that. I'm not even sure he was president yet. As I recall, he was giving a speech and some lunatic started shooting wildly from the crowd. The guy shot the Chicago mayor, who was right next to the president—standing on the running board of the car FDR was sitting in, if I remember correctly—but FDR wasn't hit. Wow. How lucky can you be? I think the president likes to go down to Miami to fish. Maybe we'll run into him."

"That'd be somethin. Good thing we didn't lose him before he even got in office. Things have done started to turn around with that New Deal of his. First time we've had even a glimmer of hope in a while. And the end of Prohibition is reason for everyone to celebrate. The Depression was bad enough, but the Depression without legal liquor was downright cold-hearted."

As we drove south, the mountains loomed larger on either side of the road: sun-drenched on my left, with irregular splotches of yellow and red hinting at cooler weather to come, but shrouded in clouds and fog on my right as rain appeared to be moving in from the west. Amid the darkening skies, I heard Effie start to sing quietly.

> Single girl, single girl
> She's going dressed so fine
> Oh, she's going dressed so fine
> Married girl, married girl
> She wears just any kind
> Oh, she wears just any kind

I grinned. "What's that you're singing?"

"Oh, just a Carter Family song I heard recently. Everything they sing reminds me of home, just like them mountains do. I love it here. It just feels like a warm embrace to me."

> Single girl, single girl
> She goes to the store and buys
> Oh, she goes to the store and buys
> Married girl, married girl
> She rocks the cradle and cries
> Oh, she rocks the cradle and cries

We were approaching the Tennessee line. I don't think it was the song. I really don't. I think it was just seeing her so happy. And somehow I knew that I wanted to capture that happiness and hold on to it for a lifetime. I'd made so many mistakes. Been fooled so many times. Been caught up in the exuberance of the moment. But this felt different. It felt like something enduring. Something I could really hold on to. Something I didn't want to lose.

"Effie, let's stop in Jellico and get married. What do you say?"

She stopped singing and looked at me. "Lawsy. What brought that on?"

I glanced over at her. "I love being with you. I love having you sitting next to me. Let's make it official. That's all I'm saying. We can take care of it this afternoon. Far as I know, Tennessee still doesn't have any impediments to two crazy lovers wanting to tie the knot in a hurry, for whatever nefarious reasons."

She laughed. "I don't know, Lyons. I done been married twice. I'm not sure I'm a good bet. My husbands ain't fared none too well. You think you wanna cast your lot with me? Ain't you a confirmed bachelor?"

I set my jaw and swallowed hard. Maybe I needed to come clean this time. Maybe I owed her a full reckoning before I dragged her into my life. If I really loved her, shouldn't I show my hand? Let her know who I really was? But somehow all that seemed superfluous right then. I always felt like I could change the future if I just put my mind to it. I could discard the past like a bad hand of cards as long as I still had hope that the next draw was a winner. What did it matter, where I'd been or who I'd been with? It was just the two of us now. The two of us and the open road.

I managed a grin. "Maybe I just hadn't found the right woman. Maybe I've been waiting for you, ever since those early days in Middlesboro. But now that I have you in my clutches, I'm ready. It seems like such an obvious thing to do." I checked the road ahead and then turned and looked at her. "Effie Mae, will you marry me?"

She giggled. All the times I'd uttered that question, and that was the first time my plea had been met with laughter. Seemed to be a good sign.

"Oh, what the hell, cuddlebug. Guess we might as well. Let's make this proper. If you're willing to team up with me and my bad luck, I reckon I can go along with your crazy plan. I kinda like you, after all. Maybe we can write a different ending this time."

My smile felt like it stretched all the way to my oversized ears. "That's my girl. Stick with me. The world won't know what hit it."

WHEN WE GOT INTO town, I pulled up to the courthouse to make some inquiries. The folks in Jellico were used to us northerners crossing the state line and showing up desperate to get married. We were simply another couple in a steady stream of either starry-eyed or blinded twosomes carried away by the moment. Justices of the peace abounded in the tiny town. The clerk I cornered told me we could run in the local bank and ask for Mr. Hargrave, the septuagenarian vice president. Or we could stop by the grocer's a little farther down Main Street and let Mr. Ogleby marry us right there beside the pickled pigs' feet and the lamb fries. The clerk assured me that Mr. Ogleby was always careful to put on a clean apron before the brief service.

Now, I have not led what one might call a conventional life, but those options seemed a little too unorthodox, even for me.

As I pondered what to do, an older gentleman who had been standing off to the side watching my exchange with the clerk called out. "I'll marry you, son. You don't look like a lot of the folks who come down here in a big rush. I expect most of them have realized their mistake by morning. You look a little more sober-minded, like you may have thought this through. You've got some wear on your tires, if you don't mind my saying so. You didn't get the young lady in trouble, did you?"

I felt my face redden. Then I had to laugh. "I beg your pardon? Of course not. Effie Mae and I could have grandchildren, if we'd gotten started at the age most do."

"A late bloomer, eh? Been scared away before? Well, you're not the first. I've married hundreds and I've seen it all. I'm the pastor over at the Presbyterian church. Why don't you and the missus grab some lunch and pop over there about three o'clock? The corner of Cumberland and Kentucky. I'll bring the paperwork. See you then."

I thanked him and turned to head out to Effie with the good news. Then I wheeled around and called back to the clerk.

"Is there anywhere nearby to stay for the night?"

She sized me up again. "I reckon Mrs. Floyd might have a room for you over on Welch Street, a couple of blocks off Cumberland, up from the church. Tell her Ruby sent you."

THE PASTOR WAS AS good as his word. We found the quaint little white chapel with its simple box steeple and three distinctive stained glass windows on the hexagonal façade. I had the sense that some Puritan preacher had rolled the clapboard church from New England to the hills of Tennessee after finding the piety of his freethinking congregation lacking.

Effie was tickled pink. She worried she wasn't dressed properly for a church ceremony, but I convinced her the Lord didn't care one whit what clothes we wore when we stood before him. We took care of business and then headed to the Victorian home of Mrs. Floyd. It had begun to rain, and we were happy to take refuge in her rose-colored parlor that reminded me suspiciously of a popular Toledo brothel—which I had frequented only to hear Art Tatum tickle the ivories, of course. After a cup of tea and an exchange of pleasantries, Mrs. Floyd led us up to a modestly-furnished garret room that smelled of rose-water and mothballs. Effie and I looked at each other and promptly disappeared into the cavernous feather bed.

Effie Mae
Friday, August 7, 1942

I was kneeling in the little dirt patch behind the house wrastling with the tomato stakes when I heard the screen door slam. I looked up and saw Lyons carrying a couple of glasses. He took a seat in one of the rusty green metal lawn chairs on the small stoop.

"You wanna take a break and come join me? I made us some lemonade."

"Let me finish tying off this scraggly vine. It's been so hot and rainy this summer you'd think them tomatoes would be thriving, but I reckon it's just been too much of a good thing."

I put down the scissors and twine and pulled a few stray weeds poking up around the plants. I wiped my forehead with the back of my garden glove and pushed myself up to a standing position. My knees couldn't take much of that kneeling no more.

When I looked up at Lyons, I felt myself go dizzy. I teetered the few steps to the chair and grabbed both arms, my head hanging low.

"What's wrong, Effie? You OK?" Lyons put the glasses down on the stoop and stood up and grabbed my elbow.

"Yeah. Yeah. I think I just stood up too fast. Let me set in the chair a minute."

I managed to turn around and slump into the seat. I kept my head down a few moments longer, but I could feel the fog beginning to clear.

"Have you been having dizzy spells like that?"

"Oh, just once or twice. You know, when I get up too fast. And the heat don't help none. It ain't nothin. I'm good now. Whaddya say you had in them glasses? I could use something cold."

"Lemonade. Fresh squeezed."

"You found fresh lemons? Did we have any sugar left from our ration, or will it pucker my lips?"

"I think I sweetened it just enough. See what you think. I may have used a little of your canning allotment. Don't tell anyone." He grinned.

I took a sip. Perfect.

"That hits the spot. I think I'll live now. Is it ever going to cool down, you think? How many days has it been in the 90s? I sure miss that breeze we used to get off the water."

"Yeah, the air's pretty stagnant here. Let's just hope we don't have any more 100-degree days like we had back in July. What a summer. Too bad gas rationing kept us from going to the Virginia mountains to see Logan and his family. You would have enjoyed that trip."

I let the thought of cool mountain mornings and towering trees on the hillsides quiet my mind. I was feeling a little better. I settled into my chair and took another sip. "I sure am glad they left us these old lawn chairs. You cain't get these kinda metal chairs no more. They've gone the same way as steel pots and pans. You know, I didn't really care to live through another war."

"I guess it's better than the alternative, as they say."

"At least they still haven't called up Doug. I'm just keeping my fingers crossed." I finished my lemonade and set the glass down beside my chair.

"You starting to feel better about this place?" Lyons asked.

"I suppose so. Fritz and Sofie sure have been nice. I guess they ain't spies, after all." I tried to smile. Lyons knew I was embarrassed by my initial reaction to our neighbors. I don't know what come over me that day we first visited the house. I think I was just scared about everything changing again. I wanted the old and familiar, not the new and different. But I also wanted Lyons. So here we sat.

"You think they'll really give them Germans the chair tomorrow over in D.C.?" I asked.

Lyons nodded. "Sounds like it, unless there's some sort of appeal tonight. According to the news reports, they planned a lot of destruction, taking out railroads and bridges and electric plants. Just wreaking havoc. I read that the locks on the Ohio River outside Louisville were a target. I know that area well."

"But, you know," he continued, "for some reason I don't trust that we have the full story. Two of them are American citizens, and the others had lived and worked here for years. They had wives and girlfriends here. Were they just stooges hoping for a big pay day or some sort of Nazi glory? It doesn't add up for me."

I brushed some dirt off my Bermuda shorts. "Reading stuff like that makes it easy to be suspicious of anyone with an accent, I reckon. And now we're rounding up all them Japs and even some of them Germans and Italians and putting em in camps somewhere. I almost wonder if the govment's just trying to stoke more fear. *They're so dangerous we have to corral em in pens.* What are we supposed to think? But then I see how kindly Sofie treats us, and it just don't make no sense."

We sat in silence for a few moments, soaking up the sun. Then I saw Lyons look at me outta the corner of his eye.

"I was at the hardware store the other day, and Irvin Klein started telling me about the rumors he's hearing from family he left behind. You know, about what the Nazis are doing in Europe. I wanted to believe it was propaganda—like they spread about the Germans during the last war—but it sounds like this might be true." He was shaking his head.

I felt my face flush. I had seen a little article in the paper a coupla months before, but I didn't know how to process it. I let my thoughts wander to our neighbors. "You know, I go to work next week for Mrs. Katzenberg. I have to wonder what she's heard from her family."

We was quiet a bit, as the weight of the war threatened to smother our thoughts.

Lyons finished his lemonade and leaned back in his chair, squinting at the sun. "I know I'm not around here much, but I like this neighborhood. I like going in the bakery and talking to Max Pfueller or chatting up Louis Schluss at that little neighborhood bar. Or running into Anna Salavitsky while she's out walking her dog and asking about the new cars in her showroom. I like hearing about the horses from Leon. Everybody's interested in something different. Everybody comes from someplace else. It's not all about steel and warships and airplane parts. And I like feeling like we're part of a real neighborhood and not some town manufactured by the industrial warlords."

I let him rip. I had to agree. It actually was a pretty good place to live. I was getting used to it. It was still a little lonely, but I was finally meeting some of the neighbors. And starting a new job next week—even if it was only part-time—was gonna help me get out and about. Not that I didn't miss some things about the Point, mostly seeing Doug and Mr. Fowler ever day, but we was getting along fine. It appeared I would survive this change, too.

On Monday, I got up early and made the half-mile walk over to the Katzenbergs on West Rogers Avenue. Their live-in maid had decided to move to D.C. to be closer to her grandchildren. Mrs. Katzenberg—or Selma, as she kept asking me to call her—had decided they didn't really need full-time help now that their children was grown and out of the house, so she had put out an ad for a part-time maid. Lyons saw it in the paper and thought it might be just what I needed to fill my days while he was working. When I met with her, we agreed to three days a week to start. She was even willing for me to work my schedule around Lyons' so I could be off some days with him. That just seemed too good to be true, and I jumped at the opportunity.

The first time I walked in their house I felt like I was on a movie set. It seemed magical. I kept opening doors and finding another handsome room with bookshelves lining the walls and thick rugs carpeting the floor. What did two people do in all that space? There was at least two enclosed sitting porches looking out over the narrow lawn and giant trees. The dining room alone felt bigger than our whole apartment over at the Point. The ceilings was so high on the first two floors that I didn't see no way I'd ever get up there to clean the cobwebs. Up the grand staircase, on the second floor, there was four bedrooms connected by a wide, curved hallway. Only one was being used. A door off that hallway led up a set of narrow stairs to the third floor, where there was three more bedrooms. I suppose that had been the maid's quarters—and probably a cook and maybe a gardener at some point. It sure was a different way of living. Ever since Charleston, I had made my home in rambling boardinghouses jam packed with working men. This place felt as removed from that as Hollywood was from Yellow Creek.

Walking up the short sidewalk that morning, past the high hedges lining the street, I noticed the home's beige stucco and big windows. It didn't look quite as imposing from the outside, but I knew now what awaited me on the inside. There was a lot of rooms to clean. I wondered if I might need four days a week to keep up.

Selma musta seen me coming up the sidewalk cause she was there to open the door for me. A slight, dark-haired woman, she was a little taller than me and a few years younger, I guessed. She had a warm smile and a welcoming manner. She was dressed rather smart, in a skirt and blouse and a string of pearls at her neck, as if she had someplace to go. But she offered me coffee and a warm applesauce muffin. We sat at the table at the back of that immense kitchen, surrounded by windows high above the backyard, as we discussed my responsibilities. I sensed some loneliness from her, as if she was just happy to have someone to talk to. Or maybe it was sadness, or grief. I didn't know her, of course, so it was hard to decipher. When we had finished our coffee, she walked me through the whole house again, pointing out trouble spots and showing me where she stowed the cleaning supplies. It occurred to me that I could be there all day and never run into her.

When I got back to our little house late in the afternoon, my feet was aching and my back was tired. I hadn't been working like that for a few months, and I could tell I was gonna have to get used to it again. I'd gotten soft piddling around our place and playing in the patch of dirt I had dug up out back for my tomato and pepper plants. But I finally felt useful again. And needed. And that was a mighty fine feeling.

The nights was hard when Lyons was over at Aberdeen. I'd fix myself a little supper, maybe turn on the radio for some company, but all the war news tended to trouble me. The summer had made the long nights easier, though, cause I could sit out on the steps and wave at the neighbors if they was out. Occasionally Sofie might stop over and visit. I had gotten to know her two young'uns, the twins Lizzie and Bert. They was born in Germany, but their English was already better than their mama's. They had trouble understanding me at times, so I tried to think hard how Lyons might say something when I was talking to em. We all worked to help each other along. Mostly we found ourselves laughing and giggling a lot. Especially me and Lizzie. We got to be real close by the end of the summer. She'd help in my little garden, and I'd walk with her down to Meyer Fishman's for a sody pop. We'd teach each other songs and make a terrible racket. I realized what I'd missed not being around my own grandchildren much.

I expected I'd be more lonesome after the kids went back to school and had homework in the evenings. Then the days would get shorter and the nights longer. Maybe I would look for some volunteer work nearby to fill a few hours.

When Lyons was here, though, usually a coupla days a week, it reminded me of when we was just married. Despite the war howling all around the world and the sacrifices we was all making, we felt as carefree and easy with each other as we ever had. Deep down I reckon I had forgiven him for all them secrets he'd kept from me, although I tended to bring up that whole business whenever I needed to put him in his place. But it was as if talking about it had released some of them demons that had made him run for all them years. He seemed content when we was together. If it was a Thursday, we might listen to Bing Crosby's Kraft Music Hall. On a Tuesday, it might be Burns and Allen. I was always twiddling the knob trying to find some station where the Carter Family was singing, hoping to catch "Wanderin Boy" or "Poor Orphan Child" or, my favorite, "Keep on the Sunny Side." That music would just take me home. Sometimes I could even get Lyons to whistle the harmony. I never heard nobody who could whistle like him.

It was a quiet life, different from anything I'd knowed before, but I guess it was more like what other couples was used to. Instead of chasing wild dreams or taking care of everyone around us, when we was both home we tended to lean in toward each other. There wasn't nobody else around. We tuned out the war. We forgot all the slights and the hurts and the cross words we had slung at each other. We tried to forgive our own careless blunders. And those nights that we could spend together, we'd hold each other close and remind ourselves that whatever was raging beyond our walls, we could still find comfort in each other's arms.

And that sure was a nice way to live.

Lyons
Sunday, October 18, 1942

I was lying on my narrow bunk, blowing smoke rings into the stale air above me, wishing I could be lying on the sofa with my head in Effie Mae's lap later that evening listening to Jack Benny. I loved hearing her laugh, feeling her belly rise and fall with each guffaw or chortle while she ran her fingers through my hair. Nights I was home we had gotten in the habit of settling in front of the radio, listening to some silly program. It was decidedly a better diversion than obsessing over the war news or pining for a sweet after-dinner treat paired with a cup of coffee—two standards of civilized society that we had sacrificed like all other Americans.

Being away from home three days in a row had proved more discomfiting than I had anticipated, but I would never let on to her how much I missed her. True, working ten or twelve hours a day in the officers' mess didn't leave much time for daydreaming or carousing, and it did help the days go by and keep me out of trouble, more or less.

The barracks-like dormitory we occupied could be accurately described as Spartan, despite its contemporary construction. Tight quarters and a communal bathroom demanded a certain conviviality among the men. My roommate, Jack, was a good sort, who found his way to Camp Rodman from a greasy spoon on the Delaware coast. Thankfully, our rigorous schedules prevented us from frequently stumbling over each other in our tiny room, and I'm not aware that either of us snored with enough gusto to keep the other from a much-needed night's sleep. If we both happened to retire at about the same time—abandoning an engaging evening in the lounge where we had perhaps wagered on a low-stakes card game while relentlessly tormenting the young men trying to write to their sweethearts—Jack and I might challenge each other to the daily crossword puzzle. Our evening routine combined elements of high school hijinks and military tedium.

I'd heard there were 25,000 lucky men training here. It was hard to tell, given how everything was spread out over more than a hundred square miles. Working in the officers' mess, my only interactions, limited as they were, were with the brass. We fed about two thousand ordnance officers every day, following a rigid military schedule. Shortages of meat, butter, eggs, cheese, and sugar forced us to be creative in preparing meals that satisfied these ultimate taskmasters. Thankfully, each one of the motley staff working in the kitchen brought different skills and experiences to the job, and with regular improvisation and experimentation we served some damn good meals.

Most afternoons, like today, I could steal away from the bedlam in the kitchen for an hour or two before we started prepping for dinner. If the weather was inviting, I might saunter around the proving ground, past the Colonial Revival stone buildings that housed the original ordnance school and the hundreds of wood-frame temporary buildings that now served as barracks and mess halls and applied training centers for the constantly expanding forces. Occasionally I might catch a glimpse of outside drills, watching boyish young men making sure artillery weapons could satisfactorily remove the heads from enemy soldiers, or practicing the niceties of defusing bombs before they turned you and your buddies into a thousand colorful jigsaw pieces. In another section of the proving ground I discovered, to my dismay, the structures where skilled technicians had, nearly twenty-five years before, manufactured the poison gas that my fellow soldiers had lobbed at the Germans, frequently turning a once fecund French field into a noxious valley of death.

I couldn't attest to any resemblance between the training I observed at Camp Rodman and the training I had enjoyed at Camp Zachary Taylor in the spring of 1918. We did calisthenics and practiced marching, drilled with wooden bayonets and tossed harmless hand grenades. The YMCA made sure we were entertained on weekends. Some of us took French classes. After a few weeks, we were shipped overseas ready for hand-to-hand combat with the Prussians. Maybe the U.S. military learned something after sending us doughboys to Europe so ill-prepared. Maybe a less casual approach to sending men off to war would mean fewer casualties.

I recalled a conversation with Doug back in the spring. He had come out to the house to check on me one Sunday afternoon and, I imagine, do a little reconnaissance for Effie. She hadn't yet acquiesced to join me, and he knew we were both miserable. We sat quietly in the living room, smoking cigarettes and sipping beer—bourbon being yet another casualty of war. The federal government had decreed that the nation's distilleries could only produce the sort of alcohol needed to make synthetic rubber and anti-freeze, not the spirits the rest of us relied on to endure the incessant barrage of bad news. Thankfully, perhaps sensing our desperation and fearing a domestic rebellion, federal propagandists were simultaneously promoting beer drinking as a way to boost the nation's morale. I couldn't argue with that.

"What's Effie doing this afternoon?" I asked, trying to start some sort of conversation.

"She was in the sitting room playing spades with some of the fellas when I left." He paused. "We have to figure out how to get you two under one roof."

"Yeah."

Problem was, neither of us had any inkling how to break through her stubbornness. I knew she had to come to that decision on her own. I decided to change the subject rather than face my failure to sustain conjugal bliss.

"Saw where Doolittle finally managed to drop some bombs on Japan. You think that's a turning point?"

"What I know about the Japanese, that'll just steel them for something worse. And I think we killed some civilians during that raid, too. That'll fire em up."

"We needed some kind of win after losing Bataan," I countered. "Wonder what Pacific island paradise the war will introduce us to next."

Doug shifted in his seat and took a sip of beer. "I guess we knew we couldn't keep a lid on this tinderbox forever. But don't nobody ever think about the lives lost, the families destroyed, the suffering these damn wars cause? Ain't it obvious? And for what? Is it just ego at the top? They have no idea..."

He stared out the window. He and I shared the frustration of uncompleted business. We'd both been on the fringe of war. Neither of us felt we could claim we had made a difference. We certainly hadn't done anything to prevent repeating this inanity on an even bigger stage. But we had been close enough to see the horror. To smell it. And we had no idea what to do about the holes those nonexistent bullets had gouged in our psyches. At times we wallowed in a helplessness that seemed to render all action absurd. When that feeling lifted, only intense action could medicate our wounds. We were trained to fight back. But sometimes we could only run, sprint from whatever was threatening to consume our very will to fight.

I blew one last smoke ring and then twisted to my left to put out my cigarette in the overflowing ashtray between our two bunks. It was that damned helplessness that had nearly cost me the woman I loved. I had run again because I didn't know what else to do. I didn't know how to fight for what I believed in. The Army never managed to teach me that.

I picked up the Agatha Christie mystery I had recently purchased in the PX, but before I could divert my attention from Effie Mae to Hercule Poirot there was a sharp rap on my door.

"It's open," I called.

A very young serviceman opened the door a little hesitantly and stepped in the room. He stood right at the foot of Jack's bed.

"Sir, are you Lyons Board?"

"I am."

"I have an urgent message for you."

He handed me a piece of paper. My heart began knocking violently against my ribs. I unfolded the note and read, "Effie Mae Board admitted to Sinai Hospital in Baltimore this afternoon. Situation serious. Mr. Board has permission to leave the premises immediately."

I looked at the young man. "Do you know anything more?" I demanded, knowing full well that he didn't.

"No, sir. That's all I have, sir."

"OK. Of course. Thanks." He turned and exited the room, closing the door softly behind him.

I stared at the paper another moment before the adrenaline nearly knocked me off the bed. I put on my shoes, grabbed my jacket, wallet, and car keys, and ran out to start Bessie. Someone else would have to tell Henry that he'd need to find another ride back to Baltimore tomorrow.

It was Sunday afternoon, so the cars that were on the road were not in much of a rush. I was. The hour-and-a-half drive made me feel like a convicted man waiting on the governor's pardon. Sinai Hospital was in our neighborhood, just on the other side of the Pimlico race track. That's the hospital where Fritz worked. I wondered if he knew Effie had been admitted.

But admitted for what? I had no idea why she was at the hospital.

The note said it was serious. Was there an accident? If I recalled correctly, I think she was supposed to help Mrs. Katzenberg with a reception at her home that afternoon. Had something happened there? Had she fallen ill? I had seen her suffer a couple of dizzy spells over the last few months. I tried to convince her to call a doctor, but I knew that was futile. I couldn't remember her seeing a doctor anytime since we had married.

I stared at the road ahead, but I couldn't focus. I couldn't imagine any time or space beyond sitting by Effie's bedside. Somehow I had to bridge the temporal and physical gap between the two of us. I hoped she'd be alert when I finally got there, able to tell me what happened. I needed to see her smile. I needed her to squeeze my hand and tell me everything would be all right. I needed her. She was why I got out of bed in the morning.

I wasn't paying any attention to the 35 mph speed limit. I figured if a cop stopped me, maybe I could get an escort to the hospital. But it was Sunday, and the police appeared to be home enjoying a quiet afternoon with their loved ones.

I squealed in the parking lot and slammed the car door before I raced to the main entrance. I ran up to the front desk, nearly out of breath, and gave the clerk Effie's name. She pointed me in the direction of the ward.

I slowed my pace as I rounded the corner and approached the nurses' station. I gave the grim-faced nurse Effie's name and she led me to the third bed on the left in a ward of about twelve beds. They weren't all full, but nurses were moving among the patients amid occasional low moans or coughs, like apparitions in some low-grade hell. The air smelled of antiseptic and soiled bedclothes and decay. I briefly froze in my tracks, recalling huddling in the mud against the cold with dozens of dirty men trying to stay alive.

I squeezed my eyes shut for a moment, and when I opened them I stepped to the side of Effie's bed. She was lying on her back, eyes closed. There was a bandage around her head, an IV in her arm. I stopped the nurse as she tried to dart back to her station.

"Can you tell me what happened? I don't know anything."

"She had a fall. There may have been a stroke. We're waiting for the doctor. He should be here within the hour." Then she marched away.

I sat down in the folding chair next to the bed and took Effie's hand. I murmured to her that I was there, that everything would be OK. I thought I detected a very slight smile on her lips, but I couldn't be sure.

I remained there with my head bowed for several minutes. When I heard the clack-clacking of a lady's shoes on the hard floor, I looked up. A slim, attractive dark-haired woman was approaching me. Despite the anguish on her face, she seemed too vital to be in this ghostly gallery, as if she were the only figure around with coursing blood and the determination to stay alive. I reluctantly let go of Effie's hand and stood up.

"Are you Lyons?" she asked in a whisper.

I nodded, and finally croaked, "Yes."

"I'm Selma Katzenberg. Effie Mae's been working for me. I'm so sorry. This is just devastating. I don't know what happened."

I pointed to the chair. "Would you like to sit down?" She seemed to accept my offer without thinking. She glanced over at Effie as she took the seat.

I started to put the pieces together. "Was she at your house when this happened?"

I saw her discreetly wipe a tear from the corner of her eye. "Yes. She had helped me with a reception for my garden club at the house. The guests had left, and we were starting to clean things up. I was in the kitchen, and..." She stopped. I could hear the catch in her throat. "And I heard a loud thud. I ran into the front hallway and I saw her at the bottom of the stairs. She must have taken some of the flowers from the table up to our bedroom, because I found them there later when I grabbed my purse after the ambulance left. I don't know whether she tripped coming down the stairs or what. It was just horrible."

She dropped her head and put her face in her hands. I didn't know what to do. I put my hand briefly on her shoulder.

"It sounds like an accident," I found myself saying. "She's been having some dizzy spells lately. She may have just lost her balance coming down the stairs."

I tried not to think about Effie lying in a heap next to the bottom step. "Do you know anything about the extent of her injuries?"

She had dropped her hands, and her face was as pale as the light reflected from a new moon. "The doctor who initially examined her was amazed that she hadn't broken anything. Maybe she didn't fall very far. But she did hit her head, I guess on one of the steps when she fell backward, and there was an ugly gash. There was a lot of blood."

She caught a little sob. "Oh, Mr. Board, I am so sorry. I wish I could have prevented this. She has been so good to Bernie and me. This is just awful."

I looked over at Effie Mae again. Her expression had not changed. I could barely see her breathing.

"The nurse said something about a stroke. Do you know anything about that?"

"No. When I got to the hospital, she was still in the emergency room, but I didn't see the doctor. They pointed me up here after they had moved her. I wanted someone to be with her, so I stayed with her for a while, then I went to the cafeteria for a cup of coffee. That's when you must have arrived. I had told the staff you were out at Aberdeen."

I didn't know what else to say. I walked to the other side of the bed and gently rubbed Effie's arm. I had never seen her so still. She was always moving, talking, doing. I hardly recognized her.

Mrs. Katzenberg stood up. "I'll leave you alone with her. I know this has to be extremely hard. I am so sorry. Let me give you our phone number in case there's anything we can do for you. I'll stop by tomorrow and see what you've learned."

She rummaged in her pocketbook and found a business card with her husband's name on it. She pulled out a pen and scribbled their home number on the back and then handed me the card. I thanked her and put it in my pocket.

"Will you be OK getting home?" I asked.

"Yes, of course, it's just a few blocks down the street. I would have walked if I hadn't been in such a rush to get here. I'll be fine. Please take care of yourself, Mr. Board. And, again, I'm so sorry. I hope when I come by tomorrow I see her bright smile again."

I nodded and watched her turn and walk along the row of beds, trying not to look at the other patients. Then my eye caught a rather large man moving hurriedly in my direction. Fritz.

He came right up to me and pulled me into a quick embrace. He pulled away before either of us could be embarrassed.

"Lyons, what's going on? I was going through the admitting paperwork and I saw Effie's name. What happened?" He looked down at her with a face full of chagrin.

I explained all that I knew. Effie hadn't moved. We chatted just a minute, then he said he had to get back to work. He put his arm around my shoulders and tugged hard one more time before he left.

"It'll be OK. This will be OK. She's a tough lady, you know. She'll get through this."

He squeezed my shoulder and walked away. I was left alone. I sat down in the chair and waited for the doctor.

I FELT MY HEAD jerk up. I must have nodded off, sitting there in the chair. By the light coming in the windows, it appeared to be just past dawn. I reached over and took Effie's hand. I didn't like how cool it was. I wrapped both hands around it trying to warm it up.

The doctor had finally stopped by about seven the night before. He told me preliminary tests indicated she had a subarachnoid hemorrhage—bleeding in the brain, probably from the blow to her head. He wasn't sure yet how she would respond to treatment or what steps they would take. He was going to stop by this morning with a team of doctors to further evaluate her.

She hadn't moved all night, as far as I was aware. Her expression hadn't changed. I felt her slipping away. I talked to her softly, asking her to hold on, for me. I told her I loved her. I held her hand. I didn't know what else to do.

A few minutes later, my head was lowered when I heard a sound like a raw gulp. Maybe a gasp. I looked up in time to see her eyes open briefly, But I didn't see Effie there. Then her eyelids flickered and closed.

"Effie! Effie!" I called her name several times, pleading with her to come back to me. Her hand grew cold.

WHEN I SAW THE notice pinned to the bulletin board in the dormitory lounge, I knew what I would do. The U.S. Army was looking for cooks for the troop trains that were crisscrossing the country. Bereft, with nothing left to hold me in Baltimore, I thought I might as well head west. My cousin Caroline had moved from Louisville to Oregon when her husband had accepted a job with the railroad out there. I hadn't corresponded with them in ages, but I figured I could look them up if I made it that far. Thinking of her reminded me of the watery disaster on Stoner Creek the day of the boating party, when I first met Nell—and all the unpredictable turns my journey had taken since then.

There was a train leaving for Seattle the following week. I called the number and convinced the fella I was just the man he was looking for.

Nothing was the same without Effie Mae. All joy had left me. The burial had been hard. Doug was a mess. He had made it to his mother's side just after she died. He'd been working the night shift when he got my message and couldn't get away. She had never been conscious, but it hurt him badly that he hadn't been able to say good-bye. I didn't know how to help him through his grief. I couldn't manage my own. I had never felt so lost, so empty. All I knew to do was hit the road.

When I boarded the train—a drab-green smoke-spewing beast that had seemingly swallowed a teeming mass of drab-green servicemen happily headed to Alaska or some godforsaken island in the Pacific—I recalled my own trip to New York more than twenty years before. We were so young and foolish. We had a sense of anticipation, almost of excitement, about what it meant to be a soldier and what we were capable of doing. We celebrated our good fortune as we headed off for a grand adventure. Our illusions were dashed soon after we landed in France. Looking around the Baltimore station at the bright-faced young men in their crisp uniforms, I wanted to tell them to run. To take their chances. To go live a good life somewhere else. But, of course, their fate was sealed. Just like Effie's. Just like mine.

I had made it home, of course, unlike so many. Who among these young men would get a second chance at life? What would that look like for them?

I had no idea what lay ahead for me either. I just knew I had to keep moving. If I stopped, if I stayed too long in one place, I might get rooted again, like my parents had. I might settle. I might get comfortable. And I didn't see how I would ever be comfortable again without Effie at my side.

I boarded the train and stowed my duffle. When we finally started moving, I watched the reflections of the other men dance in the window as we slowly left the city behind.

1991

I helped my mother settle into the armchair near the cherry cabinet that held the familiar heirlooms. Sun streamed in the glass door leading to the small patio. Earlier I had sat with her outside under the plum tree as she tried bravely to smoke what would be her last cigarette. The cancer had rendered her nearly mute, and I knew time was short. If I wanted answers to the questions I had never asked, I needed to ask them now.

One by one, I removed the precious items, glancing at her to encourage whatever story, whatever memory the object might stir. Crystal, china, silver—all remnants of a bygone era, a life abandoned, a world lost. I madly scribbled all that she remembered in a little spiral notebook. She weakened visibly. I had to capture what I could, knowing it would never be sufficient.

Over a lifetime, she had carefully transferred all these things from home to home, up and down the East coast and inland again, always a reminder of the father she had never known. The champagne glasses that he and her mother had received as wedding gifts in 1920. The crystal goblet his father had won at a card party in 1904. The tea set that had been hand-painted by his great-aunt in the 1880s.

Every holiday, when I was a child, we pulled out the more useful items, washing the cut-glass bowls to be filled with cranberry sauce, shining the silver platters that would be laden with turkey and dressing, admiring the silver julep cups that would brighten the table. She had cared for them all, these precious artifacts of her father's life, for decades after he had disappeared.

As she surveyed the mementos of a more graceful time, as she shared what she could, she never once uttered his name. I never dared ask. His absence silenced us both.

In loving memory
1921–1991

Made in the USA
Columbia, SC
27 September 2021